About the Author

Adam Tyler was born in Kingston, UK, in 1982. He started to write back in 2009 when he had ideas inspired by things he had read and seen; he started to piece them together, and they then became this book. He currently lives in Surrey with his wife and house rabbit. This is his first novel.

I'd like to dedicate this book to my family and friends, especially to my grandfather Professor Jim Green. He sadly passed away before I could show him the finished product. He was a huge inspiration to me and he will never be forgotten.

Adam Tyler

THE BEGINNING

AUSTIN MACAULEY
PUBLISHERS LTD.

A CIP catalogue record for this title is available from the
British Library.

ISBN 9781784558505 (Paperback)
ISBN 9781784558536 (Hardback)
ISBN 9781784558529 (E-Book)

www.austinmacauley.com

First Published (2016)
Austin Macauley Publishers Ltd.
25 Canada Square
Canary Wharf
London
E14 5LQ

I would like to thank Austin Macauley for publishing my book, for without the people who had a hand in taking my work from a simple word document to a real life book; no one would have the opportunity to read this story.

I would like to thank my friends and family who liked what they had read and encouraged me to finish this book. I give thanks to my Grandpa; Professor Green, my cousin Rebecca, and her other half; Paul who took the time to edit my work for me.

I'd like to give special thanks to my lovely wife Kelly who has been my biggest fan and my biggest critic. Without her, I'd probably still be writing the first part of this story.

Chapter 1

Adam and Eve

John got out of his car and looked up towards the sun; he closed his eyes and a smile crept across his face. The warmth on his face and absence of breeze gave him a sense of peace. He stood there for a few moments. The weather was perfect; he felt he could stay there all day. 'Right' he said quietly, adjusted his glasses, closed the door and turned to face the reception windows. Every morning he followed a set pattern. He parked in the same spot, closed his car door and in the same motion turned round. He took the usual three steps and pressed the central locking button on his remote. The immobilizer beeped as he walked towards the glass door, he opened it and walked over to the security desk.

"Morning, Neil", John said as he walked through the glass turnstiles. Neil looked up from his paper, nodded once and went back to reading. *Money well spent here,* John thought.

Working here had been challenging. The new project he had started was now an old one. 'Adam and Eve' was now five years into development and had shown very promising results. John had not asked where the two subjects had come from originally; he thought being out of the loop on that, would make working on them easier. And it did.

He worked with a team of scientists who had seen promise in his ideas on gene alteration, something he had worked on previously at the university. The money here was better, much better, and the funding behind him seemed endless.

He did find it difficult when he asked what they wished to use his results for; if he got an answer, it was very vague. John was in two minds most days when it came to the work he was doing. On one hand he got to fulfil his dreams and take full advantage of this opportunity to find out what was actually possible. But working for a goal he was not aware of was a daunting prospect. He only knew the person he worked for, Colonel Bartlett. If there were others who owned this facility; he didn't know them or even hear about them. He did wonder if this was run and funded privately or if it was a government project. Either way, he was tired of asking questions. This project and his staff had made the years interesting. It was not hard to separate genes but what was challenging was modifying them. No documentation he studied had showed any scientists managing this step in gene therapy, only that others who had tried had failed. Today was the day after implanting the new genes in the subjects known as 'Adam' and 'Eve'. He had studied what little they had given him about them and learned their real names, which were Jack and Claire. After a while they became part of his everyday life and he started referring to them by their names rather than the names given by the project. It was mildly comical that Claire's middle name was in fact Eve, so Eve she remained. He was anxious to see if their bodies would accept the changes, or not, after all his struggling and hard work. He was confident that today would have the end result he'd dreamed of for so long. He had arrived two hours earlier than normal after giving up on sleep at home. No amount of tidying or counting sheep had helped. He had given in and decided that calling in his staff would be out of the question, given the long hours and hard work they all had endured. They had asked so many questions about the purpose of their work, he himself couldn't provide them with many satisfying answers. Their pay was exceptional but that did little to keep them from asking things he couldn't tell them. It was unfair to him at first but the level of focus they had, he felt, was because they didn't really know. After a while; they had learned to stop asking. This morning he had decided getting an early start was all he wanted to do.

John walked past the security office and made his way to the lift at the far end of reception. He swiped his card on the access reader to use the lift. The doors opened and he stepped in. Inside the lift were 'open', 'close' and 'call' buttons along the bottom and the four floors it stopped on were listed individually above. Three of these buttons were only accessible by key and John had the B3 key. Every time he used the lift his thoughts were the same; What was on levels B1 and B2? No one on his floor knew, security didn't know, or at least those who answered him said so. They weren't the friendliest security guards he had met. It seemed they used a different company for each section. One company for the guard hut you drove past, one company for the patrols and another that kept an eye on those inside the building.

He inserted his key and turned it anticlockwise, which felt quite unnatural. He pressed the button and the doors closed. The lift moved quickly and smoothly with no judder like you found with shopping centre lifts. These you could sleep in while people travelled.

The lift doors opened revealing the brightly lit hallway he had become accustomed to. The lift was at the back of the floor and opposite his laboratory, the corridor just off to the left was narrow and well lit, on the left were the toilets and shower rooms and the last room was the break room.

John walked toward the double doors, swiped his card and pulled one door open. Inside was his brightly lit, white tiled laboratory, which would fit well in any Hollywood film. This environment took him a while to get used to working in, having come from an education background. The other scientists were waiting for him on the other side of the door. The first to greet him was Luke.

"Good morning, John!" he almost shouted. Luke was a skinny lad who John liked; he was exceptionally bright with ambition and a decent sense of humour. He was clutching a clipboard in one hand and a cup of steaming coffee in the other. John stopped in his tracks and looked around. *I should have known better*, he thought.

"Good morning, Luke," John said, taking the clipboard and scrolling through the information.

"Colonel Bartlett has asked how long it will be before we can them moved from The Tank and into Quarantine," Lisa said as John had barely got to the middle of the first line.

John stopped and looked over his glasses at Lisa. She was a very pretty girl who didn't wear makeup or dress in any way to draw attention. She was more intelligent than Luke and had a similar since of humour. She did have a lack of common sense though, which amused the others. "Sorry," she said looking down at the floor. John half smiled and continued reading until he got his office. He opened the door, walked in and sat down in his black leather chair which was next to his desk.

"No rejection shown at all?" John looked up. The others now occupied the free space in his office.

"None," they said in unison.

"When was Colonel Bartlett informed?" John looked up at Lisa who was standing next to him trying to look apologetic.

"About an hour ago," she said.

"Thank you. Okay, guys, I'll call him. Go away." John had a childish grin on his face now; he was glad he'd come into work two hours earlier than normal. Looking at his staff, he realised that they were all wearing the same clothes as yesterday. Alex had the coffee stain on the bottom part of his coat that Jean had caused at lunch yesterday. She still had on the mismatched socks which had amused John. "She must have dressed in the dark," he mused. Looking around, there were signs that gave everyone else away: Chris had a bit of hair sticking up where he must have slept at some point and then forgot to sort his hair out. Brian's T-shirt, which he must have changed at some point, was inside out and Vince was limping still from where he had walked into the coffee table and fallen over. The rest looked tired, worn out, yet still went along with their duties with the same conviction as always. John was proud of his team. They worked hard and managed to keep the facility a good place to be. John turned around, breathed in and out deeply; he picked up the black phone that was a direct line to the project head, Colonel Bartlett.

"Hello, John."

"Good morning, Colonel."

"Lisa told me this morning that everything worked. Congratulations."

"Thank you, sir. It is going to mean a lot more testing before we can think of waking them up."

"I know, John. I would like you to give me an idea on time, though."

"I'll be able to tell you by the end of the day."

"Okay, John. Call me when you know more." The phone line went dead. John sat back in his chair to reflect for a moment before he asked how far along his staff had gotten. He knew that telling Colonel Bartlett that his staff had been working nearly forty hours straight would have been a bad idea. They worked hard but when his staff worked this long without rest, they did not have a history of producing astounding results.

"Lisa, Luke. Come here a moment," he said without looking up. Their heads popped round from behind a piece of equipment used for gene splicing and they wandered over, a little sheepishly.

"John, we are sorry that you're the last to know, but he had been calling all night and we didn't want to lie to him," Luke said from behind Lisa's shoulder.

"Today I don't mind. If it had been like last time then yes, you would all be in trouble. You've done very well today. When was the last time anyone here got some sleep?"

"We learned from last time, John. We have been getting forty-five minute naps when we get too tired. To be honest, everyone is so focused that we have decided working like this is producing good results. All that's left to check are their meta functions."

"Bring me everything you've got and I'll go through it."

Lisa and Luke smiled and went off collecting folders off desks.

John waited patiently. His staff had potentially outdone themselves. The last time a breakthrough had happened and Colonel Bartlett had been informed before John had gotten there had proved embarrassing. Two tests had been incomplete and the gene samples had to be destroyed. Colonel Bartlett had been furious and that was something John did not want to experience again.

"I think you'll be happy with these results," Lisa said, handing him a large stack of folders.

John took them, put his glasses back on and began reading the top sheet. Lisa was hanging around. She was far too eager for the time of day. John looked up at her as if to ask what else she wanted.

"Yes?" he asked when Lisa didn't say anything.

"When do you think we can start?" Lisa said, almost bouncing on the spot now.

"I'll come find you when I'm finished," John said, trying to hide the impatience in his voice.

She nodded and left. John kicked his door closed. It swung into place, barely making a sound. He had become good at that. His staff had gotten used to coming and going freely from his office, usually without knocking. He sat back and started reading the top sheet again.

The morning passed into late afternoon. John had gone through everything twice. The tests had been completed, checked and then rechecked. No wonder the vending machines were almost out of caffeine drinks and chocolate. They were right. Nothing had been left out. All the results were what he had hoped for. John now saw his staff with an almost beaming sense of pride. The past five years were leading to the breakthrough he could only have imagined before working here, and he had a dedicated team to thank for making his dream become a reality.

"What do you think?" Jean asked from next to the lunch-room door. John was enjoying his favourite coffee; mint latté with one brown sugar.

"I think it's time to tell Colonel Bartlett that everything is ready," he replied. He stood, finished his drink in two gulps and threw the empty cup into the bin behind him.

"When was the last time the Tank and Quarantine rooms were screened, Jean?"

She looked into space for a second and John could have sworn he saw her enter a day dream. She blinked, muttered something about Lisa and left for the doorway. John smiled and started walking after her, she was now running through the laboratory door and almost took Simon out, who was standing inches away.

"Lisa, when did we last screen the Tank and Quarantine rooms?"

"Tuesday, Alex screened them Tuesday," Lisa said just as John walked through the door.

"Good, let's get things started then. Lisa, please go and get Luke ready to move," John said and watched Lisa almost start to skip as she went to find Luke.

John went over to Alex's desk and looked at the screening report for Tuesday. "A hundred per cent sterile." John nodded to himself, turned and walked back to his office.

Inside he sat down and picked up the black phone.

"Hello, John," a heavy voice said.

"Colonel, we're ready to move them into quarantine."

"Fantastic. Have them moved, and call me in the morning with details when they are responsive."

The phone went dead.

John met Luke and Lisa at the opposite end of the laboratory and went to what they had come to call 'The Tank'. John swiped his card on the reader outside a pair of white security doors covered with 'Warning' and 'Authorized access only' signs. They walked into the airlock, which had clean suits, sets of pyjamas and various other things stored and wrapped in airtight bags on the walls and floor. There were signs on the wall that stipulated that all staff wear the clean suits at all times. Luke pulled the door closed behind them, sealing it shut with a pop. They each put on a suit, and checked one another's for damage and open areas. Once happy with the conditions and breathing equipment John pressed a button with 'sanitize' imprinted on it. Air and smoke began filling the room, Luke jumped at the sound and Lisa laughed. John shook his head. They had to go in and out of the tank once a month to set things up and take readings from the tanks and every time he sanitized the room Luke would jump and this always caused Lisa to laugh at him.

Once the room was full, a vacuum began sucking the air and smoke out, a green light came on once the vacuum had turned off and the room was clear. John pressed the 'Open' button on the inner door, picked up two sets of pyjamas and stepped through the opening door.

Inside was a large room, the three walked in as strobe lights blinked on. Two large glass containers stood in the centre of the room filled with liquid, a man and a woman were inside. They were in their early twenties. Both were unconscious, with tubes coming from various parts of their heads and bodies, which ran down and connected to a computer in between the containers. Behind them was a large door with 'Quarantine' written above it. Several leads ran from the computer to a very sophisticated desk that was directly in front of John. This had seven glass monitors, showing various vital statistics above a large keyboard. Lisa sat down and started typing. There was a small cupboard on the left hand side of the room, which John made his way towards. Luke sat down next to Lisa.

"Lisa, start the sequence to get them ready for moving, please. Luke, check the vitals while I get things ready to transport them."

"I've started," she replied. Lisa enjoyed coming here to work. The equipment was top of the range and was constantly working on updating its software while keeping everything here as they had designed it. It worked faster than any computer system she'd worked with before and given how quickly she liked to work, it made her very happy to come here once a month.

John took out two stretchers that were in the cupboard. He wheeled them over to the containers and put a set of pyjamas on each. After she was done, Lisa started the draining sequence while Luke monitored the vitals for changes.

"It always gets to me, being in here," Luke said while sitting in an uncomfortable-looking chair.

"Just keep an eye on the screens and stop being a sissy," Lisa joked as she was working.

He looked at her and smiled. She punched him on the shoulder and went back to work.

The containers started draining and the people inside started floating downward. Once the containers were empty, a green light flicked on one of the screens Luke was monitoring.

"The containers are empty, Lisa. You can release them when you're ready," Luke said.

"Thanks," she replied sarcastically.

The keyboard Lisa was working on had two large buttons that had once been labelled 'Adam' and 'Eve'. Over time they had started calling them by their real names and someone had put new tabs over them. She pressed the button that had been re-labelled 'Jack' and raised her arm with her thumb up. John looked up and nodded. The glass started rising towards the ceiling. Once the glass had stopped, John started carefully removing the tubes from the man's nose and throat. The man took in a breath when this was removed, which made John jump a little.

"Bloody hell," he mumbled to himself and chuckled, he started taking the tubes out of the man's body. "I'm glad I'm not a surgeon," he mumbled and when he had removed all the tubes he could find, he took the pyjamas, opened the bag they were in and started to dress the unconscious but breathing man. John looked at the stretcher and looked back at the desk.

"Luke, give me a hand, please." Luke nodded and made his way over to help John and as he walked past Lisa laughed.

"I'll just stay here and do everything," she said. John looked up at her and smiled.

"Multitask, for a moment." he said. Lisa mumbled to herself about being left out of playing dress-up with the boys and positioned herself so she could work both sides. John and Luke put Jack in the clothes and once dressed, they put him on one of the stretchers and secured the straps in place. Jack was breathing by himself but still didn't look quite alive.

"Thanks, now please take over from Lisa." Luke walked over to Lisa who had pressed the other button labelled 'Eve.' John began removing the tubes from her and did the same procedure; Lisa helped remove tubes and dress her. Once Eve was dressed and secured on the stretcher, Lisa looked up at Luke.

"You can start the standby sequence now, Luke."

"Okay, the system will take a few minutes. Can you come over and monitor the sequence while I start shutting down?"

"Sure." She tutted and made her way over to the desk while John checked them both over for anything he might have missed.

When the system was in standby, Lisa and Luke left the desk and helped John with the stretchers. They moved past the containers and went to the door labelled 'Quarantine'. Next to the door was a numbered key pad. John put in his security code and the lock popped. He pulled the large door open and held it while the others pushed the stretchers through.

Inside the room was a small open space with two doors in the middle of the wall. John walked over and unlocked the doors by putting in his security code on the key panel and pressed the 'A' and 'B' buttons.

Inside each room was a bed, which was really a metal box secured to the floor, with a mattress and pillows to make it more comfortable. There was a plastic toilet with a drinking fountain on top and a bin on the side. This was located in the middle of the back wall; the unit was stocked with food and toilet paper inside. The bed, floor, walls and ceiling had heavy padding underneath Kevlar lining. The rooms had two small security cameras positioned in adjacent corners. The cameras were in the walls and almost impossible to see if you didn't know where to look. Lisa pushed Jack into the 'A' room. Once inside, John unstrapped him and carefully put him on the bed, Lisa then left and helped Luke with Eve. Once they had left and taken the stretchers back into the tank, John sealed them inside. They made their way back into the tank and John sealed the quarantine door while Lisa and Luke returned the stretchers to their place in the cupboard.

"Now it's the waiting game," Lisa said to Luke as he fumbled his attempt at putting the stretcher back into the cupboard. She found his struggle amusing, but didn't offer to help him. She smiled and walked towards John who saw this and shook his head.

"Little help, Lisa?" John said as he walked past her. He unhooked the trapped clip which was stopping the stretcher from returning to the cupboard and patted Luke on the head. He looked at the clip and back up at John. He was a little embarrassed. Without saying a word John walked over to the computer between the now empty containers and activated the sensors inside the quarantine rooms. The glass lowered over both containers and sealed back in place. The desk Lisa was working from changed between monitoring modes. The new mode was designed to record and document everything the sensors within the two quarantine rooms picked up.

"Luke, Lisa, we're ready to leave now," John said to them as they walked towards him. Lisa was teasing Luke about the stretcher. "They will wake up in a few hours and when they do, I will call Colonel Bartlett."

"John, we don't know how they'll react when they wake up," Luke said. He looked back to the large door with a nervous look on his face. Lisa just stood there smiling, almost bouncing on the spot with excitement.

"Can I speak to them first?" Lisa asked once they were back in the airlock.

"That might be a good idea. They will most likely be frightened. Remind them that they are safe and try to just explain the basics to them," John replied. He had wanted to speak to them first, but hearing a soft female voice might help to keep them calm. After all, they had new genes and there were no possible ways to know what would have changed about them. They could only determine that the genes had given Eve an altered thinking pattern. Jack, on the other hand, now had mental tissue altered to be more adaptable, and his skin had a different texture to it. How the genes would affect them was completely unknown and they couldn't do any further testing while they were in the tanks, and the measures they'd put in place for security prevented them from doing tests while they were unconscious and exposed to treatment. The only way they could find out now was to wake them up.

They stepped back into the airlock and Luke pulled the door closed behind them sealing it shut. John pressed the 'sanitize' button again. From the corner of her eye, Lisa watched Luke, only he didn't jump in the usual way. His mind was elsewhere and hadn't heard the pop. Lisa looked disappointed. John was watching them and simply tutted in his suit. Once the vacuum took out the air and smoke the green light came on. They took off the suits and put them back in their original place. John pressed the 'open' button on the door that led back into the laboratory.

"How did it go?" Brian asked, before John had time to step through the door, causing him to jump. "Christ," he half gasped. No one else reacted. They were all too anxious to hear how it went. Once Lisa and Luke were out and the door closed, John turned to the impatient looking group of tired and curious scientists.

"Brian, it went well; we drained the tanks, unplugged them, dressed them and put them to bed. It's just a question of waiting now. Okay?"

Brian nodded and a slightly nervous smile crept across his face. The others all did the same and turned around.

"What now?" Jean asked as they walked back to the laboratory.

"It's been less than half an hour. Their bodies have to get used to being outside the containers, they have been in there for well over a year. They will not be in the best of moods when they wake up, let's hope we can get through the rest of the day without incident. I need everyone here monitoring their stats and let me know the instant something changes." Jean nodded and ran off to bark orders at the others. Luke and Lisa had become John's right and left hand, but Jean had appointed herself in charge of the others when they weren't around, she did a good job and was always able to keep up the morale.

John went into his office and switched on the monitors above his desk. The screens warmed up and after a few seconds, all four cameras were showing a good picture of Jack and Eve sleeping in their beds.

For the next three hours, the staff monitored everything inside the rooms, from body temperature to noise levels. The tests that John had reviewed earlier had shown that

Jack and Eve had lost very little muscle tissue and their brain waves remained at an impressive level.

The black phone started to ring; it interrupted John's train of thought. He picked it up and coughed before putting it to his mouth. "Colonel Bartlett," John said, trying to keep his voice even.

"Hello John. How are they?"

"Fine, sir. Just waiting for them to -" John stopped mid-sentence, in his peripheral vision he had seen Eve move, on camera. John moved his head closer to the monitor.

"What? John, is everything Okay?" Colonel Bartlett sounded concerned.

John saw Eve move again, her hand moved to rub her eyes. "Lisa!" John shouted from his chair, three seconds later Lisa was at his side. A few members of staff rushed from where they had been working to stand in the doorway.

"Colonel Bartlett, one of them might be waking up."

"Keep me on the line, I want to hear everything."

Lisa moved to a microphone base unit sitting on John's desk next to his keyboard. John pressed the power button and the base unit beeped into life. Lisa pressed the button labelled 'B', which John had done earlier that week.

"Good morning," Lisa said in her soft Irish accent. Eve juddered at the sound; her eyes were still not fully open. The lighting inside the room was soft so as not to harm their eyes and the microphone volume was on a low setting.

Eve started to move again, she raised a hand to her eyes while the other pulled at the sheet she was lying in.

"Hello?" she said, barely above a whisper. She swallowed a few times; her eyes were trying to blink now and her throat was dry. She raised her hand so it was shading her face. "Hello?" she said in a dry croaky voice.

"My name is Dr Lisa Bennit. You are safe. There is no need to worry. Everything is fine."

Eve looked around the room, her hand still shading her eyes. "What? Where, where am I?" she asked, her voice sounded a little clearer, but still barely audible.

"My name is Dr Lisa Bennit. You are safe and there is no need to worry. You are in a medical facility. We have been helping you get better. What is the last thing you remember?"

Eve laid her arm back on the bed, closed her eyes and started to snore softly.

"That was interesting," Colonel Bartlett said. "When they wake up, call me." John put the phone down and laughed.

"Well, that was interesting indeed," he said.

Everyone was smiling.

"Okay everyone. That was the start of things to come. We need to be ready for when they wake up." They all left to continue what they were working on. John got up and walked out of his office. He and Lisa made their way to the row of desks now dedicated to monitoring the sensors inside the quarantine rooms.

John looked at the monitors and noticed that there hadn't been any change in their stress levels. Alex was sitting on the desk monitoring the sensors. He looked up at John with a smile.

"The room temperature rose a little when she started moving."

John looked at him, nodded and went back to his office, where Luke was waiting outside.

"Did Jack move?"

John shook his head. For the first time in a long time, he didn't know what would happen next. There were no 'do overs', this was it. What were they capable of doing, and when would they find out? Had they done the unthinkable or had they changed two people in ways that would benefit mankind? John went to his chair and sat heavily. He smiled. He didn't know just how wide a smile he had now.

Luke looked at John, smiled and moved to get a closer look at the screens.

The others started to gather in the once spacious office and before long it was full. Most of the scientists had gathered inside when Jack started stirring in his sleep. It had been almost two hours since Eve had briefly woken up and everyone was now focused on when Jack would do the same.

"What time is it, John?" Brian asked from where he was hiding at the back of John's office.

"Almost nine o'clock, Brian. Five minutes after you last asked me."

Lisa was sitting on the corner of John's desk, staring at one of monitors that showed Jack sleeping uneasily.

"He has to wake up soon," she said.

John looked at her. His patience was wearing thin, even though his staff had been working near on three days with little to no sleep and had done so without complaint. The number of people now hanging around in his office was starting to irritate him.

"Why don't you get some sleep, Lisa?" John said, trying to make it sound like a suggestion rather than an order.

She looked at her watch, trying to think of the last time she had a nap. Had it been twenty-four hours? She had lost count by now. She and Luke had taken it in turns napping through the night, seeing as one of them had to be awake, but since the first time Colonel Bartlett called, asking how things were going, neither of them had the chance to rest.

"If you don't mind, I would like to wait until one of them is awake, John," she said in a tired voice. She was determined to get some rest, but not just yet.

"If she passes out on my desk -" John began to say to Luke and noticed Luke was looking a little more tired than Lisa. Luke nodded slowly at John. He then let out a yawn that made everyone look in his direction. He remained as nonchalant as possible, stretched, crossed his arms and continued to stare at the monitors, focusing on one at a time taking very long blinks as he did.

Lisa let out a yawn of her own and she was the last to see Jack start to wake up. Everyone, including John moved closer to the screen but Lisa, as tired as she was, was able to beat John to the microphone button.

"Hello?" Lisa did her best to sound awake. "How do you feel?"

"A bit tired but okay, I guess." Luke said, almost like an automated reaction, which caused everyone in the office to laugh.

Lisa did laugh but quickly turned back to the microphone. "You're safe. Do not be afraid, my name is Dr Lisa Bennit. You are in a medical facility where we have been treating you."

Jack looked a little more awake then Eve had earlier. His eyes had not opened yet but he looked like he was becoming more aware of his surroundings. He rubbed his eyes, tried to blink and started moving as if to sit on the side of the bed.

"What's happening? Where am I?" He was still trying to open his eyes so he could look around. He started to realize that he was in a strange padded room, he managed to force his eyes open and tried to look around but he couldn't focus properly. Jack started to think of what could have happened to him. How had he ended up in a place like this? He felt quite weak, but put it down to having just woken up.

"How long have I been here?" he asked. The questions he had asked repeated in his head; he almost didn't hear the voice return.

"Let's start off with how you are feeling?" Lisa was sounding more like herself now. She didn't feel any more awake but she wanted to make sure that Jack felt okay and remained calm.

"What? Erm, I guess I feel okay" Jack looked at the drinking fountain. His eyes had not quite adjusted yet but he could see what it was. Instinct took over and he moved off the bed and fell to the floor in a heap. John's office went deadly silent, nobody reacted to what they saw. Jack let out a soft chuckle. Walking was not an option so he decided crawling would be safer. He made his way slowly over to the drinking fountain and with a little effort got into a seated position on the toilet, so that he could get a drink. Jack pressed down on the button and the water hit him in the face. This surprised him and he started to laugh. It was a pleasant feeling and it did help his eyes. He got another spray to the face, before realizing he had to move his mouth over the fountain. He took a big mouthful and started coughing. How long had it been since he'd last had a drink? He couldn't remember. He tried taking another, with more success. He rubbed the water trickling down his face into his skin. It felt good and he bent back to the fountain and began drinking.

The water was soft and pleasing to his dry throat. He had not realised how dry it was until now and it felt good to quench his thirst. He looked around the room while drinking, there was no food laid out. In fact, there was not a lot in the room, apart from the toilet/-cum-drinking fountain thing and the bed. *Where the hell am I?* he thought.

After he was done with the fountain, he wiped his face on a pyjama sleeve, fell again to the floor and slowly made his way back to the bed; he pulled himself back up and collapsed.

"Can I get some food, please?" he asked quietly. He was looking around for something to focus on. His eyesight was getting better but it was only gradual improvement.

John picked up the black phone.

"Hello, John," Colonel Bartlett said after three rings.

"Sir, Jack's awake. His muscles are a little weak but he is responsive and hungry."

"What about Eve?"

"She's stirred a few times and, as you know, she's spoken but she's not regained conscious yet."

"Okay, see if he will eat something. Have you told him anything?"

"No, sir. He has been made aware that he is in a facility and that we are here to help him get better."

"Okay, make sure you tell him that his memory loss is due to his sleep and that is why he is in quarantine. When Eve wakes up, call me."

"Yes, sir." The phone line went dead.

"Lisa, let him have some food," John said.

She nodded and pressed a button on John's keyboard labelled, *Food for room A.*

Jack heard a noise coming from the toilet and sat up. The section of the toilet that the water fountain was on started rising. It revealed a flat tray. On it was a loo roll and a tray of silver packets. Jack put his feet on the floor and eased himself to a standing position. He took a step forward and swayed into the nearside wall. *Got to get used to walking again,* he thought. He got himself back to a standing position and slowly walked to the corner of the room. He made it to the toilet and sat down. The silver packets had labels on them. One had *chocolate* written on it. The others had *biscuits*, *sausage roll*, *fruit roll* and *potato* written on them.

"Thanks, I feel like I'm in a psycho ward now. Careful of the sleepy guy in room one. He can't see properly yet and has to learn how to walk again," he said with little humour in his voice.

Lisa smiled and leaned towards the microphone.

"It'll be no time before you're running around again. We just need you to get more rest. We've a few more tests to complete but don't worry; we will explain everything in due course."

Jack put his hand up and gave a thumbs up. He removed the silver packets and stacked them on the toilet in edible order. He looked at the loo roll, picked it up and thought, *just in case.* He put it on the toilet seat and leaned back with the 'potato' packet in his left hand.

Lisa pressed the button again and the fountain started lowering, until it was back on top of the toilet.

"Thanks," Jack said and opened his potato.

John was enjoying some of his favourite music. He was sitting in a red leather chair, which looked like he'd had many years use out of it.

The library was located in the corner of the house, as it gave the best isolation, which came in handy in the once-hectic house he had shared with his wife and kids. He was all alone now, nothing but his work kept him busy. His wife had passed away; his children had their own lives now and only visited on the holidays, they knew well that their father was a busy man. They knew he enjoyed them visiting, though it had been years since the last real visit.

The room he sat quietly in was circular. It had a great many shelves stocked with many more books, all of which he had bought, read and shelved once finished. He seldom read a book twice. There was a single ladder on a brass rail, which was the only way to gain access to the higher level books, though he'd not used it in years so there it remained, gathering dust behind his desk. He'd updated his desk in the early nineties, when technology started getting to a point where it was common in most households. He had updated his equipment so often it was at the point now he had almost too much high-tech equipment on his desk, buzzing with life. Most of the equipment was the latest edition and had been personalized so he was completely unrestricted and could work just as well here as he could at the office. The down side to this was it did ruin the early Victorian look to his library.

John was day dreaming; he was so far gone that it was a full minute before he heard his phone ringing. He snapped out of his dream and picked it up, answering without bothering to look at the display.

"Good evening, colonel," he said, once he had cleared his throat.

"Good evening, John," a familiarly husky voice said in response. "How are things going with the project? I see one of the subjects has gone back to sleep after being fully awake, if this report is accurate."

"Everything looks promising. Both subjects have taken the alterations well and are in recovery."

"Good. Have your staff ascertained when we can move on to stage two?"

John picked up the report, which had slid off his lap and was now in between the chair and its cushion. "They should be ready to be moved in ten days."

"So on the fifth we can move on, correct?"

"That's right, sir. Everything is ready, we just need them to be calm and used to the environment before we can move on. Due to the unprecedented success we have had, there is no way of telling what changes have occurred while they are in recovery."

"I'll look forward to the next report then, Doctor. When they've been moved and settled in, I'll look forward to meeting them."

"Yes, of course, sir."

The phone went dead.

"Four thousand years of human development; now comes the next chapter in our evolution," John said, stood up and walked out of the room. He was heading back to work.

Lisa was sitting in John's chair. He had gone home initially to get a change of clothes. He'd spent hours talking with Jack and after dropping a cup of coffee on himself, he decided it was time to go home for a bit. Lisa had taken over after she had gone home and changed. John had ordered everyone to go have a few hours away; he was the last to leave.

Lisa had taken charge and in the middle of her conversation with Jack, she noticed Eve moving and told him she had to answer the phone.

"Sure, I'll just wait here then," Jack said and lay down on the floor.

Eve was just waking up; she felt the sheets she was lying on and realized she didn't know where she was.

"What the...?" she said, quite startled.

"Good morning, you're safe, don't panic. My name is Dr Lisa Bennit. How are you feeling?"

"Where am I? What do you want?" Eve was trying to shift around on the bed, trying not to look weak.

Lisa looked at the image of Jack improving on his press-ups in the room next door.

"You're safe. This is a facility full of doctors and scientists. There is nothing to worry about, we just want you to feel safe, please stay calm. Are you hungry?"

Eve did not feel the slightest bit calm. She looked around at the white room she was in and tried her best to focus her eyes. "How long have I been here? Why do I feel like this?" She held back the tears she felt coming and tried to sit up.

"There is a water fountain at the end of your bed, if you are thirsty? Please be careful, your eyesight and muscles won't have their usual strength yet."

Eve's blurred vision did show that this strange woman, who avoided answering questions, was right and she was thirsty. Slowly, she moved until she was lying on her stomach with her legs hanging over the edge of the bed. Her weight lowered her until her knees touched the soft padding on the floor. *Great, it's a mental asylum,* she thought.

Her lack of vision was annoying her but she was trying her best to move forward. She crawled towards the fountain and pulled herself onto the toilet. She reached around trying to find a way to activate the fountain and accidentally pressed the button, causing the water to spray her forehead. She let out a cry, put her hands to her eyes and began rubbing the water in. It felt like it was helping, she opened her eyes and noticed the improvement. Once her eyes had focused enough, she saw the button, activated the fountain and began drinking.

She didn't realise how thirsty she was until she started to take in bug gulps of the fresh cool water. She kept drinking until she felt slightly bloated; it was strange, but having a full stomach made her feel better. She sat back on the toilet and closed her eyes, almost in a daydream. *How am I going to get out of this place?* she thought.

Her head was almost resting on the fountain; it was not comfortable but she didn't mind. The realization fell upon her, she was in a place she had no memory of getting to, she didn't know where she was and there was no foreseeable way of getting out. A tear appeared at the corner of her eye; she leaned forward, put her head in her hands and wept until her eyes could cry no more.

Chapter 2

The Reason We're Here

It had been over a week since both Jack and Eve had woken up. There were no issues with Jack to begin with, but when he asked questions and they weren't quite answered in a way with which he was satisfied, he became frustrated and then angry. He had lashed out at the heavy padding against what he had learned was the door and even though there was no damage or fear of him breaking though, all the staff were on edge when it came to talking with him.

Eve got her frustrations out early; the third day was spent crying and screaming, which echoed around her room and through the speakers in John's office. When the fifth day came, she was calmer, but at the same time, wouldn't talk much. The fact that there was nothing she could do to get out had upset her, but soon she came to accept the fact that whoever they were, they had no interest in hurting her. She was clothed, warm and whenever she asked for something it wasn't long before her request was granted. "It's only a matter of time," she said to herself that day.

The staff had been busy while Jack and Eve were getting used to their rooms and their moods had given them a lot of information on any changes that occurred. All tests came back neutral on the environment; nothing about them changed, regardless of their stress levels. Neither of them could do anything out of the ordinary as far as they could tell, so the staff got more nervous as the days and normality continued.

Day nine arrived. Tomorrow, Jack and Eve were to be moved from their rooms and taken to level B2. John had only learned this when he was passing security that morning and was given a key. The man who gave him the key was very large. His muscular build and his many scars led John to think he was ex-military. John only knew his name was Patrick and that he was head of security.

"Dr Duncan, you're to go to B2 today before you start work and familiarize yourself with the area." Patrick then turned around and walked outside, lit a cigarette and began a routine patrol.

The key was brass and a little heavier then it looked. John didn't ask him any questions, he simply added the key to the rest of his bunch and pressed the lift button. The doors opened and once inside, John put the key into the B2 hole, turned the key anti-clockwise and pressed inward. The door closed and the lift started moving.

The lift doors opened to a room in which the walls, ceiling and floor were all a very soft blue. It reminded John of the Caribbean Sea as he'd once seen it from an aeroplane window when coming in to land. In front of John were two large glass boxes, which went from ceiling to floor and were the main part of the room; a narrow aisle was to the left and looked like a walkway. Two computer desks were in front of the boxes; both computers were on standby. John made his way over to the boxes and looked inside. Each contained a bed, which was bolted securely at the corners. There was a state of the art weight lifting machine and a running machine, along with a table and chair in the opposite corner of the room. John saw that there was another part of the boxes in the back, which looked at first like the back wall, and when John opened the door, he saw a shower, a sink and a toilet. *Wow, they'll be happy moving here*, he thought. In fact, John wouldn't mind staying here himself; only if the boxes weren't see-through, of course.

John walked out of the box he was in and made his way down the narrow walkway.

This part of B2 was lit in a darker blue. There were two much smaller boxes with a sturdy-looking black chair inside; it looked like it was either part of the box, or secured through it and into the building itself.

John walked into a box and tried shaking the chair; it didn't move at all. The metal was cold steel and John could see that it had been modified with upper and lower leg and arm restraints, made from the same metal. From the inside, John could see that the frame around the boxes was very thick and like the chair, could be a part of the building itself. John could see a large rectangular table, with two chairs at the sides, at the other end of the room. He walked over to the table and noticed it was a touch screen computer. The screen was showing a flower bouncing around the screen, changing colour as it moved. The picture quality was the best John had seen. He touched the screen and the flower disappeared; in its place was a login box. John walked around the computer and went to the far end of the room which had three small doors labelled 'Quarantine'

John smiled and said quietly. "Here we go again."

John jumped as he turned around. Stood directly behind him was Patrick. He had a slight smile on his face; one of amusement.

"Quite a sight, isn't it, doctor?" He mused.

John caught his breath and looked at him with an amused look of his own.

"Quite. Now, it's not nice to sneak up on people, Patrick."

"Sorry, old habits," he said, leaning toward John and winking.

John laughed. "What brings you here then?" he asked.

"Just making sure you're not breaking anything," Patrick said then burst into laughter. "You're introducing this place to its new inhabitants tomorrow, right?" he asked.

"Er, yes. But how did you-" John began

"I'm head of security, doctor. There isn't much that's kept from me. The only thing I don't know is what you've done to those people or what's going to happen when you move them here." Patrick lowered his voice and said, "But I'm looking forward to finding out."

"Tomorrow will be the next step to what we've been working towards." John replied.

Patrick smiled and turned towards the lift. John followed him and when he got the lift, Patrick stopped him dead in his tracks.

"Doctor. You get this one, I'll get the next." He stepped aside and motioned John to go first.

"You're going to B1, I assume, then?" John said, stepping into the lift and putting his key in the B3 hole.

"Have a nice day, doctor," Patrick said as the doors closed.

The lift doors opened on B3. John stepped out and saw Luke and Lisa, who were standing so that he could not step out.

"Good morning John," they said in unison.

"Morning," John said, looking at them to suggest they move, which they did not.

"Your car was outside and you didn't come straight here," Luke said as John moved past him.

"Luke, I was on B2. No, I cannot talk about it yet so please do not start telling everyone or bothering me with questions. Everything will become clear soon, mate. How have things been?"

Lisa looked at Luke in excitement then began talking at high speed.

"Well, Eve is doing more sit-ups, lunges and press-ups, while Jack is keeping his usual routine. If you're asking if anything else is different, then, no." She looked at Luke who was trailing back a few steps and said, "Someone is in your office." As John turned around she had turned towards Chris, who was working on a computer and trying not to eavesdrop.

"Wonderful," he said and opened his office door.

"Good morning, John." A husky voice said from the leather chair which was facing the screens on his desk.

"Good morning, colonel, I thought you were coming to visit tomorrow."

"I was, but I decided that I'd come today. I see nothing exceptional has occurred, there's nothing new to report and that they are acting the same as any normal people that are stuck in a ten-by-eight-foot padded cell would. Tell me, John, what are we expecting from them?"

The chair turned to face John and sat there was a man of experienced years, dressed in an immaculate navy blue suit, white shirt, black tie and black shoes. He was a heavily muscled man, who in his prime would have given Patrick a run for his money. As he stood, John closed the door behind him, all the while keeping eye contact.

"We can move them today if you like, sir. The abilities that lie within them must be in their minds, there is limited danger in moving them. May I suggest staff with knowledge of the site move them, just in case they try to escape?" The colonel moved past John and opened the door.

"The skinny lad and the girl he follows around like a lost sheep. I'll be waiting on B2."

"Yes sir," John said while taking the key off his bunch.

John saw his staff hide away or try their best to look busy as the colonel walked towards the lift. Once inside, with the doors closed behind him, John went to where Lisa was stood with Luke at the desk behind her.

"Get them ready to move now," John said to them while the others looked around and almost all of them smiled at once.

Luke turned to Chris, who was now grinning from ear to ear. "I told you," he said.

"Just get them ready. Luke and Lisa will move them, I'll talk to them and the rest of you work on updates and everything we have that could suggest it's too early."

"Already done, John," Chris said, while standing so quickly he almost lost his balance.

"Lisa?" John said while looking Chris in the face.

"Chris is right, we've been going over the data taken from every day and checking with everything we have. Nothing will happen physically. The alterations in Eve are mental while Jack's appears to be circulatory. That's what the information available is telling us.

"We didn't put it in your office because the visitor was in there and none of us wanted to disturb him."

"Okay, that should have been given to him, but not to worry. Get everything ready."

John gave Lisa and Luke quick instructions and the key for the lift. He went back to his office and sat down in his chair, leaned forward and pressed down on both labelled buttons.

"Good morning; this is Dr John Duncan, if you haven't gotten used to my voice yet. I'm happy to tell you that you'll be getting moved to a new room today. Two

41

members of my team will be down shortly. The man that I work for is here today and he will be able to answer some of your questions. I've got to get things ready for you now, I'm sorry I have to be brief."

John released the buttons and looked at the monitors. Jack lay on his bed and smiled for the first time that John had seen in days. He mouthed the words, "Thank you," and put his hands behind his head

Eve didn't say anything. She smiled and began tidying around her bed. When she was done there, she started cleaning up the wrappers and food she had been collecting and started putting it all in the bin hole that was in the side of the toilet.

Lisa and Luke decided to move Eve first. She seemed calmest.

Lisa took a plastic bag from a shelf in the airlock and Luke did the same. Luke pressed the 'sanitize' button and jumped when the noise started.

"Thankfully, that's the second to last time we do that," Lisa said and turned to Luke. "I'll do the talking, as you're a bundle of nerves. And I do wish I'd known about this before," she said. She was holding a blindfold, which she put into her back pocket.

"Why?" Luke asked. He looked at Lisa and it suddenly clicked; they just so happened to be wearing almost identical clothing. He shrugged and continued, "It will be weird going in there without the suits on. And I'm just a little excited, that's all." Luke looked at his blindfold and decided to copy Lisa.

The green light came on and they entered the tank. They made their way to the computer stations and began the necessary sequence to shut down security and allow them to move Eve from quarantine.

Inside the open area, they moved to Eve's room and Lisa input the code.

"Ready?" she said and before he could answer she pressed the button and the door began to open. Lisa stepped inside.

Eve heard the door open and spun round. She took one look at Lisa, dressed in her denim jeans and red shirt, and began laughing.

"Ah ha, people! Now, where the hell am I?" Eve shouted with excitement and a touch of anger in her voice.

"I'm Lisa and this is Luke," Lisa said, pulling him inside the room. Eve saw the skinny man Lisa pulled inside and saw that he was wearing the same colour shirt and jeans.

"Are you twins or something?" she asked.

"No." Luke said, looking at the floor.

"He copies me," Lisa said.

"I can't tell you anything and I don't expect you to trust me, but I have that ask you wear this," Lisa said, taking out the blindfold.

"Two minutes and we will be on a new floor and on our way to the boss, who will answer your questions. Is that okay?"

Eve allowed her to put the blindfold on and then she noticed something.

"What did you say, Luke?" Eve asked.

"Er, nothing," Luke said quietly.

"No, you said something about Lisa, or … I think so." Eve opened her eyes once the blindfold was on and was upset that she could not see through the material.

They led her out of the room and to the left. Lisa got out the key she needed to enter a staircase. They had not known about this until John told them not ten minutes ago. She put the key in the now obvious lock and turned it. The door opened, revealing a small staircase. *I can't believe I didn't work out this was here,* Lisa thought.

"Nice to see I'm not the only one in the dark," Eve said.

Luke looked at the blindfolded girl.

"Sorry?" Lisa said, turning to her as well.

"I'm in some strange staircase that you had not been told about. It's nice to hear that I'm not the only one that doesn't know what is going on," she replied.

"Ah, crap. She's a telepath," Luke said.

Lisa and Luke took a step back.

"What?" Eve asked.

"We'd best get you upstairs," Luke said. *Quickly*, Lisa thought.

"What the hell have you done to me!?" Eve cried. She started to fight back against the two people holding her arms. They held on tight and Eve started to relax. She had a sudden realization that they had done something to her but there was a boss up the stairs who would answer her questions, and she would plan on really letting go on them, for everything that had happened to her since she woke up. The two people here didn't know much and were therefore not worth her wasting energy on. The person upstairs was responsible for her life being ruined. Eve could now taste the adrenaline in her mouth.

"We're not going to keep anything from you. Our boss is upstairs and he will explain everything," Lisa said, trying not to hold on tight.

They started walking her slowly up the stairs. Eve only cooperated because she knew there was someone responsible only a few moments away and that she would demand her answers. If she was now what they said she was, it would be impossible for this man to lie to her.

44

Round the corner and up another narrow flight was a door with a key pad. Lisa put in the code that John had given her.

"I'll remember that code, thanks," Eve said.

Lisa and Luke shared a look.

They pushed the door open and walked onto the blue floor. They looked around in amazement. As difficult as it was, they didn't see their boss. Then he was standing, waiting for them. He was waiting for them to leave when they'd only just arrived.

"Thanks," he said. His voice interrupted their trains of thought. "I'll take it from here."

He motioned for them to leave and they did so, without a word.

Just as they were closing the door the colonel stopped it. "Please give me an hour, OK?" He took Eve's hand and with the other, removed her blindfold.

The door closed.

"Hello Eve, I am Jim Bartlett. Follow me and I'll explain what is going on." Eve stopped and snatched her hand away. He stopped and turned to face her. "I hope you don't mind, but for now can I call you Eve? We've grown quite used to calling you that name up until now." She ignored him.

"Wow, he's not too nice today," Lisa said as they made their way back to the lab. She and Luke walked back, securing everything they'd opened while discussing Eve's ability. They walked into John's office and saw him sitting in his chair.

"John, we've got an hour before we can go and get Jack." John nodded and pointed to the monitors, which now showed B2 and what was going on. Patrick had called and informed him that the CCTV permissions had been changed. He could access cameras there now. John had the speakers on and they listened intently.

"How did...-" Lisa started to ask. John hushed her and pointed to the screens.

Eve sat down on the edge of her new bed, in what Jim had said was to be her new room for now.

"So, what is this place?" She made herself more comfortable and listened intently to what this man had to say. She was a bit scared of him, he was physically intimidating, but she mostly feared the level of authority he had.

"It's a facility that I own and run for human experimentation. You and a man called Jack have been here over seventeen months."

Eve looked at him in shock and tears began to form in her eyes.

"I know this will be hard to hear but I'm going to be honest with you. If you'll allow me to finish, then you can ask whatever questions you like."

Eve nodded and breathed in hard enough to stay calm.

"I've been working all my life to be the perfect soldier. Years ago I started training men and women to become the best they could be within their field. I did all I could make them reach their full potential.

"Ten years ago, I heard of something called 'The Human Genome project'. This was a project where scientists theorized that humans could possibly speed up the evolutionary process. If successful, we could alter mankind, giving additional abilities to people so they could make a difference, set an example that others would follow. So we began. We started working with the project. Five years ago I separated and set up this facility. John and the other scientists are the ones I chose because they're at the top of their field. They came to the conclusion that a certain type of person - you and Jack - had a specific genetic structure. This would serve perfectly as a template. The two of you were not the only match, there were a handful of people we found around the world. You and Jack were the only ones we could make disappear, with minimal effect on others."

Eve couldn't hold back any more, she began sobbing and pulled the pillow up to her face, trying to hide and dry her tears.

Jim continued. "Eve, we found you in a hospital bed. You had been admitted from a car accident. You were in a coma; you'd been there almost six months. Both of your parents had passed on before your accident, you had no close family and your visits slowly dwindled. I'm sorry, but we simply took you and brought you here. You still have a chance to see those you love again one day. I'm sorry, truly I am. It won't seem like it at the moment, but we did you a kindness.

"We have succeeded in altering your genes. All I ask is that you remain here and we can see your true potential. It's truly unfair to have taken you away and for that, again, I am sorry. No one could predict if you would ever recover from your coma. Here, we have managed to help you."

Jim lowered his head to her height. He waited for her reaction.

Eve's eyes were now red; she'd been rubbing them furiously, trying to calm herself and dry the tears that had now fully opened the floodgates.

"I would have made it through! How dare you deny me the chance to fight for my own survival! My friends would have been distraught. You've taken my freedom and played around with people's feelings. When do I get out of here?"

"We can't discuss that now. Your body has been repaired using growth techniques and your DNA has been modified in ways that I have no idea how to explain."

Eve's head snapped up when he said this.

"I feel different. I can't explain it. When the woman I saw just now put the blindfold on I could hear the guy she was with, talking. But somehow his voice was different. Like an actor's voice during a monologue. I could tell where he was but not through seeing him. He fancies her, so far as I can make out." She closed her eyes, as if in discomfort. "Is there more to come? How do I control this? When the blindfold came off everything went back to normal."

"We will help you, train you. This isn't a government building. I'm the only one who has any say in what happens here." Jim put a big hand on her shoulder.

"Eve, can you please close your eyes and see if you can hear my thoughts?"

She closed her eyes; her eyebrows frowned in concentration. "I can't really see or hear. Something about a house, a wooden house and there is a woman sitting in a rocking chair -"

"Open your eyes." Jim had gotten out of his chair and was holding her hands.

She jumped and opened her eyes at his touch.

"I saw everything!" she exclaimed. "You were in your chair." She was eager to tell him what she'd seen. "I was following your thoughts. I felt you getting out of your chair and when you touched me I saw the whole memory. It was your old house in Texas. Your wife was sitting on the porch, watching you walk up the driveway. You'd just gotten back from Vietnam where you'd -

"That's great, Eve." Jim interjected. His voice was elevated. "You're telepathic! When you close your eyes you can tune into other people's minds, their thoughts are open for you to read. It would seem that when you touch them, somehow it becomes amplified or you have more focus on their mind. We'll help you train your mind so that you can develop and control it."

Eve looked him in the eye and smiled. "Perhaps you've done me a sort of kindness after all; but I'll never forget what you've done. I would have fought through. I'm stronger than I look." She stood up. Eve looked keen to learn about this place and what she could now be capable of. "I'll stay, I'll help you and when I'm done, I get my freedom." She put out her hand and Jim shook it without a word.

They conversed for a while about what had happened. Jim had a device on him so that Eve could look at how the people she knew were doing, what they'd been up to since she'd been unconscious. The vast majority were settling down with their partners and having children. Eve didn't want to go and see them until she was better. She wanted more control over herself. Jim told her she could have far more potential but it could take a while before she would have complete control over her ability. She talked to him about her time in quarantine and they moved on to her name. "I think I'd prefer being called Eve. My old life has been cut short for me and now I'm here, in this place full of people who know me literally inside out". She took in a big sigh. "I just want to be happy and I think if I start fresh, I have more chance." Jim nodded. He could see the tears well up in her eyes, but chose to ignore them. He smiled at her and thought a change of topic would be in order.

"Eve, in your new room there is a shower and a toilet. Would you like to make yourself at home while I go and see the head of research? You'll be alone, there are cameras in here and microphones, so if you need anything, just ask. I'll be back in twenty minutes." Jim half grinned. Eve turned to get a good look around her new room. She saw clean clothes and food packaging had been left on a table in the corner. She noticed that there was a running machine. *When was the last time I went for a run?* she thought.

Eve turned around and saw only an empty chair. "Maybe he has an ability, too," she joked to herself; she got off the bed and walked over to the running machine.

"She's a telepath, John," Jim said.

The two men were in John's office with the door open. The other scientists were working within earshot of their conversation.

"How is she taking it?" John asked while glancing at the screen picture of Jack, sitting on his bed playing drums on his thighs.

"How do you think, John? It's a pretty big shock but she's handling herself well. Why wasn't the report on your desk about this earlier?" Jim was reading the report Lisa and Luke showed John just before heading to B2.

"Colonel, you scare the staff. They didn't want to disturb you."

"So, it's circulatory? What could be his ability?" Jim said glancing at the screen John was half watching.

"It could be anything. But we think it might be a sort of replication ability. Like an energy sponge perhaps," John said.

"So he could absorb energy from those he touches?" Jim closed the file and looked at his watch.

"It's possible," John said, taking the file as Jim handed it over.

"Get him ready. I'll meet him on B2," Jim said walking out of John's office.

"Lisa?" John said, knowing full well she could hear him without raising his voice. "Can you and Luke go and get Jack, please? Be careful not to touch his skin, so you'll have to wear these." John gave them rubber gloves to wear and they went off to the tank.

"I wonder what he can do." Luke said as they cleared the airlock.

"Well it's something John doesn't want us taking any risk over," Lisa said. "Ready?" she asked as she was putting in the code, and as before, she opened the door before Luke could answer.

The door opened and Lisa went in first.

"Well, it's about time!" Jack said as Lisa walked into the room.

"Hi, I'm Lisa, this is Luke," she said as she pulled him through the door, again.

"Hello. So, am I being set free or just moved today?" Jack said jokingly, holding out his arms in a gesture for them to put handcuffs on.

"There is no need for that but you have to wear this because security -"

"I'd just like to play along. Sorry for interrupting, but I just want to know what is going on here," Jack said before Lisa could continue.

"Okay. Please turn around." Luke said, holding out the blindfold.

They walked him out of the room and towards the staircase. Lisa and Luke each kept a hand on his forearms. Their long sleeved shirts and gloves kept Jack's skin away from theirs as John had asked. Inside the staircase, Jack started to try and walk faster. The blindfold didn't seem to hinder his pace. Lisa and Luke increased their pace to match his.

"Please wait here a sec," Lisa said as she turned to input the code.

The door opened.

"Thank you, I'll take over from here," Jim said as they stepped into the room.

This time, they just turned around and went down the stairs without a second look. Jack was standing there with his blindfold on, his arms cupped together in front of him.

Jim was wearing a pair of gloves, like Luke and Lisa. He had taken off his suit jacket, allowing his own long sleeved shirt to cover the remainder of his skin.

He walked over and removed Jack's blindfold.

"Hello, Jack. I'm Jim Bartlett. I'm sure you've got a lot of questions. First I'd like to apologize for the formality but for the time being I'll call you Jack, as that's how we've come to know you. I hope that's okay?"

Jack shrugged his shoulders. What did he care what they called him? He looked at the strange blue room he was in. In front of him, he saw Jim.

"Sir, I would -" Jack began before Jim quickly raised his right hand, stopping him in his tracks.

"Do you remember anything?" Jim asked.

Jack looked him in the eye. "I remember everything, sir. The last thing I remember, before this place, was sitting on London Bridge. I looked up when I heard some guy say something to me, but I didn't quite hear. I went to stand up and then - nothing, just black. The next thing I know, I woke up in a padded room, half expecting to be tied up with a gag in my mouth. It was a padded cell, nothing to do and no one to talk to. I heard a voice. It came out of nowhere. What did you do to me? I've had fantastic luck, ending up in a fancy rehab clinic or the government had taken me and I'm now some sort of guinea pig. Which is it, mate?" he asked. All the humour had gone from his face.

"Neither. But your first guess is the closest," Jim answered.

Jim ran through the details as he had with Eve. Jack had no sadness, as his life before was empty. He had no family that he could think of and no friends. He had fallen into a life of poverty. After college, he had landed a job in investment banking. He was good at his job and it took over his life. He had everything; money, friends and the woman of his dreams. One bad decision ruined his life. He lost his job, his girlfriend left him. His friends deserted him after he lost everything. He was a broken man. He sold everything he could and drifted around the world for a few years. The money ran out and he returned home. He had lost the will to work. The travelling had kept him happy but his broken heart had taken away all the fun he'd had. He returned home. He had nothing to his name. Not even friends. He went and tracked down his ex-girlfriend only to find her happily moved on. She barely recognised him. He'd drifted off and spent a few months living off his wits around London, before deciding to sleep on London Bridge, the last night he could remember. Jack sided with Eve on starting afresh.

"Eve is in the room next door, but I would like to find out exactly what ability you have before we go any further." Jim stood up and put his arm around Jack's shoulder.

They walked into the smaller box and Jim sat down on one of the chairs that had built-in restraints. The clamps closed when he sat down, securing him to the chair by his thighs, ankles, upper arms and wrists.

"Okay, that's pretty hard core," Jack said, taking a step back. He started admiring the chair Jim was now securely fastened to, from a distance.

"Would you mind closing the door?" Jim said in a calm voice. The fact that he was now trapped in the chair hadn't bothered him at all.

Jack turned and closed the door and when he did, a glass pole shot up, effectively sealing them inside.

"The room is now secure. Nothing gets in. Nothing gets out."

A wave of panic shot through Jack like he had just been electrocuted.

"Another locked room!? At least the other one had a bed and a bog! Why, oh why are we stuck in here?" Jack was shouting, trying to push the door and when that did nothing he tried pulling the pole down, with the same result.

"Jack, you have a kind of ability that affects others when you touch them. We don't know what exactly it is that you can do. This is only a precaution. I would like you to touch my face with your hands. I'm secure here so that whatever happens, you'll be protected from me." Jack leaned against the glass, sweat now coming from his forehead.

"But what protects you from me?" he asked. Jim smiled. "So I touch you, and no one has any idea what's going to happen?"

"That's about it, yes." Jim said.

Jack stood still for what seemed like an eternity. He shook his head and looked down at his hands.

"It's going to be okay" Jim said.

"Sure. And Hell is just a sauna." Jack said.

He looked at Jim, who still looked calm. "Well, nothing to lose I guess. Are you ready to begin?" he said to probably the only man to be happy with what was going to happen. Jack's hands were shaking. He clenched his fists tight, opened them and walked towards Jim, his right hand outstretched.

Chapter 3

Thresholds

Jack stopped a few inches from Jim's face. He didn't close his eyes or flinch in any way and it was almost as if Jim had no fear of the situation he was in.

"Look, I don't know if this is a good idea and I don't want to hurt anyone," Jack said nervously. His fingers were outstretched and his whole hand was trembling.

Jack was taken aback by the realisation that he had not been in human contact, at least with anyone's skin, since he had been awake and now he wasn't sure what would happen if he touched this man. He had rubber gloves on, as did the two scientists who had brought him up here.

"Relax and try not to think." Jim said. A strange smile had crept into one corner of his mouth and his head had relaxed against the headrest.

Jack put his right hand on Jim's face. The connection was like nothing he had ever felt before. The feeling was similar to the pins and needles that most people felt when a part of their body had gone to sleep, only this feeling was running up his arm and into his body. Jack focused on the skin he was touching and could feel Jim's pulse. It was very strong, such as might belong to an Olympic athlete after a competition. Jack's mind wandered for a minute. He thought that this wasn't uncomfortable. In fact, this was quite pleasant, it was then he opened his eyes. He had thought about Jim and realized he hadn't looked at the man he was touching. He saw Jim's taut frame. Jim had the look of a man who was holding onto an electric fence and couldn't let go. Jack let go of his face immediately and Jim's body slumped back into the chair, heavy breathing took over and Jim's eyes closed. Jack felt something different inside him. He sat down on the chair Jim had previously placed in the box. He couldn't take his eyes off the man who he had just seen in such pain. Jim was now fully relaxed in the restraints, and had begun to breathe normally.

Jack looked down at his hands and could feel a kind of nourishment throughout his body, like in some way touching Jim had a recharging effect on him.

"Wow, I feel pretty good," Jack said, still looking absent-mindedly at his hands.

After a few minutes Jim opened his eyes. His head was tilted back in the chair and he was looking up at the ceiling, his eyes focusing on the slight reflection of himself in the box. His breathing was calm now and he moved his head down to look at Jack.

"Did you say something?" Jim hadn't made sense of the words Jack had said while his body was recovering.

"Sorry?" Jack looked up and focused on Jim, remembering where he was and what had happened nearly three minutes ago. He started wondering if he had drifted off into a dream world. He was looking into Jim's eyes; he looked tired, like a man who had just woken up from a short sleep.

"I said I felt good. Sorry. I could feel your pulse through your skin. It's almost like I was using you to recharge. It wasn't until I saw what I was doing to you that I realised I had to let go. Are you feeling okay?"

"Yeah, I'm okay. It felt like you were, in fact, using me to recharge. I could feel my body getting weaker and there was nothing I could do about it. My mind had shut down the ability to react. I've never felt like that before."

Jack told Jim about the pins and needles feeling and how it was coming from his hand and going into his body, giving him the feeling of being recharged. Jim listened intently, remembering what that felt like.

"Do you want to try and see if anything else happens when you touch my hand or arm? You may be able to recharge people. Would you like to give it a try?"

Jack seemed eager to try this out; he made a mental note not to hold on too long and to let go the instant Jim looked in much pain.

"Ready when you are," Jim said. He closed his eyes, preparing himself for what was coming.

Jack stood up from his chair and in the step it took to reach Jim, raised his right hand and grasped Jim's left glove. He removed it and gripped his hand.

The feeling returned to Jack's arm and this time he noticed the rigidity in Jim when he took hold of him. The feeling was running up Jack's arm and into his body. Jack focused on the feeling and tried to control it. Jack felt the feeling slowly pause and eventually become neutral, staying inside the crook of his elbow joint. He had stopped the flow. He felt Jim's arm relax. Jack concentrated and felt his body react to his command, it felt almost as natural to reverse it and Jack could feel the pins and needles moving from his arm into Jim. Then Jim's arm went rigid suddenly, his body seemed to react more to the reversal and the grip Jim now had on Jack's hand was rather painful. The look on Jim's face was one of torture. He tried to break the grip but he could feel his body feeding Jim's. It wasn't unpleasant, but the grip was. After a short while of watching Jim's body, he started to loosen his grip. He thought about letting go, but decided Jim would want to play this out to the end so he held on.

After a few more minutes, Jack let go of Jim and sat back in his chair, watching the relaxed man in the chair in front of him. He didn't look recharged, even though Jack wouldn't know how that looked; nor did he look any different. As Jack was watched Jim, he started to daydream and then something caught his eye. Jim's face started to fade from view then returned to normal. Jack broke from his daydream and leaned forward in anticipation. He wasn't sure if he had seen this or not. After a few moments Jim's face disappeared. Jack leaned back in his chair in shock, if the chair wasn't against the wall of the box, Jack would have certainly gone backwards.

Jim's body was gone, His clothing hadn't moved, it still rose and fell as if Jim was still there, breathing, but there was no sign of a person. Only the suit remained.

Almost as quickly as it disappeared, Jim's face and body reappeared. Jim's eyes were open and there was a look of concern on his face.

"Jack, are you okay?"

"I'm fine. Are you okay?" Jack was sitting in his chair with his mouthy slightly open, still in awe at what had just happened.

"How's this possible?" Jack asked.

"What happened while I was out?" Jim was concerned now. He did feel different somehow. His skin had a different feel to it. Jim was now looking at his hands, wondering what Jack had seen happen to him while he was out.

"You disappeared. Only you didn't, if that's possible? I'm not sure. This is too much for me to process at the moment." Jack sat back in his chair allowing his head to relax against the glass and closed his eyes.

"Jack?" Jim asked. He wanted to be out of the restraints.

"John, please release me."

John was sitting right on the edge of his chair looking at the monitors which now showed the floor on B2. One monitor showed the main area from the lift lobby and the two boxes Jack and Eve would now be staying in. The second showed from the walkway to the back wall. John had been watching the whole time Jack and Eve had been on B2 and everything that had happened with Jim. Luke and Lisa were standing behind him watching the monitors. John looked at his computer, which had now rebooted with updated software, allowing him to access various programs. He had no idea what most of them were for but he was certain this would become clear in the near future.

John turned and slipped off the edge of his chair. His right hand slammed hard on the desk, just stopping him from what would have been an embarrassing fall to the floor.

"Wow! That was close, John," Lisa said, reaching out to him. Making sure he was okay

"Yeah, thanks," he said, sitting back in his chair, facing the computer. He opened a program labelled as 'left box'. An item labelled as 'restraints' caught his eye and he opened it. A small box opened on his screen. 'Set' and 'reset' were the only options available. He clicked on 'reset' and turned to the monitors and saw Jim kneeling next to Jack, who was now sitting forward with his head in his hands.

Jack started explaining to Jim what he had seen while he was out and Jim was trying to keep Jack calm. His speech was erratic, from what Jim assumed was a slight case of shock. Jim couldn't blame him for feeling this way.

It's not every day you discover you have the ability to alter people just by touching them.

"It's okay"

Jack sat up and looked at Jim. "What's the end game, Jim? What is it you want?"

Jim sat down in the chair next to him.

"I want to help. However, your abilities are more than I could have dreamed of. I've got to re-think about how to help out now. You and Eve are of great importance to me and the work I hope we can do together should start to make the world a better place. This has been a huge success!"

Jack looked at Jim in wonder. All the possibilities were running through his head. There was a real opportunity now to change things. Jack was very aware that he was going to be useful now. The only thing that remained to be seen was for what purpose.

Jack looked at Jim. "Can you try?"

Jim looked at Jack; he was going through the options on what to do now. His own ability had almost escaped his attention. He looked at his hands and tried to relax his mind. As difficult as it was, he managed to relax and focused on what he was doing.

"It doesn't seem to be working. I think the excitement has to pass before I can concentrate."

"Well, remember what I told you. It only happened when you were calming down, your breathing relaxed and you just started to disappear. When you woke up, you came back."

Jim nodded and remembered how he felt when he woke up. The distraction had helped him focus and he tried to relax his muscles as much as he could. Jim closed his eyes and Jack took in a sharp breath.

Jim looked down and saw his hands had gone. The feeling was apparent to him now. It was like he had put his muscles to sleep and focused on not getting excited. Jim's sight was as normal as ever but now he couldn't see his nose. It was an odd sensation. It reminded him of when he had polished one of his favourite cars and how a clean windshield, without the small triangle the wipers never reached looked. It was a good feeling. Jim leaned forward and reached for his trouser leg. He felt the soft fibres between his fingers and pulled it up, revealing his socks and he could see the floor where his legs should have been. Jim smiled and looked up.

Jack was watching with great interest. It reminded him of an old film he'd seen about a man who, through a freak accident, became invisible. He was now watching an empty suit move at will and he had to resist laughter from the very notion of what he was seeing.

"How do you feel?" he asked. A small chuckle escaped as he thought about talking to an empty suit.

"Fine. I guess. It's weird being here but I'm not, if that makes sense?" Jim stood up and Jack could resist no longer. He burst out laughing.

"I'm guessing a suit talking with no one in it would be amusing." He let out a chuckle of his own.

Jim sat down and let the feeling pass. He saw his nose once more and Jack finished laughing. Jim looked past him and saw Eve.

"John, could you please release the security locks?"

A few moments later the pole shot back into the floor. This caused Eve to jump a little. She looked at where the pole had gone, cautiously opened the door and walked over. She saw where the pole lived now. It was flush with the floor. If she hadn't seen it go back in she would have sworn it was a part of the tiling. Jim motioned for her to come in and she walked towards the chair that was in between Jack and Jim.

"'Hi. I'm Eve," she said to Jack, holding her hand out.

Jack turned and saw her. He admired the beautiful woman that was standing to his left. She was quite short, with long, dark red hair. Her ivory skin and green eyes almost took his breath away. He remembered he had to speak before she noticed he was staring.

"Hi. Jack Gibson. It's a pleasure to meet you," Jack said, shaking her hand. He could feel the pins and needles in his hand and forearm but managed to just about keep it steady. He didn't think Jim would appreciate him hurting her.

"I see the clothes fit, Eve," Jim said, standing up.

Eve was dressed in a dark pair of jeans and a white fitted T-shirt. As she walked, the blue slippers she was wearing made a slight squeaking noise.

"Thanks. I think so. It's nice to be in clothes instead of those pyjama things I spent a week in." Eve chuckled and sat down.

"Ah, so you were my neighbour?" Jack said, trying to put some of his own humour into the conversation.

Eve turned to him and smiled. She could now see Jack's features fully. He body was quite toned; his pyjamas fell loosely over his frame. He had blue-grey eyes Eve hadn't seen before and there didn't appear to be a black outline around them. He had brown hair and a strange, crooked smile on his face. She couldn't resist widening her smile in response.

"They were lined with antibacterial material, quite necessary at the time. I'm sorry if they weren't comfortable." Jim said, moving between the two chairs and squatting to their height. He rested his hands on the chair arms and looked back and forth between them.

"I don't think they are that bad." Jack said flicking imaginary dust off his shoulders towards Eve.

"That's something a homeless person would say," she said, ignoring his gesture.

"Well, I was." Jack chuckled and looked at Jim, who was smiling. He turned to Eve who had gone a shade of red, her eyes wide not sure how to react.

"Jack, would you mind giving me and Jim a minute?" she asked quietly.

Jack turned to Jim who nodded. "Sure. I'll go test out the bathroom." Jack stood and turned to go out of the room.

"Jack," Eve called out after him.

He turned and smiled. "Don't worry, I'll be back soon."

"No, I was just warning you that I've already taken the room on the left," she said back to him.

He winked at her and continued down the walkway.

"It's nice to see you two getting along," Jim said, patting her hand.

He moved and sat back in his previous chair.

"He's confused as to what you're planning on using him for. And to be frank, so am I." Eve said.

Jim looked at her and leaned forward. "I see you're getting the hang of your ability, Eve. I can't lie to you. I honestly don't know what to do next. There are so many possibilities. But you have my word, I won't ask anything of you that you would think to be wrong."

She smiled. Eve was getting the hang of how to read minds now. She was in the shower when she heard Jack going through options and scenarios. She was glad to be around him and Jim, as using the abilities for wrongdoing hadn't stayed in their thoughts long. She had been entertaining herself with all the different options she could use hers for and she was excited to find out what was next.

She was hoping to make a difference in the world; these thoughts were mirrored in what she was getting from Jim.

"We can't move on to anything before we know fully about the limits on our abilities," Jim said, smiling.

"Wow! You have to show me," Eve said in response to what Jim already knew she saw in his head.

"Okay. You can help, in fact," Jim said, sitting back preparing to use his ability.

Eve saw what he was asking and nodded.

Jim relaxed and allowed himself to disappear. A chuckle escaped from his mouth as Eve stared at the now empty suit sitting comfortably in the chair opposite her.

"Hahaha, I can still hear you," She said, sitting back proudly in her chair.

"I was wondering if it was a manipulation of people's visual equality. John. Please tell me if you can see me."

"No, colonel," John's voice echoed around the floor.

"Eve...-" Jim began.

"No, Jim. I can hear you though. Jack's singing in the shower. He has a terrible voice, in case you're interested." She smiled and Jim did too.

"Well, you can hear very well through the boxes, which is impressive. The material is very thick," Jim returned and Eve clapped.

"I don't think I'd come back if I could do that," she said.

"It's tempting but I'd find it rather rude."

Jim and Eve joked about fighting crime, then discussed helping out with court cases and whether it would be a good idea to see if psychics were real or not.

After a while Jack entered the box, dressed like Eve.

"Sorry I took so long. It's a great shower," he said to Jim, who motioned him to sit in the chair he'd placed next to Eve.

"Jack, please close the door before you have a seat." Jack stopped and looked at Eve.

"What's going on now?" he asked.

"Jim wants to see what happens when you touch me," Eve said. The smile she had worn most of afternoon was there, but it was more for show than happiness. Jack could see she felt uneasy about this experiment.

Jack closed the door and the pole slid into place.

"Great, so you've been discussing this while I was gone." Jack felt like a group had formed and he was not a part of it.

"Jack, we've done no such thing," Eve said with a look of empathy on her face.

Jack looked blankly at her. *Did I say that out loud?* he thought.

"No," Eve said. Her smile became genuine.

"Jack, she developed telepathy, I don't have a word to describe your skill," Jim said. He was relaxing in the chair he was once a prisoner of.

"Okay, that's going to suck. You'll always be in everyone's head?" Jack asked.

"I won't always, but it's fun," Eve said, unsuccessfully holding back a chuckle. "Three hundred and twenty seven," she added, bursting out in laughter.

"Crap," Jack said, sitting down.

"Eve, would you mind -" Jim began.

"Sure." Eve stood up and walked over to swap chairs with him.

"Don't you find that annoying?" Jack said to Jim as they crossed paths.

"Funnily enough, he doesn't mind," Eve said as she was making herself comfortable.

Jack and Jim shared a look of understanding and Jack shrugged. "I guess it's another something to get used to," he said, standing up.

"John, can you please secure Eve," Jim asked, sitting.

The restraints shut in place and Eve let out a startled yelp. Jack jumped at the sound while Jim remained unmoved.

"You okay?" Jack said. He was right next to her and leaned in while he asked.

"No. But I know you don't want to hurt me. I can see what happened. Only it's worse for me because I saw what Jim had to endure and I can see what you saw, just before you stopped. Think I'll stop listening now," Eve said, trying hard to stare at the ceiling and not to use her ability.

"Jim, what did you want to try first?" Jack asked, all the while looking at the worry on Eve's face.

"What happens when you recharge yourself, please?" Jim said leaning forward.

Jack put his hand out and touched Eve's forehead. Her whole body stiffened against the restraints and a noise of stress came out of her mouth, followed by a sharp scream. Jack let go and she slumped in the chair, tears weeping from her emotionless face. He looked at Jim, who nodded and he reached forward again, with tears in his own eyes. Jack tried to keep focus and kept the flow in a slow movement this time. He concentrated and felt something strange going on inside his own head. He could feel her pain from her point of view. Jack felt the flow slow even more and Eve's body relaxed. Jack didn't like the images he was getting from Eve's mind. He put his other hand on hers and made it so that the flow was going in full circle.

Jim saw him doing this and moved to stand next to him.

"Jack, what's happening?" Jim asked in a slightly worried tone.

Jim was worried about what would happen about trying too much too fast.

Jack was not paying any attention to what Jim was saying. He could feel Eve's stress leave her body and she relaxed.

Jack let go and Eve opened her eyes. She didn't look affected by what had happened; Jack had evened out the flow so that she hadn't been. *Those are quite strange,* Eve thought, looking at Jack's eyes.

"Like I haven't heard that before," Jack said.

She looked at him, dumbfounded. "I didn't say that out loud," she whispered. Eve motioned for Jim to hold her hand and he took it without hesitation.

"I don't feel the pins and needles," she said, slightly disappointed.

"John, release Eve, please," Jim said and the restraints went back to their original position.

Jack moved to sit down but Jim and Eve moved him towards the chair Eve was sitting in and once he was seated, the restraints automatically snapped on. Jack looked at them and laughed. "I'm not going to go berserk," he joked.

Jack could hear Eve repeating over and over about closing the door.

"Jack, close the door in your head. It will go away. Just focus," she finally said out loud. Jack listened; he became less confused and understood what she meant. He concentrated and shut that part of his brain off, now the only thing he could hear was his own breathing.

"That's much better." Eve said.

"Jack, do you want to try again? Only this time let's see what happens when you touch me." Eve and Jack looked at

Jim in surprise. This was becoming more complicated than they had all thought; Jim wanted to push the limits today.

"John, please release Jack." The restraints went and Jack stood up.

He moved out of the way, not saying a word, and once Jim was in place asked, "Are you sure?"

Jim opened his hands. Jack shrugged and took them in his own. This time Jim's body barely moved. Jack was concentrating on keeping a full circle going clockwise. His forehead creased from the effort and once he was comfortable with the flow and Jim's stress level he smiled. Jack relaxed and Eve gasped. Both of them disappeared. Their clothing remained and Eve took two steps back and fell into the chair behind her. Jack noticed this and let go of Jim, who reappeared and in shock would have jumped out of the chair had the restraints not been in place.

"Wow!" Jack was looking at where his hands should have been and saw only the floor. He remembered how he'd panicked when he had absorbed Eve's ability and closed his eyes, trying to relax.

"John," was all Jim got out before the restraints went and the distraction brought Jack back to the present.

Jack turned and saw Jim and immediately, sat in the chair behind him. "I'm fine Jim, please don't worry."

Jim stopped and slightly raised his hands with his palms facing up.

"Well, what do you want to do next to try and break the limits of our sanity?" Jack asked with all the humour he could muster.

Eve put a hand up to her face to hide the laughter and Jim sat back down in the chair.

John, seeing an opportunity, activated the restraints securing Jim to the chair, causing the three of them in the box and the three of them in John's office to break out in laughter.

"That's very funny, John," Jim said and the restraints disappeared.

"Sorry, sir, I couldn't resist." John's voice echoed around the floor. John released the button and leaned back in his chair.

"Well, Jack. Your ability appears to be more than meets the eye," Jim said, relaxing back in the chair closed his eyes, steadying his breathing, and vanished.

Eve looked at the suit in amusement. "Showing off now, are we?"

Jim came back into view wearing a big grin. "I think it's time we got something to eat. Don't you agree?"

Lisa and Luke brought down food from the lunch room; sandwiches and cans of Coke from the vending machines. Jim took this opportunity to properly introduce them. Eve saw that Jim had intended to get some of his staff on first name basis with her and Jack. Over the years he had maintained a distant relationship with them, due to security and the job that they had to carry out in the facility. It seemed that Jim no longer wanted the place to be a scientific facility, due to the results they had and it was to become something else, in part.

"I'm really glad to finally get to have a conversation with you two." Lisa was with Jack, discussing the past week, the strange day he was having and what work she had been doing on them.

"Well, I'm glad you let me out of that cell. A week in there was not fun at all. I don't think I've ever been that bored or confused in my life. Jim says it was for healing or something?" Jack was glad of conversation. Since he had awoken in quarantine the only communication he had had was with voices that come from speakers.

69

"We had to see what you could do before we could move you. You'd been out a long time, so healing was a big part of it." Lisa was not sure how much Jim wanted her to share with them. He was on the phone with John discussing what was next.

Luke was trying to talk to Eve about how she felt and how her ability worked. She was doing her best to look interested in their conversation but, she was picking up on what Jim was taking to John about.

"Okay, John. We'll discuss it tomorrow." Jim hung up his phone and walked over to the table and picked up his sandwich.

"I think it's time we left you to get some rest. It's been a long day and I'm sure you both need it."

Lisa and Luke seemed a little upset to be leaving so soon, but disobeying Jim was not an option, so they said their goodbyes and got into the lift with Jim, leaving Eve and Jack alone on the floor.

Both of them tried picking up what was going through Jim's head, but he was thinking in Vietnamese.

"Did you pick up anything?" Jack whispered, staring at the lift.

"Nothing I could understand. I wonder what's in store for us tomorrow," she said, reaching for another apple.

"Not sure. I'm guessing him leaving us to chat with the two who brought us here was so he could make a call," Jack mused.

Eve didn't seem to be bothered. She liked where they were and the ability was something she'd never dreamed of having. Jim wasn't a bad man as far as she could tell. They were safe and had their own place to sleep. She understood Jack's doubts, but no one could lie to them now and she was excited to see what would happen tomorrow.

"Now that I think about it, I could do with some sleep." Eve put the apple on the table and walked towards her sleeping quarters.

"Think I'll have a work-out before its time to call it a day," Jack said.

"Don't make a racket." Eve was starting to yawn as they parted company. They entered their separate rooms. Jack got on the treadmill as Eve got ready for bed.

Jim left the lift on the ground level and walked around to the right. He pulled his access card from his trouser pocket and swiped it over a tile on the wall, which was one shade darker than the rest. He pushed the wall and the small door opened to a dark void.

Inside, Jim closed the door and lights flickered into life. He was standing in a large room. To the rear was a black wall. He made his way over there, past a large black leather sofa and a coffee table, which had all the reports from the scientists on B3, along with various security reports. He pushed a door in the black wall, which led to his office. Once the door was closed, CCTV monitors glowed into life, showing lots of live camera angles from inside and outside the facility, including images from each floor. Jim could see all the scientists getting ready to finish for the day. Jim watched the images of what Jack and Eve were doing. He smiled to himself and his eyes moved to another set of images, showing a floor quite different from the ones he'd been on today. This one had various rooms; one appeared to be a gym with only three machines inside. There was another one which was very long with thick straps attached at one end, another room with blocks of metal varying from very small to very large, stacked in size and weight order. There was a gun range of sorts, a decent swimming pool, and a games room with a table at the far end, with various stick-and-block games. The final room looked identical to one of the quarantine rooms. This one had no bed or toilet. It was rectangular, covered from floor to ceiling in padding. Jim's eyes moved over each image and he sat down in a big leather chair in front of a large desk. The final camera showed a narrow walkway in between these rooms, which led to a pair of steel doors resembling a lift entrance.

Jim's mobile phone started ringing.

"Hello, Patrick. Give me a second."

Jim got up and walked over to the entrance to his room and opened the door.

Patrick walked in and went straight over to the sofa and sat down. "It's been a successful day then, Colonel?" he asked, making himself comfortable.

"Yes, very," Jim replied, closing the door and walking over to where Patrick was sitting. "Tomorrow, I'll have to decide on what is next. Jack's ability, I feel, will be extremely useful."

"When can I shake this man's hand? I don't want to be left out of this."

"I'll have to think about that also. I'm not going to ask him to just hand out abilities. You know how bad this could get if someone got something we can't control."

"Colonel, I'm fully aware. I just hope you're not going to keep me out of this. In all our years together, have I ever let you down?"

Jim looked at Patrick and leaned forward so they were only a foot apart. "No, but you're well aware of my concerns, aren't you, Captain?"

Patrick sank back in the sofa, maintaining eye contact with Jim. "Sir," he replied quietly.

Patrick got up from the sofa and made his way back to the entrance, "Colonel, that was a long time ago and if I do get carried away, you've the means to prevent things getting out of hand. I am only asking you to put me first in line for any trials."

Jim turned around, "We go back a long way, Patrick. I'll keep you at the top of the list, but one mistake and you're out."

"Sir." Patrick opened the door and headed back towards the reception desk.

Jim sat in his chair behind his desk and got out a folder with the heading *The Facility*.

He skipped to the back where there was a list of names; Jack Gibson, Eve Foster, Jim Bartlett. He sat back in his chair and thought for a few minutes. He went through various situations that could occur, some of which made him smile. Jim went back to the list and added some names: Patrick McGuiness, John Duncan, Lisa Bennit and Luke Smith.

Jim underscored the list and closed the folder. *Tomorrow will prove interesting*, he thought. *I'll have to have a chat with Eve before we start. Our chat today has proved invaluable.*

Jim moved over to the cameras again. John was surrounded by the scientists, each of them holding a cup. John had two empty Dom Pérignon champagne bottles on the table next to him. "We've had the success we dreamed of; you've outdone yourselves in every sense and I've never been more proud to be a part this team. I'm not a big talker so - cheers!"

John raised his coffee mug, which was mirrored by the group. "Cheers," Lisa said, which was echoed in unison.

John looked up at the camera that was overlooking the event and raised his cup, as if he knew Jim was watching. Jim's grin widened, he nodded his head as if John could see him through the camera. *We'll get started tomorrow, John. This could prove to be the real test*, Jim thought, leaning back in his chair. His gaze moved over to a monitor which showed the reception desk. Patrick was sat there, mindlessly flipping through a magazine. His feet were up on the desk. Jim knew what was bothering him. The other security personnel were giving him a wide berth, which wasn't unusual.

"Perhaps finishing tomorrow with you would be best," Jim said.

Chapter 4

The Beginning

Jack's eyes opened sleepily, something had disturbed his slumber. He blinked a few times to try and wake himself up, noticed something in his peripheral vision, and looked sharply left. Eve was kneeling beside his bed. "Good morning."

"There isn't anything good about it yet, Eve."

Jack turned to face her and began rubbing the sleep out of his eyes. Once he'd done so he looked down to where she was. *God, she's pretty*, he thought.

A good night's sleep had worked wonders on her. She seemed happy this morning. She had her chin resting on her hands; it made her look exceptionally cute. He lay back on the bed and closed his eyes. "GET UP!!"

Jack held his ears but the shouting didn't stop.

Then Jack's head was full of laughter. "I just wanted to see if you were in my head. You really aren't with it this morning, are you?"

Jack turned and saw Eve grinning at him. "You look like you got a decent night's sleep. How are you this morning?"

"I feel so much better, thanks. Are you okay?"

Eve could see he looked refreshed today, despite the unusual way he was woken up. She enjoyed flirting with him; he wasn't really the type she normally went for but the connection was something she couldn't ignore. "I'm good, thanks. The wake-up I could have done without but I'm sure I would have slept all day if you hadn't woken me. One thing though, could you not scream inside my head again? My brain is still bouncing around inside my skull."

She burst into laughter and Jack laughed along with her.

They heard someone clear their throat. "Good morning, I'm glad to see you're both up."

Jim was standing in Jack's doorway. The suit was gone. In its place was a T-shirt which looked like it was painted on, along with a pair of black jogging trousers that were clinging to his legs. "Good morning, Jim. Have you been out jogging?" Eve had turned to face the doorway. Jim still intimidated her but she figured there were only a few people who didn't find him this way. He clearly looked after himself and for a man of his age, he did look fantastic. *Yeah, I wouldn't want to get on the wrong side of him,* Jack thought.

Eve turned to face Jack. He was looking at Jim, the look on his face suggested that they had the same opinion.

Jack looked at Eve. "Please stay out of my head."

Eve smiled. "Only if you do. Good morning Jim. How was your run?"

Jim walked into the room and as he did, he disappeared completely from view. "It was interesting," Jim's voice replied.

"Hey, what the ..." Jack and Eve leaned from their sitting positions, away from where they last saw Jim.

"Relax. As I was out this morning I checked to see if there was any difference to my fitness and when I looked down, everything had disappeared. My sweat must affect my clothing."

Jim came back into view. He had a smile on his face that almost went from ear to ear. "I've got to invest in a pair of those then!" Jack said, his own smile mimicking Jim's.

"Not around me," Eve said instantly. "Not that I'm not happy for you both. But I wouldn't feel comfortable showering and everything. Not knowing where the hell you guys were. It's not a trust issue. It's just -"

"Eve, don't worry. I just came to show you what I discovered. I've got my usual attire upstairs. I understand what you're saying. Really, it's okay I'll be back in ten minutes. We have things to discuss. Jack, please get ready."

Eve looked back at Jim; he nodded and turned to leave.

"Can I have five minutes, please?" Jack said.

"Sure. I'll wait at the large table/computer thing." She patted his shoulder as she stood.

Jim was back within ten minutes, he joined Eve and Jack by the computer table. He was dressed in a nice blue suit, white open shirt and beige shoes. Jack and Eve were dressed in the same blue trousers and white tops.

"Jim, I think we should start with the lead scientist, John." Eve was playing a version of solitaire on the computer, while Jack was playing a game of chess.

"I'm starting to get used to our open conversations, Eve. I'm guessing you and Jack know what I am asking of you today." Jim sat down on a chair opposite them.

"Well, I'm a little in the dark. But from what I understand, you've four people in mind for experimenting with and we're here to help." Jack said, looking up from his game.

"Correct. John, Lisa and Luke, the people you met yesterday. Patrick you've not met yet."

Eve's eyes widened as she scanned through Jim's thoughts on his second in command. Jack looked at Jim, with doubt filling his mind. "As you've seen, he's a dedicated soldier, who misses war. I can't hide his past from you. And I shouldn't be thinking of his bad attributes. We've been through a lot together and he's been an invaluable colleague. He is also my friend."

"Jim, we're looking at this from a fresh perspective. He has what you call a happy trigger finger, hardly any remorse and sees almost anything as a challenge. He could possess an ability that we can't control. Who knows what he will want to do. I see the benefits. But I'm not sure it's a good idea," Eve said.

Jack was nodding all the way through. "It's important to you so if we see what happens with the others first," Jack was leaning on the table now, keeping eye contact with Jim and trying to reason with him.

"See how we get on," Jim said. He shared a look with Jack and Eve. He didn't want to deny Patrick the chance to fulfil his potential, but he was more aware than them of the problems he could cause.

"I'll go get John. He's excited to take a more practical part in this, as is Lisa. Luke wants in but I can't blame him for being overly nervous. I'll be right back." Jim got up from his chair and walked towards the lift.

"I hope you get something from them that can help control this guy. I'm not sure about him at all and we've not even met him yet."

Jack felt the same as Eve but they both trusted Jim and if he said no, he wouldn't be challenged by anyone. This Patrick guy could be a problem if he saw fit.

"John? It's time, are you still sure about this?" Jim put his arm around John as they walked from the rest room, back toward the lift.

"Colonel, I've never wanted to become a member of something more in my whole life until now." John was smiling, but his whole body was trembling from the adrenalin.

"Luke can work the computer while we do this. I said he can go before Lisa." Jim selected B2 and the doors closed.

Inside John's office, Luke was wiping the sweat from his hands on his trousers. The nerves were getting worse.

"Relax, please, Luke. You're making ME nervous. And I really don't want to be, any more than I am already." Lisa was sitting on the desk next to Luke who had taken position in John's chair.

"I'm sorry. I have no idea what to expect from what's going to happen to me."

"And I do?" Lisa stood up and moved to the arm of John's chair. She knew if she was close it would help him relax. She didn't feel the same way for him, but as a friend she would always be there to help.

Luke took in her scent and felt himself relax. He felt like leaning against her but he knew she didn't like him doing that.

"It's going to be okay" she said, putting her forearm on his shoulder.'

That seemed to help him more and a smile crept upon his face. Luke took hold of the mouse on John's desk and opened the files he would need.

John and Jack were having a talk inside one of the boxes; John was standing by the chair Jim and Eve used. They were given a moment alone so Jack could talk John through what to expect.

"Okay, let's do this." John sat down in the chair and jumped a little when the restraints snapped in place.

"John, are you ready to begin?" Jack asked. John nodded, but Jack could hear John's brain going a thousand miles an hour.

Jack took his hands. He let the pins and needles feeling flow from him into John and with his other hand, he took the feeling into himself. John snapped against the restraints for a moment and once Jack had a steady flow, he began to relax.

"Eve, can you see what's happening?" Jim asked quietly.

"I can see the thoughts in his head. He's not in discomfort. Jack is starting to get a hand on controlling this; whatever it is."

Jim kept his eyes on the box. The two men both had their eyes closed. They weren't still but they weren't moving either. You could clearly see that something was going on between them. He and Eve remained quiet.

A few minutes passed and Jack let go. "Luke, he's okay," Jack said. Jim took a rushed step towards the box, but Eve put a hand on his arm before he could overreact. The restraints came off and the pole went back into the floor.

John retched in the chair and Jack did the same. A look of panic shot across Jack's face. John looked like he would be sick at any moment. Jack grabbed John and rushed him out of the box towards the first room they could get to. Jim stood there watching the two men run. He looked confused. Eve still had a grip on his forearm.

Jack and John got straight into the shower, just in the nick of time.

"What's going on?" Jim said sternly to Eve. He'd kept out of the situation, as directed, but now he wanted answers.

"Jim, it's to do with John's ability. All I saw from Jack was panic followed by humour. He could feel his body change and he knew that they needed to get somewhere before they both -"

Jim could hear the noises from the bathroom and knew they were both throwing up. "So John's ability causes him to be sick? I don't see how that could be helpful."

"No, Jim. Jack is trying to inform me as we speak. His body is changing. Apparently it's reset itself to when it was at its most healthy, the same as John. Their bodies automatically had to reject all bodily fluids that were not needed, or were harmful. Jack said its best we don't go in there. He said they need a bin bag for their clothes."

She let out a giggle. Jim looked confused. "Jack said it's the first time he's been naked with another man and he has decided it's not the way forward for him."

Jim laughed and looked towards the noise of running water.

"Jack said it's not funny," she said, holding back a laugh of her own.

She tutted as Jack was talking to her in their private way. "Men!" Eve said. "I'll go get a bin liner. John's told Jack where I can find them. Apparently I'm not allowed to be here for this. He's asked for you to go in and see them."

Jim tapped Eve on the shoulder as he walked towards the sound of running water. Inside he saw what Jack was keeping Eve from seeing. The floor in the shower was a mess of fluids and clothing. "We need to move from here to Eve's shower," Jack said.

Jim looked the two men over. Jack didn't look too different. A bit more muscular and a little slimmer, but he looked good.

John, on the other hand, looked the healthiest a man his age could be. If John wasn't ten years older than his body looked, he wouldn't have been mistaken for a man in his early sixties. "How are you feeling, John?" Jim asked.

John spat out a mouthful of phlegm. "I feel fantastic, sir. I've not felt like this in years!"

"I think you'll have a little shock when you look in the mirror, John," Jim said back. "Eve has gone to get a bin liner; I'll see if I can find a shovel for this mess. How do you feel, Jack?"

"I'm naked with a sixty-year-old man, sir. It's not my finest hour."

The three men laughed. Jim got a few towels for the floor and for the men to dry off, before going off to the other shower so that they could clean themselves properly.

Luke came down with Eve, equipped with a few heavy duty bin liners and a small shovel. Jack got to shovelling while John held the bag. The air conditioning system had been activated by Lisa and there was no trace of the incident after they had everything secured in the bags.

"I'll get one of the guys to put this in the furnace out back." Jim said, carrying the bags to the lift.

Eve went over to Jack and sat down next to him on the box he'd gone back to. "How are you feeling? It didn't look like something I'd like to go through. Your body does look good though," she said, prodding his chest and shoulders.

"It was not fun in the slightest, but I do feel fantastic. I used to feel his way all the time when I was working out. But that was a long time ago. It seems like it's reset back to then. My tattoo has gone," he said, pulling his shirt sleeve over his shoulder to reveal his plain skin. "My scars have gone, too. I had one on my leg from when I was climbing as a kid. The aches I used to have from my bones have gone. It's the strangest feeling. Well worth the experience."

Eve ran her nails down Jack's arm, leaving pink scratch marks. "Hey, what are you doing?" Jack looked down at his arm and to his surprise, he saw the pink lines fade until there was no evidence that they'd even been there.

Eve smiled smugly and punched him in the arm. "You heal now! I wonder if there are any limitations." Her eyes widened and she looked around for John.

"Poor bastard," Jack said as he watched Eve leave the box and make her way over to John.

"John, can I scratch you?" Eve said as she walked in front of Jim who was in mid conversation. She pulled out one of her hair clips. It had a sharp edge to it.

"I'm sorry, what -" John began before Eve dug the clip into his arm and pulled down to make a single deep line down John's forearm. As with Jack's, it healed before John had the chance to finish complaining.

"Eve, that wasn't the way I'd have gone about testing, but you've answered most of my questions in one stroke. Forgive the pun" Jim chuckled.

John rubbed his arm through habit rather than any pain. "Can I expect this sort of thing from now on?" John asked.

"No, I'm done for now. Thank you, John," Eve said patting his arm and walking back to where Jack was sitting.

"She's normally like that," Jim said to John, who was looking at his arm. He nodded and looked back to Jim.

"I wonder what would happen if my blood got into someone else," John said to Jim, who had a look that suggested he was thinking the same thing.

"I was thinking the same thing," Jack said, walking over with Eve. "Although my blood is probably not worth testing, but yours could heal people. Don't you think?"

"We'll have to run tests on everyone's blood and see what's possible," John said, looking at Jim, who had a slight smile on his face.

"I think it's time we got started with Luke," Jim said looking at John. "Jack, are you feeling okay? You've started a collection of abilities now. I don't want to wear you out."

Jack smiled, that was all Jim needed to see. John nodded and walked towards the lift. "Right Luke, it's your turn now, mate," John said.

Luke was sitting in John's chair. He and Lisa were in his office. Lisa was waiting to take her turn in the chair. "Okay, just let me get things ready, first," he replied. John turned and looked at Lisa. "Luke," she said. He turned round and looked at the expression on her face. "You can go now or you can go last. It's up to you," she said coldly.

Luke sighed and stood up. Lisa gave him a quick grin and sat in his place. "Let's go, chap," John said as he put his arm around Luke's shoulder.

John came back with Luke. He walked past Jim and Eve, who were talking just outside her new room. He walked into the box and John stayed outside.

Jack walked over and put out his hand. "It's okay, mate. I'll try and keep this as unpleasant as possible," He said, trying to keep the humour light. He sat Luke in the chair, walked back and closed the door. The box locked and the restraints snapped in place. Jack walked back over to Luke, who looked more nervous than ever. Jack began to explain to him what was going to happen.

"Right, are you ready to begin?" Jack asked Luke, who had turned a slight shade of green.

A nod was all he could muster, but Luke opened his hands.

Jack took his hands and watched Luke's frame stiffen at his touch. He kept the flow slow to ease Luke into it. The last thing he wanted was for Luke to be sick on him. Slowly he increased the flow, until Luke's body relaxed enough for Jack to close his eyes and concentrate.

A few minutes passed and when Jack was finished, he let go. Luke was breathing steadily. He reached across to pat Luke on the shoulder. He made contact with Luke's left shoulder and he shook him a little. Jack put his other hand out and Luke opened his eyes. Luke moved his head away and closed his eyes, as if expecting pain, but he was still locked in the chair. Jack's hand then stopped where it was, a few inches from Luke's shoulder.

"Okay," Jack began and tried forcing his hand down onto Luke's shoulder but it didn't move. He looked at his right hand, which was still on Luke's other shoulder.

Luke then opened his eyes and saw what Jack was doing.

"Wow," Luke said and then Jack's hand moved past his shoulder at speed; Jack fell to the floor.

"What the hell..." Jim said. He ran towards the box, which was still locked. He moved round to see behind Luke's chair, where he found Jack, lying on the floor behind the chair, and saw him laughing.

"Jack, what happened?" Jim asked, tapping on the glass. He was on a bent knee, looking at Jack, a little confused.

"Luke has telekinesis," Eve replied from behind him. "He reacted to Jack going to touch him, and thought that the worst wasn't over. All he was thinking was that he didn't want to have that hand near him and for it to stay where it is was."

Lisa heard this and decided the risk was over. She reset the restraints and sent the pole back into the floor.

Jim walked round and opened the door, where Jack was getting to his feet.

"I couldn't do anything," Jack said. "I was trying to push back but nothing happened. Then he thought about it moving past him and that's when I fell over. His ability worked before I could react, I had just enough time to push myself away and miss the chair. This ability can be triggered by pure natural reaction; it could be useful as a defensive or offensive attribute."

Eve saw straight away in Jim's head that they could now control Patrick; the risk would now be minimal for them to change him.

Lisa got out of the chair and made her way down to the others. She got into the lift; her hands were shaking now. She was so excited she could hardly stop the smile on her face turn into a full blown grin. John saw her enter the floor from the lift and walked over. "Are you ready for your turn?"

Lisa looked at the others, all of whom were with Luke, asking him how he felt.

"I guess so. You're all so different. I only wish I knew what to expect," she said, walking towards the box. Jack moved from the others, his back still facing her.

"Boo!" he said turning to face her when she was behind him. She jumped and closed her eyes.

"Not funny" she said.

"Relax; I'm getting pretty good at this now. The more relaxed you are, the more it helps me concentrate. Okay?" Jack had a hand on Lisa's shoulder she was grinning again. "See! You'll be fine. Just don't floor me like the little man did," Jack said, walking into the box.

John made his way back up to his office. He sat in his chair and for a moment just looked at the others; they were talking and laughing. Lisa and Jack were in the box. John was sure Jack was going through the details with Lisa. John locked them in the box. He saw her reaction to the sound of the restraints moving into place; Jack patted her shoulder.

"Lisa, are you ready to begin?" Eve said to Jack, who she knew was listening around to everyone's thoughts still. He looked at her without turning his head and smiled.

Jack took hold of Lisa's hands. He felt her flinch at his touch. She closed her eyes and tried to relax.

The feeling was becoming normal to him now and he knew just how much effort it took to keep the discomfort to a comfortable enough level. Lisa was surprised at how little it hurt not to say she didn't feel happy when it was eventually over.

Jack let go a few minutes later. He let go of her hands; this time he decided to just wait for her to open her eyes. He wanted to be ready for whatever ability they shared. He could feel a new freedom within himself. He took his eyes off Lisa who looked at peace, resting. Jim and Eve were in front of the door, while Luke was on the other side, watching Lisa. Eve looked at Jack, concerned.

Jack heard Lisa thinking about the experience and turned to face her

She opened her eyes and blinked a few times. Jack saw her grin return. "Thank you," she said and closed her eyes. A few more minutes went by; John released the locks and the pole as per Jim's command and Eve's reassurance. He joined the others and they all entered the room. Jim put his hand on Jack's shoulder as he walked past him and leaned towards Lisa. Before Jim could get a word out, she suddenly vanished. Everyone gasped except Jack. Eve turned to ask him a question; she noticed everyone had turned and were looking at her.

Jack was in a daydream; He wasn't focused on the confusion. He had his own to concentrate on. He let his mind wander further and suddenly found himself standing at the computer table; he'd been thinking about the cheating computer and when he could have another go. Jack came back to reality and looked around in disbelief. Lisa hadn't let on to what she had, even if she knew herself; no one could have been prepared for this.

"He's at the computer," Jack heard a male voice say. He hadn't registered who it was and before long the group were around him, all asking the same question in various forms.

"This will take some getting used to," he said. Jack could hear the others talking. It was getting a little too much and he wanted to be back in the box, to be free. He closed his eyes, concentrated and when he opened them, he was in the glass box he was thinking about.

The group ran back to the box, still asking questions.

"Ssssshh," Jack said, "or we can play this game all day."

Jim's thoughts were the least garbled, so he decided to answer him first.

"I don't know where she is. I went to the computer table to have another game of chess. I'm sorry, her mind was quite quiet. I never saw this coming."

"I hope she's okay," Eve said. "The last thing I heard from her was that she missed good coffee."

No sooner had she finished speaking than Lisa tapped her on the shoulder. Eve jumped; she was just getting used to knowing what everyone was planning to do or what they were thinking. She thought the days of people taking her by surprise were over. She turned and smiled at Lisa.

"I do," Lisa said. "I was back home in Ireland at the little coffee shop that I miss. It was what I was thinking of and suddenly, I was back there."

"You came back empty handed?" Jim said, causing everyone to laugh.

"I forgot my purse," she replied quickly. They all laughed hard at the exchange.

Once everyone had finished asking questions as to what the experience was like, Jim gave his credit card to Jack and suggested that to save people recognising Lisa, he was to go and order coffee and food in her place. Jack agreed. He and Lisa spoke for a moment quietly about the place, and when he was quite happy that he would end up in the right place, Jack went round and asked what everyone wanted. "See you all in a bit," he said.

The others waited patiently, though a little worried about him coming back at all. Half an hour passed before he came back with everything that was asked for. "You took your sweet time," Eve said.

"I was having a walk. Why, did you miss me?" He asked.

"No. We've all been here, getting thinner by the minute," she replied.

"Well; dig in," he said, walking over to the table and setting the cup holders and the bag of food down.

Everyone said the coffee and food was best they'd ever tasted. Jim wondered if the odd way it was transported would have affected anything they were eating, but no one could taste anything to suggest this. John was wondering what it would feel like, being teleported, and asked if he could see for himself, so Jack and Lisa agreed to see if they could teleport him across the room. He took hold of Lisa's hand. She nodded to Jack who was across the other side of the room. He waved back to her and closed her eyes. John did the same and he disappeared. John opened his eyes and saw Lisa grinning. He was about to turn round when he felt Jack grab his hands from behind. John's eyes blurred and he was back with Lisa. "Oh, well -..." he began, when she grabbed his hands and suddenly he was looking back at her from a distance. She was laughing now and so was Jack. "Jack, can I -" he began before he was cut off once more.

After a while John asked for them to stop, as he felt like they were starting to play a strange game of catch and he was the ball.

They all moved to sit at the computer table. Jack was at the back of the group, with Eve in front of him. Seeing an opportunity, he snuck up on her. Just as he was about to slap her pony tail, she moved away. Jack, reading her mind, moved as she did; she was still reading his and moved just in time. After a while, it was like they were inventing a new dance. This provided entertainment to the group as one after the others noticed what they were doing. It seemed that no one would get the upper hand and eventually, Jack took a step back and raised his hand; Eve seemed to start floating in the air. She huffed and crossed her arms. Jack grinned at her. He could see she didn't find it amusing. Jack could hear the others start clapping.

"You've proved your point," Eve said. The others were now around her in a circle. Jack put her back on the ground and she walked toward where he was standing.

"How about we call a truce?" he said, holding out his hand. She took it without saying a word. The look in her eye said he would not hear the last of this.

There was plenty of food to go round. Almost too much but everyone enjoyed the cakes, sandwiches, biscuits and coffee until Jim interrupted the group and asked if Jack was still okay to do one last person.

"Sure. One last job and we can call it a day, Jim," he said as they got up and walked toward the lift.

"I'll go get Patrick. You can stay here and finish up. Once we're done, I'll show everyone what's on level B1."

Jack went back to the group around the computer table and told them all what he and Eve already knew.

"So what's on B1?" John asked, finishing his now cold cup of coffee. "It's some sort of training level," Eve said.

Lisa looked at John and Luke. "We've never seen it" they said almost at the same time.

"It does look pretty cool. There is a pool, a running strip, a shooting range, a weights room and stuff like that," Jack said, picking up his half eaten sandwich.

"The food is good," Luke said, swallowing the last of his biscuit. Everyone nodded and mumbled in agreement. Lisa looked over and took a cup cake from the holder.

"So, it's just the head of security left and then we can go up a level." The room fell silent. Eve looked around and saw everyone was looking at her.

"Oh, come on. I'm sure he's not that scary." She saw Luke and Lisa exchange looks.

Ten minutes later they heard the lift doors open and Jim entered with Patrick.

"Thanks again, Colonel," Patrick said as they walked towards the box.

"Don't thank me yet," Jim said and put his hand on Patrick's shoulder.

"So where is this guy?" Patrick said as Jim sat him in the chair, which everyone involved had now used.

"Right here," Jack said, appearing to Jim's left.

Jim and Patrick jumped. Jack simply winked at them. "I've asked Lisa to go up to John's office." Jack said. No sooner had he finished speaking than the pole slid into place.

"I guess she's there already," Jim replied and he looked at Jack. He offered Jim his hand. Jim took it and suddenly found himself on the other side of the box looking in. "Interesting," he said to himself.

"I'll keep this as comfortable as I can," Jack said and offered Patrick the seat. Patrick sat down and the restraints snapped in place. Jack decided not to go through all the details as he had done with the others.

"I'm sure I'll be fine," Patrick said back, smiling.

Jack looked at Eve and decided not to say his 'catchphrase', as Eve was now calling it. He took hold of Patrick's hands and began. Jack had it well under control; Patrick didn't seem uncomfortable at all. His body remained relaxed and didn't move much at all. This should be fun. I wonder how this works and what I'll get from it. Eve was listening in on Patrick's thoughts. *I hope Jack gives him nails that extend, fireproof hair or something quite useless,* she thought; it made her smile. Jim noticed this and she picked up on his thoughts. He was wondering the same thing, and he had become quite eager to see what would happen next.

Time seemed to go slowly for everyone except Jack, who was busy concentrating. When he was finished he took a step back and looked down at his hands. Patrick remained still for a few minutes while Jack sat down, almost unaware of the group watching him or the man in front of him, breathing like he was in a deep sleep.

Jack looked up at Patrick as he opened his eyes and watched as his hands started forming tight fists. He had a seemingly large smile on one side of his face.

"Now, Patrick. Don't do it," Jack said, standing up.

"Oh, that's interesting," Eve said as Jim stepped toward the box.

"Eve -" ... he began, but it was Patrick who answered his question. He pulled with amazing force on the restraints, the group watched on as they started snapping under the pressure. First the left arm bent the restraints up then with a pop, his arm was free. The same happened with the right; this one was freed with loud cracks as the restraints snapped, unable to withstand his amazing strength.

"The computer is no longer responding," Lisa's voice came over the speakers.

Jim crossed his arms and smiled. "Exactly the right ability," he said.

Patrick then snapped the restraints on his legs, using only each leg to do so and stood up.

"Thank you," he said to Jack and offered him his hand.

Jack looked him in the eye and took Patrick's hand. The hand shake started off normal but after a few seconds, Patrick's forehead creased with effort and his biceps flexed, to the point that his shirt was showing signs it might start tearing. Jack was showing signs that he was putting in more effort but it wasn't unpleasant. He winked at Patrick.

"What's going on?" Luke asked Eve. Everyone turned to hear what she was picking up.

"Patrick wanted to put a little more effort than necessary in the handshake, but he didn't know Jack has the same ability. Jack is smiling because his muscles are healing even when they're under too much stress. Patrick isn't sure how to finish this."

"That is enough!" Jim almost shouted at the box. Jack let go and Patrick looked down at Jack's hands.

Jack laughed and patted Patrick on the back. Lisa dropped the pole and the door opened. Eve looked back at Luke, who had opened the door. He looked at the floor with a guilty smile on his face.

"How do you feel?" Jim asked while shaking Patrick's hand.

"I feel fantastic, sir," Patrick said. His smile had returned.

"Good. Now I think it's time I show everyone else 'B1' and after that we will go to the residence."

Jack and Eve were already aware of the plan and were looking forward to seeing everything up close. Jim took himself, Patrick and John in the lift, while Jack took Eve, Lisa and Luke to B1.

They all met in the lift lobby. The floor, like the laboratory, was brilliantly lit in white, but with a green tinge. In front of them lay a long, narrow corridor. At the far end they could see a lift door.

Down the corridor were doors on the right hand side and each had a label. To their left was a door in a right-angled part of the wall and to the right of that, against a flat wall, was another.

"To the far left is the running area and the other door leads to the shooting range," Jim said as he led them down the corridor. There were quiet discussions between members of the group, and Jim showed them each room in turn. More excitement grew when they got to the lift at the end.

"This is the lift to where you'll be staying. It's reasonably comfortable." The lift door opened. Patrick, Jim and John got in and went up first. When the others got to the floor and went out of the lift, they walked into a blue-walled courtyard, with fresh grass on the floor. Lighting the area was a glass roof. Opposite the lift was a short corridor, with six doors on either side.

"These are small apartments," Jim said. "They have a few luxuries, but nothing to boast about. As I said, they are reasonably comfortable."

Jack and Eve sat down on the grass and stared at the blue sky. Eve couldn't remember the last time she'd seen the sun or felt grass under her skin. A tear crept from her eye and she let it roll down her cheek.

"It's beautiful," she whispered. The blue walls and the sky were close to being the same colour. It was easy for them to mistake the room for being a part of the sky.

Jack was sitting back on his hands, staring upward. He was enjoying the warm sun on his face. His smile was almost from ear to ear and he closed his eyes. Eve lay down and closed hers. Everyone silently did the same, choosing to either sit or lie down and enjoy the sun. Jim first walked over to a small box on the wall and pressed a green button. Air conditioners came into life and a slight breeze swirled around the room.

The others enjoyed the sun while Patrick and Jim wandered around the apartments.

After twenty minutes or so Jim and Patrick returned and sat down with the rest of the group.

"The rooms are all open. Choose which one you want for yourselves and if you need me, I'll be down on B1, in the gun range."

The others went about their own business for a few hours after John, Patrick and Jim went down to B1. Jack and Eve slept on the grass, while Luke and Lisa went for a look through the apartments. Each one was identical to the last. They had living quarters, sleeping quarters and a bathing area. Clothes of universal sizes were on the shelves. The living quarters had a television and entertainment system. Lisa decided to go back to B1 for a swim, while Luke watched the news.

Eve woke up on the grass a while later. The sun was now behind some clouds; her slight shivers had woken her. She got up and made her way to the box on the wall, to turn off the air conditioning. Once it was off she wandered over to where Jack was lying and knelt next to him.

"One day, I hope you will leave me to sleep, Eve." Jack said. His eyes still closed, a crooked smile on his face.

"Perhaps one day. But then where will I get my kicks?" she said and helped him to his feet.

They walked around the apartments and chose from the ones that were left. They joined Luke in his apartment and caught up on what they'd missed out on.

Jack wasn't happy with how his football team was doing, while Eve was very excited to get herself to a clothing shop she'd seen advertised.

"Are we employed now?" Jack asked.

Eve looked at him and, for a change, had no idea on what the answer to that question was.

"Jim is on B1 still, I think," Luke said, and they decided to go and ask him on how they were going to get any money from their brand new lives. They decided on using the lift and wandered over to it. Once inside, Luke pressed the button. The lift doors opened on B1 and they made their way to the gun range.

Jim was sitting on a wooden bench with Patrick, filling magazines.

"Jim, how is it were going to make a living now?" Luke asked.

Eve noticed how Jim's and Patrick's thoughts went from English to Japanese.

"It's best we have this discussion when everyone is together," Jim said, looking up at them. "Shall we meet in the first apartment on the left in 20 minutes?"

They all nodded and Luke went to inform Lisa, who, he believed, was swimming.

They were all together in what happened to be Patrick's apartment when he and Jim walked into the room. The table that was in the corner had been moved to the centre of the room, and extra chairs had been brought across from other apartments.

"Look, we have abilities now which we can all see great potential in," Jim said. "We can all agree that working normal jobs is out of the question. Patrick and I have a lot of military contacts with some government officials, who could use our assistance. Nothing too hard to start off with. We'll just see what work we can help out with. I know most of you have toyed with the idea of Eve and Jack cleaning up in Las Vegas, or starting a travelling circus." A few sniggers were heard. "I know we can make good money helping out in places where the government can't, along with some private jobs that will save the country money. There are laws in place which we will be breaking, but if it's for the greater good, I'm sure none of you will mind."

"So I guess it's individual jobs, mostly," Luke put forward. "I can help out in construction; for example; on military bases, you know, things like that."

"Something along those lines," Patrick replied.

"Okay. Well, do we have any work coming up?" Eve asked.

"In fact, yes. We know of a high profile murder case in Florida coming up, if you're interested in helping out in that, Eve."

"I'm not too comfortable with those sorts of mental images yet. How about something low key for me to start off on, perhaps?" she said, looking to Jack.

"I'll have a look." Jack replied. Eve wasn't a huge fan of blood and starting off on a murder case would be pushing it for her.

"Thanks, Jack," Jim said.

They sat around for hours, discussing various things from pay to secrecy. Costumes were joked about but quickly discarded. Being able to keep their anonymity was the most important subject discussed.

They decided on a few jobs, to be split between them, which Jim knew were available. Jack was going to help out in the murder case. Lisa was going to transport some witness protected people across the country and John was going to work on testing their blood with the help of his staff on B3, who had been given the week off. Luke and Patrick were needed on a building site the military were behind schedule on and Eve was going to sit in on a few court cases, to help out.

Jack and Eve saw that Jim was going to help out on special operations for an old friend. He wanted to keep it from the others, but having Jack as possible back-up was a good idea.

"It's nice having a job of sorts to look forward to," Jack said to Eve and Lisa, who had been doing laps in the pool.

Lisa was having a break; she was relaxing in the corner where Jack was soaking his legs. Eve came back from the middle to join in the conversation.

"It's going to be interesting. I've never sat in a courtroom before and I'm sure you've never worked in security." Eve said to Lisa.

"It'll be a quick job on my part, luckily," Lisa replied. "It's a family of four, I'm moving next week so I've got to practice a few things, but I don't think I'll have any issues."

The door opened and Luke poked his head around the corner. He was sweating; Jim had gone with him for a run in the track section on the floor. What had started off as a run had ended up as a competition, which Luke had lost.

"Is anyone getting hungry?" he asked.

Jack and the girls exchanged a look which suggested that they were getting that way.

"Jim says fast food would do for him. John and Patrick aren't picky. What do you guys fancy?"

Eve laughed.

"Did I miss something?" Luke asked.

"Jack was wondering if Big Macs were still awesome. And I have to say, I'm also curious. Would McDonald's do for everyone?" she asked, looking at Lisa, who nodded. Luke smiled, as if that was his idea all along.

Jack took the list that Luke had written, with everyone's requests on it. Jim gave him some money and John went with him to help bring it back.

Chapter 5

A Brave New World

The next day, Eve woke up to a strange noise. She'd slept well that night. After they had finished their food, the remainder of the day had been spent utilizing the facilities and discussing what would be done the next day. The last thing Eve had done before she had gone to sleep was lie on the grass and watch the sunset.

It was now morning and when she looked around, there was no sign of what had woken her up. *Right, okay,* she thought.

"Morning, sleepy," a voice said.

"What?" Eve said, looking around the room.

"I thought you were going to sleep all morning" the voice said.

"Jack?" Eve said as she pulled the covers off and spun round to get off the bed. She put her feet on the floor and suddenly felt a cold hand grab her ankle. Eve let out a scream. She stomped on the hand that was attached to her leg and heard Jack laugh. Jack's head appeared from under the bed, he was grinning.

"You didn't think about trying to find me in the new way that's open to you, then." He was laughing now.

"It's still new to me! I don't wake up and automatically search around for people hiding under my bed. How old are you?"

She didn't look too happy; she crossed her arms and motioned to kick him in the head. Jack, hearing her thoughts, moved in time and crawl out from under the other side of the bed.

"Are you ready for day three?" he asked.

Eve was already moving to her bathroom and decided to ignore him until she was fully awake. *Right, where is he?* she thought after putting on a fresh shirt and jeans she had left in her bathroom the night before, to save time. She thought how funny that her old habits were still there even now. She was in a new place, with strangers who had all entered a new chapter in their lives, with no clear future laid in front of them and she still had a habit of doing things to 'save time.'

She concentrated and could hear a conversation coming from a nearby room.

"Morning, Lisa."

Luke had woken up and decided to see her after washing his face and changing into a fresh set of clothes.

"Morning, Luke." She had gotten up early, not through choice as she'd had only gotten a few hours' sleep. The day's events had kept her awake. Her future was now uncertain for the first time in her life and this meant sleep was impossible.

"You slept well?" she asked.

He was used to seeing her first thing in the morning; years of napping at work meant that when it was her turn to get some needed sleep and when he had to get her, he'd got a great look at how she looked at her worst. To him, she always looked amazing, regardless of how tired she was.

"I got some sleep, how about you?"

He had not gotten much, though certainly more than her; but not nearly as much as he would have liked.

"I've been up most of the night. I'm sure I'll get back to my usual amount when things become clearer. I just need to get a hold on life again."

Lisa walked towards her door and Luke opened it, using his new ability. She smiled and punched his shoulder as she walked past.

"That's for being lazy," she said.

Eve didn't find Jack's voice anywhere, so she decided to go see if Jim was up. She walked out into the corridor and went to his apartment. Eve knocked on the door. No answer. She knocked again and waited.

"Poor girl," she heard from behind her. She turned around and saw Patrick, who was walking up to say hello.

"I didn't hear you coming," she said.

"Sorry, old habits," he said, smiling. *Jim and Jack have gone to get breakfast, they'll be back soon,* he thought.

"Oh? What's for breakfast?" she asked.

Patrick started laughing. "I'll never fully get used to having people around who can do that", he said.

"Well, you usually think in Japanese, so you're not what I would call unprepared," she said.

"Well, it's the only way to keep my thoughts to myself," he said, smiling still. *She's quite pretty,* he thought, looking from head to toe, before he realized she was probably listening and went back to thinking in what Eve perceived to be Japanese. She tutted and walked off.

Jim and Jack were standing in line. They had decided to go to the café close to the facility and get a variety of food for the others. First thing in the morning, the café was always busy. It was the only place close by which served anything palatable.

The café was rather small; the seating area could hold twenty people before every table was full. The walls were a smoke-stained yellow from years of customers who enjoyed a cigarette with their food. The counter was old and beaten-up wood; the owner had made it from an old work table and the till was as prehistoric as you could get. With how beaten-up the place looked, Jim was surprised that there never appeared to be a shortage of custom. People from afar would come here for breakfast or lunch, collect it then leave; the only customers that came here and sat were the staff from the facility. Jim had first come here when he had overheard one of the security staff complimenting the place while handing over to the new shift. He had decided to come here when he knew it would be quietest.

"So, what's good?" Jack asked. Jim was looking up at the black and white chalk menu board.

"Everything I've tried," Jim said, still reading. He was looking for something new to try.

The person in front of them collected their food, turned and walked away.

"What can I get for you, dear?" the little old lady asked. She was short, with curly white hair. She was dressed in an old white blouse and flowery skirt. Jack could see the years had been kind to her; she had looked after herself. *Those are strange eyes. Beautiful though,* Jack heard her think. *He's with the guy who lives in the old dairy. What he's changed that place into I'll never know.*

"Good morning. Could we get seven full English breakfasts please? Will a dozen hash browns do?" Jim turned to face Jack

"Yup, that will be enough," Jack said cheekily, reading Jim's thoughts.

The little old lady turned back to Jack and smiled. *If only I were thirty years younger*, she thought, and smiled at him. Jack winked and smiled back at her, causing her to blush; Jim saw this and smiled at Jack without turning his head.

Patrick was with Eve in the gun range when Lisa and Luke walked in. They were going over how things worked. Patrick had been thinking through the safety aspects as well as the differences between the guns in the range. Eve had been asking questions whenever she hadn't quite understood. *It is quite handy that we can stay in silence and still maintain our conversation,* Patrick thought.

Eve was admiring a magnum handgun that Patrick had already told her was far too big to start off with.

"Yup, I can never be lied to again," Eve said. Turning the gun around in her hands, she started to look around for where the bullets were kept and Patrick started smiling.

"I'll be fine, shut up," Eve said, walking over to where she had learned they were.

Eve then stopped and turned around, because Patrick had started thinking about whether he could bend the gun pipe so it would backfire on her.

"Fine, I'll start with the twenty-two," she said, walking over to where he was and the gun he had prepared for her earlier.

Patrick patted the gun and went over to get the bullets for the magnum. As they crossed paths, Eve motioned to hit Patrick on the arm and he moved along with her. She read his thoughts and came up blank. He managed to trip her up and she landed in a heap on the floor.

Patrick kept quiet and moved on as if nothing had happened. Eve got nothing from his thought, aside from how many bullets he wanted. She sheepishly got up and dusted herself off.

Lisa and Luke saw this exchange and Eve wasn't happy with being outwitted like that.

"I let him do that," she said, looking at the pair, who had not moved yet from the doorway.

Eve picked up the little gun Patrick had suggested. After a few seconds of thinking she popped on the ear defenders and aimed the gun at the paper target that was placed thirty yards away.

Lisa went to get a set of defenders which were placed on the far wall. Luke got two off the wall and almost automatically got them to his hands. Lisa smiled and disappeared.

Luke looked at where she once was, confused. He heard laugher, looked at where he had gotten the defenders from and saw Lisa with her own pair on. She was laughing at him.

"Two can play at that game," he heard her say. She was shouting like someone did when they were wearing headphones, listening to music and was trying to shout over the music.

Patrick was looking at Luke and motioned for him to send over the now-spare set of defenders. Luke sent them over and Patrick put them on just in time. Eve opened fire, striking the target in various places off centre.

The gun she was holding was the perfect weight for her. With each trigger squeeze it rose up a few inches as one would expect. Once she had emptied the clip she ejected it and reloaded like a professional.

The clip floated an inch from the ground where Luke had caught it and he put it in the shelf below Eve's elbow, next to the bullets.

Patrick walked over and inspected her handiwork.

"Not bad. Two head shots, three other fatal hits and the rest would have slowed them down."

Eve took off her defenders, as did the others. Lisa was admiring her handiwork and Luke was looking at Patrick, asking for a go.

"Luke, wanna take the next clip?" Eve said, hearing his thoughts.

"I'll prepare another clip," Patrick said, moving towards the bullets.

Patrick prepared enough clips for everyone to have a few goes and he had set up his own work station for when they were finished.

Lisa and Eve agreed Luke was to have the first go and her second.

"How long does it take to prepare breakfast?" Eve asked.

"I'm sure they'll be back soon," Luke said, clumsily sliding in his first clip.

Luke pulled the trigger unexpectedly. Lisa fell to the floor and Eve screamed and covered her ear defenders. He had not meant for it to go off. He meant to only test its sensitivity, with the safety catch off. He put the gun down, his left hand on his chest, his heart was racing. He turned to apologize, to where the girls were standing, only to become face to face with a magnum barrel.

"Never pull a trigger, without making sure what position the safety catch is in." Looking past the barrel, he could plainly see how annoyed Patrick was. "It's mistakes like that where people get killed, idiot," he said, lowering his gun.

"Right, sorry. It's Lisa's turn now," he said, turning to walk away.

Patrick grabbed his shoulder and pulled it back, causing Luke to spin.

"It's still your clip in there?" he asked. Luke nodded.

"Then continue. Just make sure people know you're going to start shooting, okay?" Patrick put his gun back in its place and took a step back, adjusting his defenders.

Eve and Lisa moved to stand either side of Luke and he made doubly sure everything was safe. He clicked the safety off and emptied the clip into the fresh target.

The gun barrel moved up more than when Eve had been shooting, showing Luke's inexperience.

Patrick moved over to Luke as the last shot went off and the barrel locked.

"It's your first time shooting?" Patrick asked, taking the gun from his hands. Luke just nodded, still embarrassed from the incident only a few minutes ago.

"You managed to hit the paper with most of your shots. It's a good start," Patrick said. He had one hand on Luke's shoulder.

John opened the door and walked in.

"Morning, John," Lisa said, taking off her defenders. The rest did the same and John walked over to look at how the others had gotten on with shooting.

"Good morning, all," he said, admiring Luke's work. "The others are back early from their time off. I've been filling them in on our results here. The blood work for everyone is upstairs being tested. We should know soon," he said, looking at Luke and Lisa who knew how things there worked and had forgotten for the moment that their colleagues had been away on a well-deserved holiday.

"I thought they had the week off?" Lisa asked.

"They made a collective decision to come back in early and get started," John said, shrugging.

Jack opened the door and put his head round the corner. "Is anyone hungry?" he asked.

The group left the range and went outside. They followed Jack, who stopped once they were all out. "Right, everyone hold hands." Eve said.

They all did. Most of them had a confused look but they had started to get used to Eve knowing everything and Jack being the one who started getting things in motion. Jack had started to be looked at by the rest as Jim's number two in charge, even though Jack did include Eve in most of his decision making.

Jim was finishing with all the paper bags and plastic containers when they all appeared on the other side of the table he and Jack had prepared for them.

"Good morning. Every dish is the same. Please sit. I hope you are all hungry," Jim said, pulling out a chair and sitting. They all said their 'hellos' and sat in no discernible order.

They ate well. When the food and conversation was finished, Luke and John cleared the table and went to throw the bags in the furnace. Eve and Patrick cleaned the table while Jim, Jack and Luke got to work planning out what was next.

"So we've a few days 'til the first job. How well do you understand your ability?" Jim asked Luke.

He looked at his hands and then looked up at Jim. "Quite well. It can be a bit tricky and I sometimes lose focus but I think, with practice, I can get well accustomed to this. I have to remember not to try and show off until I have mastered my ability, tempting as it is."

"Have you tried this?" Jack said and lifted Jim and Luke up and swapped where they were standing.

Luke started laughing. "That's easy!" he exclaimed. He raised his hands and concentrated.

Jack's shirt started unbuttoning. Once off, it slowly turned inside out. With his shirt off, Luke could see Jack was wearing a similar running shirt to that which the others had seen Jim in, a few days ago. Luke started laughing again, only it sounded strained. He made Jack's shirt fit back on to him and button itself up.

"What do you think of that?" he asked, smiling.

Jack reversed what Luke had done at similar pace and sent his shirt towards Luke, who tore it in half and the pieces went either side of him. Jack read his thoughts and made the two halves come back and wrap themselves around Luke's legs, pulling him over. Luke managed to focus and just stopped his face from becoming good friends with the floor. Luke sat down on his backside and untangled his legs, then sent the two pieces swirling around Jack and Jim, before tearing them to shreds and sending the pieces towards the table, where the others were almost finished clearing up.

Eve saw the pieces coming and moved the last bag they had, so that most of the torn shirt landed inside. She threw a look at Jack, thinking it was his idea to make a mess. Jack ignored her look and faced Jim, who after breakfast had changed into his own running suit. Jim disappeared while Jack and Luke looked on.

Jack started moving, with parts of his trousers moving in odd angles, as if Jim had gotten a poor grip on them. Luke watched the strange dance Jack was doing and smiled, as it looked quite silly. Especially as he was doing this all with his eyes closed.

Jack lost focus and Luke saw a fistful of his left trouser leg rise up, making him lose his balance. Jack teleported himself two feet back from where he was standing. Before Luke could judge his seemingly pointless action, he saw Jack grab hold and lift an invisible man. He moved to put him in a headlock and then suddenly flew.

Jack landed in a heap in front of Luke, who had seen him coming. Instead of using his ability to stop Jack's flight, he chose to simply duck. Jack, not using his ability, assumed Luke would save him. Upon impact with the floor, he realized he was wrong.

"Jim, when it's a reaction and not a thought, it's almost impossible to stop you," Jack said, getting to his feet and dusting himself off.

Jim reappeared and walked over to them.

"It's a good thing too, or no one would ever stand a chance." he said, patting Jack's shoulder.

Jack smiled and looked between Jim and Luke.

"How about a good old fashioned training session? Like people do in Dojos. The grass in the residence would provide a good surface, wouldn't it?"

Jim smiled and walked off towards where the others were talking.

Eve and Lisa were discussing their earlier shooting and how Patrick managed to outmanoeuvre her. John and Luke were in the box, looking at Patrick's destruction of the restraints. He himself was over at the computer, working.

"Can everyone come here for a moment, please?" Jim said in a loud voice so everyone could hear. They all congregated outside the damaged box. Eve and Lisa were still in conversation. "Thank you," Jim began. "How would you all feel about going back to the residence and having a kind of sparring session, like martial artists do in Dojos?"

There was a murmur of discussion before there were smiles and nods of agreement. "Like an all against all, thing?" Luke asked.

"Yes, it's good practice I think," Eve said looking between him and Lisa, who was looking quite excited.

"I'll take us upstairs then," Lisa said, taking Luke's and Eve's hands.

They took a hold and she took them all to the grass area in the residence.

Jack was first to break off, walking backwards.

"Great, thanks. You're all planning on jumping me then?" he said with a slightly worried tone in his voice.

"Pretty much," Eve said, nodding to Patrick, who smiled and lunged at Jack.

Jack heard his plan to split his midsection in half and moved at the perfect moment, sending him straight into the grass. He turned and managed to block John's own tackle before Lisa teleported to his rear, taking him off balance.

Jim all the while was standing up straight, his arms crossed. He had a reminiscent look on his face. Jim couldn't help but be reminded of his military days. He used to encourage soldiers of all ranks to sort out their issues in a very similar way.

Jack heard Eve's thought, to help Lisa take him to the floor and remembered John's ability, so he pulled Eve from her charge, sending her directly into John's side, effectively winding him and allowing Jack to regain enough balance to get one foot steady.

Jack had hold of Lisa's arm and a revelation hit him. Lisa disappeared and Jack started laughing.

Eve got to her feet and knocked Jack to the floor, then sat on his stomach. He was still laughing.

John was helped up by Patrick, who had hit the floor harder than Jack had meant.

"That looks painful," Patrick said.

John's shoulder was looking slightly out of place. Patrick tore his shirt, showing his injured shoulder.

"It's dislocated," John said, wincing.

"No worries," Patrick said and pulled his shoulder from the elbow. There was a loud pop and John yelped in pain.

Jim walked over to check on John, who was completely healed now.

"How's the shoulder?" he asked.

John smiled, rotating it without any signs of it ever being damaged.

"Lucky thing," Jim said.

"No luck at all, Jim. This git knew my momentum would take us both out, with John being the one who suffered the brunt."

Jack was still under Eve, who had made herself comfortable.

"Not bad," Patrick said walking over. "Now, what's so funny?" he asked.

"Where is Lisa?" Luke asked, slightly worried.

"Oh she'll be here in a second," Jack said, hiding his laughter.

"She's not happy with you," Eve said as Lisa appeared in a new set of clothes, with what appeared to be freshly towel dried hair.

"First, that was not funny. Second, sleep with one eye open and third, why do that to me!?" she said, walking over from the corner she had teleported to.

Luke walked over to Lisa and asked if she was okay. "He bloody teleported me over the pool." I dropped before I could react and I've been in my room. Changing and drying off."

Jack looked up at Eve, who smiled. He levitated her. She was still cross-legged on his chest. "Ah, damn it, Jack!" she complained.

Jack motioned to stand, but looked at Luke as he did. "Would you mind taking her, please?" he asked, standing up.

Luke nodded and raised a hand to take control of the floating girl; who did not look happy about being passed around like a toy.

Eve looked over at Luke, who nodded.

"No, you don't," Jack said, turning just as Luke dropped Eve on him. He bent as quickly as he could, but he wasn't quick enough this time and ended up on the floor, in an awkward angle, with Eve now sitting on his shoulder.

"Please get off me, honey," he mumbled, not wanting to use his abilities this time.

"Sure," Eve said, using his face to help her stand.

Jack got up to the sound of laughter.

"Real mature, guys," he said, trying to dust himself off but realizing he was covered in dirt now. "Okay, fine," he said, walking over.

She took a hold of his wrist.

"Fine," Jack said and disappeared.

Lisa opened her eyes and looked as if to see Jack was somewhere in the room. He wasn't. She dusted her hands and walked over to Eve's side.

They all turned at the same time as Jack appeared in the same corner she had previously, soaking wet.

"I hope this makes us even?" he asked. Jack then lost his smile. "Well, I can't really argue," he said.

Jim looked at Jack. "Lisa said 'No chance,'" and then he shrugged.

Jim laughed, as did everyone. "Luke," Jim began and as he turned to face Jim, he got a hand to the face pushing him to the floor. Luke collapsed in a heap. He rolled onto his back and lay there looking up at the sky, which was mostly cloud.

"I'm not used to physical confrontation, Jim," he said, looking upward still.

"Well, that is something we shall have to remediate, isn't it?" Jim replied. "The things we can do. It will make people fear you, if they find out. If they do, you can't be unprepared. It's never been something I've enjoyed, but being prepared has saved my live many times over," Jim said, motioning to Patrick, who nodded in agreement.

Luke got up and threw a punch at Jim, who ducked and took out his legs. Luke landed again in a heap on the floor, winded this time.

"See, it's not something that I can be any good at," he said, panting and picking himself up.

Jim helped him to his feet. "It's got nothing to do with defending yourself physically. You've the ability to stop people getting anywhere near you. Focus and react. You should be fine. Patrick?"

He ran forward. Luke took a step back and instantly put his right arm into a 'stop' sign. Patrick froze on the spot, mid -sprint. He was a few feet away from Luke, who waved his arm, palm down to the floor, and Patrick skidded along in the direction Luke made him go.

Jim smiled and Patrick picked himself up, wiping dirt and grass off his face and out of his hair.

Luke wasn't smiling. He was looking down at the floor.

"Luke? It's alright," Eve said, walking over. "None of us want to hurt people, it's just that now we can defend ourselves if need be. Jim is right. We will be feared if people find out what we can do. We have to be prepared in any case. I know you'd rather use your ability for good. But I also know you agree with us. No one is asking you to hurt people. We just have to be trained enough so we can deal with every eventuality." She raised his chin and showed him her smile. He returned it and nodded.

"Okay, it's still my turn, right?" He said, taking a few shy steps backwards.

"Everyone, now," Jack shouted and they all ran towards Luke, who smiled and raised his hands. They all stopped, frozen in place. Jack winked and Luke started to levitate.

"Wow! Easy Jack, I'm not sure …" Luke said as he raised everyone with him, except for Jack who still remained in place. Jack smiled and lowered Luke to the floor, only a few feet away from where he was originally.

"Now, is that the best you can do?" Jack asked. "When you got your ability, you were able to move my hand inches from your shoulder and I ended up on the floor. See if you can't do something similar."

"I'll try," Luke said.

The next few minutes were fun for Luke as he played around with different manipulations, while everyone ran or walked towards him and tried to grab or hit him in various ways. After seven or eight minutes, Eve stated that she wanted a go now.

She moved into the middle of the group and closed her eyes.

Eve had developed her ability far beyond what Jim had anticipated. Each attack was dodged with millimetres to spare; even multiple attacks weren't a problem for her. John and Lisa ended up in a knot after they tried to tackle her. John went for her shoulder and Lisa went for her waist. Eve moved from left to right in perfect motion to avoid them and they ended up in a heap on the grass.

"It's only when I try and attack you two," she said with frustration and disappointment. "You react, it's impossible for me to read a thought that isn't there. I just don't like being helpless with that." Jim was getting up from her last failed attempt.

"Well, Eve. We've spent decades training our reactions. As long as you don't go on the offensive, towards us or people like us, you won't have an issue with anyone."

Eve was happy enough with this revelation, but having a weakness wasn't something she was happy with.

Lisa moved into the circle without declaration. Patrick saw this and went for her. All this activity had awoken the killer instinct within him and he was beginning to get carried away, which in the past had proven fatal on a few occasions. Lisa had her back to him and when Patrick was a few feet away, she teleported behind him. Patrick carried on running, unable to stop from his commitment and went straight into a collision course with Jack, who was preparing to attack Lisa. Jack saw Patrick coming in time to react. He raised an arm and Patrick somersaulted through the air; the others all stopped and watched a now fast-flying man as he landed at the far end of the corridor, where the apartments finished. Patrick managed to stop by bracing himself against the lift doors.

Jim nodded to Jack for taking proper care of the situation and as Patrick was making his way back, jogging towards them, Jim motioned for him to run off the end of his adrenaline. Patrick slowed his jog. He nodded to Jim and turned round again, heading to the room they used for sprinting.

"John, did you want a go?" Jim asked, turning round to face him.

John smiled and let out a nervous laugh. He turned to Eve, who he knew would be looking forward to going up against a man who couldn't be damaged. Little did John know, but Eve's thoughts were mirrored by everyone, except Luke, who was happy to sit out the rest of the day's sparring.

Lisa moved forward without John having said a word.

John watched her moving forward. "Lisa, really? You want to try it?" he asked, slowly crouching down in a predatory yet mocking way.

116

"Yeah, boss," she replied and launched herself toward him. John had prepared himself for her. When she was a metre away, he moved sharply forward, but only found his shoulder barge hit nothing. Before John could turn he felt a solid punch, from a seemingly small fist, strike his lower back. He felt the area quickly spasm and his right leg gave way. The feeling was gone in an instant and John rolled defensively forward. As he stood, a forearm was coming to greet his face and he managed to duck enough that it barely made contact with his hair. Lisa wasn't happy with this so she went in with a leg sweep but John was in mid-turn. She made great contact with his leg but it was far too high up and succeeded in only giving him a dead leg, which didn't take long to heal. Lisa used her ability as best as she could and kept hitting John in different parts of his upper body and whenever he went to move, she would appear on his blind side. Not quite as painful as Lisa could have made this, but it was more annoying than he was expecting. John swung back an elbow of his own, forgetting temporarily that it was their turn to attack him and he was to only avoid, as best he could. His elbow swung violently towards Lisa's face and she reacted so quickly that due to the amount of force John had put in, coupled with it hitting nothing but air, John lost his balance and fell.

Lisa was now on the other side of John, where she had imagined it would be safest. She crossed her arms and watched as he sheepishly got up from his fallen position. John turned to face her. They were both breathing a little heavily.

"I got carried away, I'm sorry," he said, lowering his head.

"Good thing my reactions took over or I would have needed a new face," she said, still a little surprised.

Jack stepped forward. "John, if you'd like we can have a proper little scrap. I mean, you can go as hard as you like, mate." Jack raised his hands openly, inviting John to attack.

Eve smiled and put her hands to her face in excitement. "Goody!" she exclaimed.

Jack was too busy with her thoughts to see John move in and take him completely by surprise. John picked Jack up in a rugby tackle, and in mid sprint fell to the floor, effectively driving them both into the grass. The drive was hard enough that those watching in anticipation heard a dull crack. Jack let out a cry and kicked John hard in the side. Another crack was heard and John fell back, clutching his right shoulder. Both men stood up. Jack straightened his right arm, which was bent back at an odd angle. There was a pop as it went back into the socket and the bone healed. The others watched as the swelling and discolouration evaporated. John pulled his shoulder back and rotated it, with no pain and no stiffness.

"This will be fun indeed, thank you, Jack," he said. Jack smiled and half bowed.

John sprinted toward him. Jack stood up straight and closed his eyes. John's right fist came into contact with Jack's face with such force that his cheekbone broke. Jack let out a dull moan and staggered back. His head dropped and he swallowed the blood that had filled his mouth.

The bones healed perfectly and Jack turned to John, who was looking at him in anticipation. Jack smiled and as he did, another piece of bone moved and settled back into place. Jack's crooked smile was back.

"Good hit, John, how much more have you got?" he asked, standing.

Their fight lasted a while. It was so long in fact, that the others started chatting, rather than watching. John was doing the majority of attacking and Jack was giving him a few decent hits when he felt like it. They eventually stopped and shook hands. It was a funny sight; two men with ripped, bloodstained clothes and faces, smiling and shaking hands.

Jim finished his conversation with Luke and saw they were done.

"Feeling better now, guys?" he asked, walking over. They both nodded, they were no longer breathing heavily when they reached the lift. They were heading to where Patrick was still running. As they got there Luke opened the door from the back of the group. Jim's hand was almost on the handle when he did this, causing him to grip nothing and he lost his balance.

"Ah, I do wish you'd warn people, Luke," he said as they walked in. Luke smiled and nodded.

Patrick came up to them in a slow jog; he was almost out of breath. Eve and Jack could see how hard he had pushed himself.

"Wow, that's a run and a half," Eve said as he reached them. Patrick didn't smile. His was out of energy and walked past them without word. He headed down towards the lift.

"He's going for a swim," Eve whispered. The others watched as he walked into the pool room and closed the door without turning back.

"I think we could be done for the day," Jim said.

Chapter 6

Earning a Paycheque

"Get up!" Jack heard inside his head.

He rolled over and opened his eyes. Eve was standing over his bed with an impatient look on her face. Today was the day that they were going to work together on a court case that was across the country.

"Good morning to you too, beautiful," he said before rolling back over to get some more sleep, removing the covers as he did.

"Ah, damn it!" Eve cried out and threw the covers back on him. Jack started laughing.

"I'm sick of you doing that, so I decided to sleep naked until you learn that 'normal people' sleep in, when they can." He pulled the covers back over his head.

Eve punched the lump where she guessed his head was. "You're gross! You can't sleep in; you've got ten minutes before we have to leave."

Eve could hear fake snoring from the lump of bedding.

"I will set you on fire, again, I swear to God!" she said and the covers moved.

"That really wasn't funny, you know," Jack said, sitting up.

She smiled and patted his head. "Yeah, it was though," she replied cutely and danced out of the room.

Jack rubbed his eyes and got out of bed. He walked over to the basin in his bathroom and ran the cold water.

They arrived at the court house where the trial was taking place. The judge was a friend of Jim's whom they had met briefly the night before. Jim had told his friend that they wouldn't get involved with too many cases of his. This one they would because it was a murder case and the person being charged would be going to prison for life without parole if convicted. Jack and Eve arrived outside his chambers, as they'd agreed to, at the time stated. The judge opened his door and welcomed them inside.

"We can't, but thanks," Eve said. "We'll just go and see the man in question, get the information you need and report back." The judge nodded in agreement, a little confused at how they'd answered his question without him having to ask and turned to close his door. Jack and Eve heard his relief that they'd turned up and heard him sit back in his chair.

"Shall we?" Jack asked and Eve took his hand.

They arrived inside the room that was next door to the man's prison cell. The dark grey walls were old and hadn't been cleaned in what to Jack looked like years. They had said to Jim that they would sit and wait. One of them would listen to what he was thinking, while the other one would listen out for other people coming to use the room or to see him.

"You do it," Eve said and moved to the other side of the room so she could keep an eye out for people coming. Jack rolled his eyes at her and closed his eyes so he could concentrate.

"I'm bored now," Eve said after five minutes and walked over to Jack, who was still listening. He didn't say anything, simply stood up and walked past Eve, who sat down on the bed and closed her eyes. She frowned. The man's thoughts were not very nice to listen to and she could see why Jack didn't say anything to her when he walked past. She could only handle a minute of his vulgar thoughts about some woman called Rose before she opened her eyes, effectively breaking the connection. Jack was standing next to her. She could see he didn't like it but she was not finding this task easy and perhaps going back to lookout would be better for her this time. Jack repositioned himself and closed his eyes. The whole while Jack was listening to the man's thoughts, his own would come in and distract him enough so that he wouldn't teleport into the room and simply ask him if he'd done it or not. Then Jack heard what he'd been waiting for. "If only I'd have changed that sodding brake light on that heap of crap Jeep. Then they wouldn't have pulled me over and I wouldn't be sitting here. That cop had it coming. I just hope that dirty cop lost my prints like I told him. He's next if I go down for this."

Jack opened his eyes and walked over to Eve. He took her hand without saying a word and teleported to outside the judge's office once more. Jim had told them that his office corridor was nearly always devoid of people and they wouldn't have an issue teleporting back and forth. As per last time, the corridor was empty and Jack knocked on the door. Eve looked around, confused.

"You're convinced?" she asked. Jack smiled and nodded back.

After a minute, the judge opened the door and smiled at them. "So, what's the verdict?" he asked.

"Guilty as sin," Jack said. "He was saying to himself that he wished he'd had fixed the brake light so he didn't get pulled over. He said that he has bribed or bullied a police officer to lose some fingerprint evidence or he'll be next. I've got very little time for this bloke already and I've never even met him. Going away would be the best thing for everyone."

The judge closed his eyes and nodded. "I thought so," he said. Jack heard Eve take in a deep sudden breath and she took his hand. Jack kept his eyes on the judge.

"If you need us again," he said and the judge nodded. They shook hands and he went back into his office, closing the door behind him.

Eve and Jack looked around. The corridor was empty and they disappeared.

Back in the glass box Patrick had broken, Jack sat Eve down in the chair that Jim had put in there. "What did you hear?" he asked her.

"That monster is his nephew!" Eve whispered back.

"I know," Jack said. "He's been plotting on doing all kinds of nasty things to him if he gets away with it." Eve heard Jim and someone else talking behind them, so she decided that she'd forget this job and move on. Jack could go back and help if need be.

"How'd it go?" Jim asked.

"No problems. The guy did it and I've told the judge what I heard him thinking. I assume he'll call again if there are any more issues."

"Good work. Now, I've been on the phone all morning with people I used to work with and others, who have gotten wind I've put a team together. Let me run things past you two that the others have already been briefed on." Jim put his arms around their shoulders and they walked with him to the table, where the others were shifting through a bundle of paperwork.

It had been three months since Jack and Eve had woken up and things were going very well. They had done an assortment of jobs in the relatively short time that had passed; Eve had helped out with four court cases, Patrick and Luke had been building military structures around the Middle East, Lisa had moved twenty families across continents in witness protection schemes. Jim had been busy working with an old colleague and had been doing assassination work. He had not wanted to tell the others but Eve insisted he did. Jack was working with them all whenever an extra hand was needed. Today, he and Eve were going to help the FBI on a case they were working on. There was a family that had been claiming that a wealthy member had run away, years ago. They needed a death certificate to claim inheritance. Eve had her suspicions that said person was the one local police had discovered recently, in a shallow grave in the middle of the Nevada desert. She and Jack needed to help get evidence the FBI could use so that those responsible would be brought to justice.

John had been working back in the laboratory. The team had been running tests on all the blood samples and had come up with some interesting results. John's blood could be used as a universal donor, and his blood would give the person injected his ability for a short while, depending on the amount given. Alex was given a very large amount and the effects lasted for the rest of the afternoon. His body went back to when it was most healthy, the cough he had from years of smoking had gone, along with his insides emptying of anything that was poisoning his body. After the effects wore off, Alex went back to his usual self, only healthier. He described it as 'having a human oil change', which made everyone in the lab laugh.

Jack's blood was extremely toxic. All test subjects in the simulators died and after more tests, they concluded that a combination of his skin, sweat and blood caused the effects his touch produced. They couldn't replicate his ability; nor could they come up with a synthetic sample of his skin. He remained one of a kind.

Every test that they wanted to carry out on a host was performed on Alex. He was the resident guinea pig and during testing, he displayed a slightly similar ability to those he was subjected to. Patrick's made him angry but quite strong; Eve's ability allowed him to hear the thoughts of others, but he wasn't able to concentrate, he had to make do with what he could understand. Luke's blood allowed him to guide things that were already moving, which he had fun with while the effects lasted. Lisa's blood allowed him to clearly see any place he had been before with perfect clarity. He described it as 'being there and seeing everything, without having to go there'. The last blood for him to try was Jim's. It had a strange effect on his skin. The texture changed so that the light shone through it but he could still be seen if he moved. No matter how tight they could get his clothing, he was always visible when he moved. He had done this out of curiosity. When Jim had come to see how things were going, Alex asked if he could be the next one to join his team. Jim said he had enough people, but he had his word that he would first to know if they were to need another.

Jack was now able to use all of his abilities at once if he wanted to. He used this on a job he was on, helping out in Libya. Jim, Patrick and Luke were fixing a structure and Jack was helping as best he could by bending a large metal frame, while holding the roof up. He began to experiment. Teleporting while invisible was easy, as was reading minds while invisible. Jim walked into the shooting range one afternoon and saw Patrick shooting erratically, or so he thought. Jack was teleporting while invisible, but his T-shirt was on so that Patrick had something to shoot at. With each successful shot, of which there were few, Jim could see blood stains and trails until Jack healed or on one occasion where Jack thought he would try and slap a bullet away, which ended up in him having to sit down while his body slowly grew a new hand. "Right, I know now not to do that again," he had said to Jim, who was questioning his sanity.

Jack and Luke did some crowd control for the American president, who went for a walk one day. It had been going well until Jack got bored and tripped one of the president's bodyguards and Luke got a little annoyed with a guy calling him names. Jim had been watching, unknown to them, because Lisa had taken him there. He waited until they were no longer needed and after a grilling about being unprofessional, Jack took them back and Jim banned them from working for the president again, unsupervised.

That morning, Jack and Eve were going to meet up with agents from the FBI. They had gotten ready and Jack was going to take them to the field office. Jack was waiting for Eve at the grass area on the resident level. He was wearing a dark blue suit with a lighter shirt. He'd gone tieless that morning. It wasn't usually something Jim allowed him to do, but today Jim was in a shareholders' meeting with the company he used to own, so Jack decided he'd dress more comfortably today. Eve walked out of her room and could see him standing there, studying his watch like it would somehow speed up time. *How cute*, she thought. Jack looked up and saw her coming. He could see she'd had the same idea as him, as she was in a blue suit, the same shade as his, only she was wearing a black fitted shirt underneath.

Lisa came out of her room, just in time to see Eve walk past. "Aw, don't you two look cute dressing the same," she said as Jack took hold of Eve's hand. He pouted a kiss at Lisa while Eve scratched her cheek with a middle finger. "Charming," she said after they had disappeared.

They reappeared in a corner of the office Jim had shown Jack yesterday.

"Right, so we're to sit in during an interview each, get what we can use and pass it on, okay?" Eve said.

Jack nodded. It was his first time on an FBI case. He'd not gotten on with the secret service previously and had pre-tarnished the FBI with the same brush. But this was a case he wanted to help on and today he would be professional around Eve. They both put on a pair of dark glasses they'd started wearing, to help them use their abilities.

Special Agent Johnson walked in. "Right on time, I see," he said and walked over to them.

"I've been told not to ask questions," he said. "Apparently you're here to help. I've been assured we'll get to the truth, so I'll listen and take what you say without question, correct?" he asked, shaking Eve's hand. They had met once before, when Jim had taken Eve to an office, where he and a Korean man had the full meeting and only in his native tongue. Introductions afterwards were the reason for Eve to have been there at all.

"That, Special Agent Johnson, was a question," she said, smiling. "This is Jack." The two shook hands without a word and he motioned for them to follow him outside.

"Jack, could you go into the room on the right? Eve, we are down the hall." Jack walked into the room without saying a word and Eve walked down the hall with Special Agent Johnson.

Jack walked in and a man in a suit similar to Agent Johnson turned around. Across the table from him was a man not much older than Jack. He was dressed in casual clothing; a plain, open shirt and khaki trousers. Next to the man was a woman who Jack assumed was his lawyer. She was dressed in a dark suit, with her briefcase on the table in front of her.

"Who's this?" the lawyer asked.

The man turned round to her without acknowledging Jack. "Agent Smith. He's new and only here for training purposes. Any objections?" he asked, raising one hand off the table.

She looked Jack up and down then faced the agent in front of her. "I suppose not," she remarked. *New guy's kinda cute, though,* she thought. *He's got beautiful eyes, I wouldn't mind him being here instead of this guy, as he seems to be missing a personality.* Jack heard her think. He ignored her thoughts, put his glasses back on and tried to concentrate on the increasingly nervous-looking man she was representing.

"Mr. Buckmore, can you tell me where your father is?" the agent asked.

Mr. Buckmore frowned and looked at his lawyer. "My client has already answered that question," the lawyer said.

"That's a 'no' then?" he remarked. *Yeah, about twelve feet under, next to highway fifty,* Mr. Buckmore thought. The comment was almost enough to make him smile though he resisted it.

"No," he replied. Jack was going through the man's thoughts. He was thankful for the dark glasses he was wearing or it would have been obvious that he was staring at Mr. Buckmore. After a while of deducting relevant information from useless, Jack pinpointed roughly where the body was. Jack was grateful Buckmore didn't look at the body much. It must have been in a grotty condition when they'd dug it up. Jack decided he no longer needed to be there, so he stood up. The agent turned his head slightly, smiled and looked back at the two people adjacent to him.

"That's all the time he needs to be here for? He's only been sitting there five minutes," the lawyer mocked.

"Bathroom," Jack said, opening the door. He walked out and went to where he had last seen Eve walking; she was standing outside another interview room, jotting on a note pad. "Can I make a note on that, please?" Jack asked. Eve put her left hand into her trouser pocket and pulled out another pad with a pen attached to it. She winked and handed it to him. "Thanks. I should have thought of that," Jack said, opening a fresh page and began jotting down what he had seen.

A few minutes passed with them both in silence. "I got a look from the wife's perspective," Eve said, not looking up from her pad. "You didn't get a good look at the state of the guy's body," she shivered. "I'm looking forward to getting these people charged. They should be locked up and have the key melted down, then thrown at them!" She looked at Jack, waiting for his opinion.

Jack looked up at her, and nodded in agreement.

"Or we could do to them what they did to their relative," he said, looking back at his pad.

Eve punched him. "We're not executioners. I'll never take a life." she said.

"Unless it's your only option?" Jack corrected, looking up now from his notes.

"Of course, only then," she replied.

"Right, so we've got the location, the depth of the grave and who did what to him leading up to before he died," Eve said comparing their notes.

"What's next?" Jack asked.

"Follow me," Eve said.

She turned and walked down the hall towards Agent Smith's office. When they got there, she knocked on the door and a voice asked them to come in.

Inside the office, Agent Johnson was talking to someone sitting in the big chair opposite his. He had a large wooden desk; the person he was talking to was facing the fireplace. Only their hands could be seen.

"How were the interviews?" Jim said, standing up from the chair so they could see him.

"So, Lisa sent you here?" Jack asked, walking over. Jim nodded and looked over to Eve.

"Everything went fine." She handed him the notes they'd made. "We got everything they need, right here, they can serve some justice now," she said looking at Agent Johnson. He nodded at her after taking a quick glance towards Jim.

"Can I have those, Colonel?" Agent Johnson asked. Jim lifted his left hand with the index finger raised. Agent Johnson sat down in his chair, crossed one leg and picked up an open file on his desk.

"They should do, indeed. This is very good, nice work," Jim said, turning to Agent Johnson and handing him the notes.

"Right, let's go," Jim said and shook the agent's hand, as he stood. He turned and walked away from the desk. Eve turned with Jim, and Jack stuttered his turn before moving away, halfway between about to acknowledge the agent and just walking away like the others. The three walked out of the room and headed towards a door which looked like the women's bathroom. Eve opened the door and all three walked in.

"Couldn't we get a special telephone box, you know, like Superman. As opposed to me teleporting us from the ladies' bog?" Jack said once the doors were closed.

Jim looked at Eve, who shook her head.

"Jim, I checked that no one was here before making my apparently unfunny joke," Jack said, a little offended.

"I'm sorry, Jack," Jim responded. "Can we go back, please?" Jack nodded and took Eve's hand, who in turn took Jim's.

Back in the residence, Luke and Patrick were arguing.

"But you shouldn't have been showing off, Mr. Muscle! We shouldn't use our abilities against people for fun. It's an advantage I don't think we should exploit," Luke had just finished saying when the three appeared in the room.

Jim walked over to them; Patrick was just about to respond when he noticed the others had come back.

"Patrick?" Jim said when he was closer.

"It's nothing. He's annoyed that I got bored and wanted to show off with the guys in the base we've just finished building."

"So, arm wrestling or boxing?" Jim asked.

"Both," Eve said from behind him. Jim turned to her and then automatically back to Patrick.

Jim motioned for Patrick to follow him which he did.

"Never again. If you want to show off then I'm sure Jack will only be too happy to help," he said, stepping closer to Patrick once they were just out of earshot. "We shouldn't draw attention, and you know that," he said.

Patrick looked over to Jack who was cracking his knuckles. "I'd rather hit a bag than him. It's not fun hitting a man who could snap me in half if I pissed him off," Patrick said to Jim.

"We'll get you a bag then," Jim said.

Lisa turned to Luke. "Look, be grateful it was only that. It could have been much worse, we've all got huge temptation to show off but we must do our best to work hard, in order to avoid temptation," she said and he smiled half-heartedly.

"Right, what's next?" Lisa asked.

Due to Patrick's nature, Jim sent him on the next assassination mission; only he and Jack knew about it and upon his return the anger and frustration were gone. He did have to get an injection of John's blood, due to a nasty encounter with a machete on his way out of the building he was sent into. The shot was of such a small amount it was only enough to close the wound. It healed in front of his eyes and he smiled as he thought about the amount of possibilities that were before him, as long as he had some of this blood with him.

John had decided that they needed to use his blood to do more than earn money, so he'd spent much of his time getting samples to take for just that reason. When it was ready, he left. John spent three weeks away with Luke in Africa, where a civil war had erupted. He was using his blood to help people who needed it most, and Luke was using his ability to remove things that surgery would make worse. The work was tiring and John's doctorate was not in this type of medicine, but he did what he could. A school building that had been evacuated due to the trouble had been his choice at first to set up; there was only one entrance and this was also the exit. Jack and Luke had set it up so that it was not possible to get in or undo any of the metal sheeting that they had secured to all sides. The entrance was small enough to get people in and out. Jack and Luke did their best inside to keep it perfectly stable. Lisa was on duty to get as many people in as she could without raising suspicion. John and Luke were primarily there to get those badly wounded, or near death, healthy enough to be sent to the Red Cross without rousing suspicion.

"Right, I think that'll be enough," John said one day. Lisa had come to take him and Patrick, who was helping out that day, back to the facility. "I can't do any more here, I'm out of our supply and giving out my blood directly is beginning to have an effect on me. The people there can manage now."

They arrived back at the facility, where Jack and Luke were doing something on the computer table. They had both taken the morning off and had only been back a short while before the others were due back.

"They were off to the right, Jim," Eve said in a low voice.

Eve and Jim were in a remote part of Scandinavia. They had seen on the news that there were missing people there. The family members had reported them missing and search parties were not proving successful. The part Eve and Jim were tracking was because of information Eve had gotten from a member of the lost party, who was found in shock along a beaten trail. He was cold, wet and couldn't speak. She'd gotten as much as she could from his thoughts.

"No one would ever think of coming here to look," Jim said.

An hour and a half of searching later, Eve heard a voice in a language she didn't recognize. She could see roughly where to go.

"Jim, they are on that cliff. I think we need Jack to get them off." Jim looked over to where she was pointing. He saw a part of the cliff that looked accessible and took out his satellite phone.

John answered the phone.

"John, it's Jim, can you put Jack on?"

"Here," John said. Jim relayed their position and asked Jack to come right away. Jack nodded, gave John the phone, closed his eyes and disappeared.

"Missed me?" Jack said behind Eve.

"Very funny," she said. Eve looked into Jack's face and could see he was hiding something. She didn't need her ability any more with him; all she had to do was read his face.

Eve gasped. Jim grabbed her arm in alarm. "How come I haven't developed that?" she asked herself. Jack flashed a cheeky grin and disappeared. He went off to where she had shown him in her mind.

"Eve, what's wrong?" Jim asked. She looked at him blankly.

"Jack wants to show you when we get back," she said and a smile appeared on her face, which put Jim at ease.

Jack appeared in front of them. "All done. I've put them at the beginning of the trail and told someone searching near there I heard crying, they should be fine in an hour or so."

"Good work," Jim said.

"Come on and I'll show you," Jack said, taking their hands.

Jack went out to get coffee that morning; he was growing tired of helping out in court cases, doing personal bodyguard work, and building structures for private contractors, along with government requests. It had been just over four months since they had begun using their abilities. Jack was in a little coffee shop in the south of France. Someone had been thinking highly of the place on one particular job he had been doing in a United States congresswoman's office. Jim had been securing some work for her that needed doing. A bloke in a cheap-looking suit was looking bored and fantasizing about a waitress he had seen in this restaurant. After a few minutes of listening, Jack couldn't tell which the man liked more; the waitress or the food at this place.

It was well worth the visit. Jack had filled himself with delightful coffee and pastries, most of which Jack had never heard of, but they were exceptionally tasty. The others would want theirs bringing back soon, but Jack wasn't in any hurry. He figured most of them were working today, but he was having a day off.

He walked inside to order a variety of things to take back.

"*Bonjour*", a pretty woman behind the till said.
"*Bonjour, parlez-vous Anglais?*" he asked.

"Yes, how can I help you today?" the woman replied.

Jack placed his order, with a few back tracks on things he didn't think the others would like. The woman responded kindly to his ever-increasing order and started preparing everything after he had settled the bill.

It was quite quiet today. Jack saw it was almost ten in the morning and he was surprised at how quiet it was.

There was a man having an argument with a female Jack guessed he was with. It was all in French, so he could only get a word here and there but he walked over to see if he could calm them down. As he approached, the man saw him coming and diverted his anger towards Jack. He didn't understand a word the man was shouting at him but it didn't seem friendly.

"Sorry, mate. What seems to be the problem?" Jack asked nicely.

"It's not your concern," the man said, waving Jack away. Jack stepped forward and the man moved to an aggressive stance.

"You don't want to do that. You want to calm down and apologize." Jack pushed from his mind by accident, rather than on purpose. The man stopped. Looked between Jack and the woman he was arguing with, then turned to face her. He looked deeply into her eyes, picked up her hand and kissed it.

She looked confused and started speaking quickly in French to him. Mid-sentence she turned and pointed to Jack.

"I'm sorry," the man said. He then turned and started leading her away. The woman gave Jack another confused look before she turned and started speaking even quicker in French to the man as they trotted away.

Jack stood there a moment and then walked back into the café. He made his way over to the woman, who had most of his order packed for him. She was carrying a container of drink he had ordered. Drop the cup, he pushed from his mind.

The woman opened her hand and the container fell. Jack put his hand out automatically and the container stopped in mid-air, it began floating up and once it was in his hand he placed it into the multi-cup holder she had placed on the counter. She gasped as he did this and rushed forward. You didn't see a floating cup. You placed it in the container yourself, he pushed.

The woman blinked and looked slightly confused. Jack took the hand she had put on the counter and kissed the top of it.

"Thank you, so very much," he said, picking up the hefty bag along with the drinks.

"You're welcome," she said back as if nothing had just happened.

Jack began laughing as he walked around the corner to the alleyway he had teleported to originally.

"Wait 'til Eve sees this," he said quietly to himself.

Jack got back to the residence and nobody else was there. "Hmm, okay," he said and teleported to B1.

Luke was standing around the table, with Lisa; he was trying to beat his top score on minesweeper. Jack moved from the box he had teleported to and walked over to the table.

"I've coffee and pastries if anyone requires sustenance," he said.

Luke stopped and looked up.

"Thanks Jack, where from today?" he asked and leaned over. With one hand he took hold of the bag, which tore under its weight. Luke raised his other hand in time and the bag stopped. There was a pastry half out of the bag which remained at an impossible angle if it were allowed to obey the laws of gravity. Luke looked like he was concentrating a little harder then he should be, considering how good he had become at using his ability. The bag moved towards the table where it landed.

"Thanks, Jack," Luke said, smiling. Lisa laughed at how much effort it took him to hold a cup and to move a bag.

"Well done," she said.

"It's French, today," Jack said. "I'd try the green square ones, if you like chicken and leek." He looked at him and smiled. The bag was torn completely open by them taking hold of different sides. The contents spilled out on the table and they took in the delightful smell that spilled out with the food.

"Wow, smells good," Luke said, moving to take a chicken and leek pastry that Lisa had her eye on. She got to it before him and he picked up a chocolate pastry instead.

"Help yourselves to coffee, they are labelled on top. Where are the others?" Jack asked.

"Crap," Lisa said, looking at her watch. She finished the pastry in two bites and moved away from the table. Her cheeks were protruding out like a hamster. Jack put two thumbs up. She smiled back sarcastically and disappeared.

Jack and Luke got busy tidying up the pastries. Jack used most of the napkins he had brought to place them on. They had just finished putting them into order, from meats to dairy when Lisa reappeared with Patrick and John.

Luke looked up. "Welcome back! Jack's outdone himself today," he said opening his arms, showing the variety of food on display.

Patrick patted Jack's shoulder and moved over to the table.

Lisa looked over and teleported the few feet to the table. She wanted another chicken and leek pastry. Luke looked at her as she grabbed one and took a bite.

"They are good, are they?" he commented. She shook her head while taking another bite. He smiled and took one. She watched as the pastry went into his mouth and he bit into it. Luke looked unimpressed and motioned to put it down after swallowing his mouthful. Lisa looked at him with a look that if it were possible, would have killed him.

"You will not waste that," she said under her breath. Luke looked guiltily at her and looked at the teeth marks he'd made in the pastry.

"Here, I'll gladly finish it," Jack said and the pastry quickly moved from Luke's hand and in less than a second, was in his. Lisa watched it dart across and looked over with envy.

"Lisa, there are two more, the rest are yours," Patrick said, taking a cheese one and helping himself to a drinks container without bothering to looking at the label.

Jack concentrated and two containers came away from the holder and moved towards him. He and John had started discussing the work he had been doing today in Africa.

"Here, your favourite, I believe," Jack said, handing him the one with 'mint Latté' on the label. John took it gladly.

"Cheers," he said, taking a sip.

John's satellite phone started ringing.

"Hello, colonel," he said. A short conversation ensued and Jack listened intently. John passed the phone to Jack, who just listened. He gave John back the phone and he put it back into his pocket. Jack finished his coffee and started trying to imagine the place.

"Lisa, where did you drop them off earlier?" he asked. Lisa just pointed to her head.

"I'm not Eve, I do have it turned off most of the time," he said. She smiled and pointed again. Jack rolled his eyes and looked at where Lisa was showing him.

"Thanks," he said and threw his empty container towards the bin they had added to the room. It was about twenty feet away and it hit the corner of the bin, went straight up into the air then slammed into the bin. Jack looked over to Luke who was grinning.

"Nice rebound," he said. "I've something to show you all when I get back."

He closed his eyes and disappeared.

The others gathered around the table and started talking about what Jack could possibly want to show them when he got back. It was then five minutes before he reappeared with Jim and Eve.

"Welcome back, how did you get on?" Lisa asked. Jim walked over to the table.

"It went well. They will be safe now." He picked up a container of coffee without looking at the label and took a mouthful out of it. "Jack, that's very good. Where did you go today?" He picked up a chocolate pastry and took a bite. "French pastry, Jack you're beginning to outdo yourself," he said turning round to face the group.

Jack took a step forward towards Eve, who was looking strangely puzzled at John.

"Eve, you've got to relax and push it out. You look like you're trying to fart," he said and almost got away before her fist made contact with the back of his head.

She relaxed and closed her eyes, focusing on John's mind.

John looked puzzled. "What is she doing?" he whispered to Patrick.

139

"I'm not sure," he replied. Eve then smiled, opened her eyes and fixed them on John.

Before anyone knew what was happening, John turned to face Patrick and punched him straight in the gut. Patrick stumbled back in more shock than pain and moved to respond.

"Ha! You didn't see that one coming!" Eve shouted at him. Patrick stopped and turned to face her. John looked around, confused, and Jim started laughing.

"That's fantastic!" he exclaimed. "How did you learn that was possible?" he asked Jack, who was looking rather pleased with himself.

"I went to stop an argument in the cafe I was in and it just happened. It must be something that manifests after a while. Like a sort of healing process after getting injured. It starts off with reading minds then somehow we are able to control them. Who knows what the limit is?" he said, looking between Jim and Eve.

"You hit me, through John?" Patrick asked, pointing from Eve to John and back again.

Eve smiled and nodded. She was very pleased with herself.

"Well, at least you've found a way," he said and walked over to get a pastry. John walked over to Eve. "Please don't do that again, Eve. I saw what I was doing, but had no control over myself." He put his hand out and she shook it. She was still smiling when they let go and she walked over to the table where the refreshments were.

"I'm not going to get away from her using me as a toy now am I?" John whispered to Jack, who looked at him and shrugged.

"I'll do my best to keep her from abusing everyone," he said. John patted him on the shoulder and they joined the others at the table.

Lisa and Eve were having a stare-off as to who would get the last chicken and leek pastry.

"I've had four now, so I guess you can have the last one," Lisa said, eyeing up a dairy pastry instead. Jim looked across to Jack who looked back and shook his head.

He mouthed the words, "She gave it up willingly." He scanned the remains on the table and decided on a chocolate pastry. Jim smiled and took another coffee.

Chapter Seven

Changes

John had gotten up early and decided a refreshing swim was first on his agenda. He opened the door to the pool and walked over to the changing room.

Inside he got undressed, he had already put on his swimming shorts and hung the bag with underwear and deodorant in and walked out to the pool.

The water was clear and warm. He dipped his foot into the water and felt how nice it was.

John half looked and threw the towel over his shoulder. It missed the chair and landed in a heap on the floor.

John closed his eyes and braced himself for at what he'd envisioned to have been a perfect dive into the pool.

Lisa jumped up, grabbed John's waist band with both hands and kicked with her legs, which she had propped on the pool wall. John was helplessly pulled at full force. He let out a sound of pain, while he was catapulted a safe distance into the clear warm water, hitting it at what felt like a thousand miles an hour.

John twisted his body round and after a moment of confusion, recognized which way was up and burst out of the water.

Lisa was leaning back on the ledge of the pool, giggling.

"Good morning to you, too," John said, half spluttering out water. Lisa waved back at him.

"Good morning, John," Jim said from behind him. John turned round and saw no one. He looked at the water and could see where it was breaking around a shape of someone who wasn't there.

Jim reappeared and John could see him now, standing straight, arms crossed against his bare chest.

"You know, that would have seemed like perfect timing to an observer if only you hadn't have come back, Jim."

"I know, but my laughing would have given it away," he responded.

"I think I'll just get on with my morning swim now, but thanks for the laugh," Lisa said, pushing off the pool wall again, swimming backstroke. She glided past John and Jim who could only admire the way her technique and seemingly perfect figure helped her to glide effortlessly through the water.

"Right," Jim said and moved to the nearest wall. "I've got to get Jack up and see what we can get for breakfast this morning. Do you have any preference?"

"I thought Eve did that?" John asked.

Jim pulled himself up out of the water and seemed to almost land straight on his feet.

"She burned his sheets again last night. So I promised him I'd do it this morning. Turns out she's still a sore loser."

John closed his eyes and shook his head. "She should really give up playing him at chess."

"What she should do is learn not to keep setting his bedding alight. This is the third time now. I just don't want a joke ending up with the whole floor catching ablaze. Even though hearing him scream is funny," Jim said, half smiling. "No, she really has to stop that," he added with his face set quite serious.

"We both know what she's like," John said to him as Jim picked up a towel that was behind the chair that John had thrown his next to.

Jim draped the towel over his shoulders and half shrugged back at him.

Jack got up without injury or fire damage, much to Eve's amusement, and went with Jim to get breakfast. Today they went to a place outside London that Jack remembered was very nice. They had pre-ordered what the others had wanted from the all-day breakfast menu the lady had read to them over the phone. Jim had set up an international diverting system so it would appear to the party concerned that it was a local number calling.

They were only gone a short time and enjoyed the feast that was provided. Everyone was fed and the now well customized dining table was cleaned, they started discussing the next job, which was to include everyone.

"It's the day we look after the American president at the theme park," Jim began. Luke looked at his watch, then excitedly at Lisa, who rolled her eyes and smiled back.

Luke had heard Jim on the phone a month or so ago. Jim had let slip that one of his contacts within the secret service had mentioned that they would come in handy when the president had planned to go out with one of her goddaughters to a theme park for her birthday. Luke was very much looking forward to meeting her, as he had voted during the election and he thought his vote helped get her into office. Lisa still found his logic amusing and would look forward to teasing him about it if the day ever arose.

"We will have to liaise with the secret service team tonight and help with cordoning the area. Patrick and I will be off this afternoon, to catch up with the head of secret service and I'll call you when it's time for you to meet them."

The past few weeks they had been training harder to see where their abilities had limits and to try and develop them. John's ability was the only one that they had finished testing weeks ago. One result had been hidden from everyone apart from Jack, who was called by the team. They had discovered that the ability John and Jack shared was slowly taking over their entire bodies. Every cell was continually replacing itself and so eventually, they would effectively stop ageing. This was kept from Eve, only because she and Jack had developed a way of shutting out their thoughts from each other completely. The team had said that their ageing would stop completely within a year. Jack wasn't sure how to tell Eve about it and so he thought it best to keep it from John until he had a way of telling her. They had gotten closer over the past few weeks, all the training and working together had developed a bond with her he could no longer ignore. He felt complete when she was around. The way she was with him kept him smiling, even though she'd now set his bed on fire three times, she'd woken him up with shouting or throwing water on him while he was sleeping in it. He had found that she didn't enjoy him moving her food while she was eating. The reaching for something that was no longer there was irritating. Once he had taken the food directly from her and she almost bit into her hand. The humour was short lived when Eve took Luke hostage in retaliation. He was only guilty of finding Jack's actions funny. She made him throw the food he was enjoying at Jack. The first handful made perfect contact but the rest was stopped inches from his face and diverted toward the bin. Eve, not enjoying her retaliation being short lived, took over the rest of the table, each having no choice but to obey her wishes. Jack was outnumbered and could not stop the barrage of food strikes he sustained. Jim was not too happy with them. He had been finishing a conference call when he heard the commotion. He saw the back of Jack's head, covered with food, and what he had managed to stop from making contact with him was all over Eve. This caused her to increase the hold on the others and started making them try and hit Jack. Before Jack could take the easy way out and vanish, Jim came into view and shouted out in the loudest voice they had heard from him.

After the mess had been cleaned up and Eve was back to her normal self, she apologized to the others and Jack promised not to do that to her again.

Patrick had developed his ability as much as he could. The increased strength also had an effect on his bones. The force he could exert would be too much for a normal person's, but his could cope easily. He could now jump further, hit harder objects, land from great heights without hurting himself. He could now run harder and much faster.

Jim could now turn clothing and small objects invisible with enough concentration. A chair was the biggest he could manage. The range wasn't much but it was more then he or Jack had thought possible.

Eve had focused on her ability more after Jack discovered before her that they could control other people's minds. She was now able to control multiple persons and animals. She learned how to do this when a robin had tried to fly away before she was able to stroke it. She had it on her finger for a few moments before allowing it to go about its business completely unharmed.

Luke was happy with what he could do and only worked on his accuracy. Objects of size took a lot of concentration. Small objects he could handle easily and he enjoyed seeing how many he could control at once and in different movements. Tidying up the leftover casings and magazines in the range he found fun; he told the others to leave the place in a safe mess so that he could practice. Jack observed him tidying up while reloading clips at the same time. This inspired him to join in. Luke was happy to share and they had the range in order quickly, every magazine was full and stored safely. With the casings, they focused on seeing how small they could make them. This was something neither of them had thought of trying before. After a while they could make them into little balls of metal and they decided to keep them in a container they had in the corner of the room.

Lisa was now able to teleport very quickly and there didn't seem to be a limit as to how far she could go. Keeping focused on where she wanted to go was easy now and she could take up to five people a few hundred miles. Her ability to teleport other people while she stayed put was the same. A few miles were all she could manage. Jack helped out with the experimentation and he couldn't do any better.

"I think in the six months that we've been together, our full potential has been reached. Accuracy and speed is pretty much all I can see any of us improving on now," Jack said.

"I think you're right," Jim agreed.

"Where's Luke?" Jack asked.

"I saw him heading to the pool room this morning," Patrick said from behind the paper he was reading.

Eve was curious as to how the team on B3 had been doing and seeing as she'd not been there since she and Jack had first been allowed to roam freely, she decided to go and see how they were and what they were working on. She got up from her bed and walked out of her room. She had gotten the information about where the key was kept from Jim previously. She helped herself to it and went towards the lift. The doors opened as soon as she pressed the button and walked in. She inserted and turned the key, pressed the button and the lift doors closed.

The doors opened and she was greeted by the same white room she remembered and walked towards where she could hear the team working. As usual, they were all working on various machines; she had little interest in what any of them did and walked over to Alex, who had now become the head of the team.

"Hey Alex, how have you been?" He turned around.

"Hey Eve, I'm very well thanks, how are you?"

"I'm very well, thanks. Have you been keeping busy?"

Alex shrugged his shoulders. "We were busy with what Jack wanted to look into. John hasn't come up to ask questions, yet. Has he been busy?"

Eve was curious as to what they had been working on and went through Alex's thoughts. A few seconds passed and Alex could see what she was doing to him. She quickly learned what Jack had been holding back from her.

"Eve -" Alex said quickly but she was already walking back to the lift with the intent of exploding on Jack. Her mind was moving a mile a minute when she suddenly felt Alex's hand on her elbow.

"Eve, I've been thinking." She turned round and glared at him. Before she could force him to leave her alone he started talking again.

"I've been curious as to whether it is possible to make someone like John. His blood is the only one out of everyone we've been able to determine will give his ability to people for any period of time. If we could take some samples from you, we can see if we can give you John's ability. You and Jack were the templates for the whole project and I'd just like to see if it's possible."

Eve thought through for a minute about what he meant and she could hear in his head what the plan was. The team would need samples from her as she was now. The samples they had were used up.

"New samples sound quite painful, Alex," she said. He thought for a minute and she went through what would be done and what the possibilities would be. His thought process was so quick she was finding it hard to keep up with. The fact that there were words he was thinking that she'd never heard of before didn't help either.

"Alex, what are the main points? I'm having trouble keeping up." She said and it interrupted his train of thought. He saw her face and stopped.

"Sorry, Eve," he said and began telling her what they would need from her. John's samples were new and so they would be able to start work straight away.

Jack walked into the pool room and found Luke sitting under water. He didn't much like invading people's thoughts any more but curiosity was getting the better of him.

Just as he started to get something from Luke, he got up and looked at Jack. Luke stood up and made his way to the surface.

"Hey, Jack," he said, quite out of breath. Jack kept out of Luke's head and tried to work out for himself what he was trying to do.

Luke regained his normal breathing after a few large breaths and just as he was about to go back under, he saw the look on Jack's face.

"Should I bother?" Jack asked.

"I'm trying to see if I can lift the water. Combined molecules might be susceptible to alteration this way. I've been here a while. See?" Luke said, showing Jack his pruned hands. Jack simply gave him a thumb up, smiled and turned for the door. As he opened it he heard Luke take a deep breath and dive under again. *Well, at least he's keeping busy*, Jack thought.

He decided on going to see how John and Lisa were getting on with the map they had for the theme park.

John and Lisa had the blue print map of the theme park on the table, they were looking at the area and trying to look at points Jim had said they would need to find.

"It's a large area. Given our abilities, shouldn't normal security be a moot point now?" Lisa asked, half looking at the map and half thinking of going for another swim.

"Jim said that there will be points that we will need to keep clear in case their security needs to evacuate them at a moment's notice," John said, pointing to an escape exit on the map.

Lisa saw Jack appear in the room and took the opportunity to leave. "You and Jack look it over; if you need me I'll be in the pool."

John half looked up to say something before she disappeared.

"So, how's the planning going?' Jack asked, looking over the map upside-down. He looked up at John, who wasn't looking too impressed.

Lisa appeared in the ladies' changing area by the pool and got a fresh swimsuit from the pile. There was now a nice collection of suits, all within a size of each other. She and Eve could pretty much wear any of them that they wanted as they were close in size. She opted for a purple suit that she'd yet to try on and got changed.

Luke came up for air again and decided that this was not quite the best way to go about lifting the water. He got out of the pool and stood on the edge. He was trying to feel the water as a whole when his concentration was interrupted.

"What are you doing?" Lisa asked. She was standing by the pool, watching him hold his hands above the water; there was a small stress line on his forehead. The one she always saw when he was thinking too hard.

Luke opened his eyes and saw her standing there; she was wearing a blue/purple (depending on which angle was in the light) swimming suit that fitted her perfectly. The swimming and running she was so keen on was keeping her figure perfect. He wasn't sure that he would ever get used to seeing her like this and decided to jump into the pool.

Lisa saw his reaction and his half awkward leap into the pool and shook her head. If they were in the first few years of high school, this behaviour would be acceptable. She then decided that she would accept the compliment, as her hard work was paying off.

Lisa dived into the pool and swam over to where Luke was; he'd swallowed some water down the wrong hole and was trying not to choke.

"For goodness' sake, you big baby," she said and gave him a smack between the shoulder blades.

Luke's face went a little red due to the effort she had put behind the slap and he choked out a mouthful of water. Slowly he began breathing a bit easier.

"Good boy," she said and gave him a hug.

Patrick had left Jim to his phone call and decided to go have a walk around B3. It had been a while since he'd been around there and was curious as to what the scientists would be up to, now that the main part of their work was finished.

The lift doors opened and he walked onto the floor. There were four of the usual people working on machines and taking readings from various printouts. They didn't notice him walking into the room. Things seemed as busy as when he'd last walked onto this floor.

He overheard a conversation two of them were having about Eve.

"We'll have to compare these with what we have on file. It looks pretty similar to me, though," a little guy said to his female college. She turned round and nodded, there was a strange smile on her face. Patrick wasn't aware that they were working on Eve and Jack again. Then he saw the guy he knew was next in line to be supervisor. He walked over.

"Alex," he boomed. The man turned round. Patrick walked over to him. "Long time, no see, chap." He saw the frightened look this guy always had whenever they were in the same room.

"Patrick. Yeah, it's been a long time," Alex said. He had been afraid of Patrick before he became like the others, seeing him here now made his fear worse.

"What are you guys and gals working on? I thought the 'Adam and Eve' project was finished now?"

Alex looked around to the others who had all left the immediate area and were trying their best to look busy. He turned back to Patrick, who was still looking around at the equipment.

"The main part is, yes. Now were just taking more samples, you know, updating our systems."

Patrick turned back to him. "Your systems and samples are up to date, Alex. We each had some samples taken and given to you guys here. I don't see why you'd be working on Eve and not on Jack. Tell me what's going on, now." Patrick said the last word, leaning forward until he was a few inches from Alex's face.

Alex looked down at the floor and decided it wasn't really worth keeping things from this man.

"We think Eve might be able to take an additional ability." Alex started from where he thought would invite fewest questions.

Jim finished with his phone call and went for a walk outside. They would be working again soon so this was a good opportunity to walk around the facility. He didn't bother walking quickly; a leisurely half hour stroll would be nice. Outside was rather pleasant. It had been raining this morning but now that the sun was out, the day looked to be rather promising. He went out into the main reception, nodded to the security guards who stood up as he walked past and made his way outside. The sun was warm and refreshing on his face. Jim took a moment to enjoy it. A bird calling from his left distracted him from the sun and he decided to walk that way round the facility.

John and Jack were still looking over the plans when Lisa and Luke joined them.

"You guys really haven't moved since I left, have you?" she asked.

John looked up. "We've been quite busy, actually. Jack and I have looked over the prints, decided on what areas we think Jim would want looking at and the areas that need keeping clear and now we're thinking about what to have for lunch."

Luke and Lisa had been thinking about lunch as well, so the four of them decided to get a few ideas then run it past the others.

Jim finished his walk and went back to see the others who he assumed would be around their table and that was exactly where he found them, discussing lunch options.

"Ah, Jim," John said. "Have you any thoughts on lunch?"

"I'm happy to go with the majority or make a decision for you later on. Where are Patrick and Eve?"

"Last time I saw; Eve was in her room. But I looked earlier and she's gone walkabout," Lisa said.

"Patrick went for a walk after reading the paper this morning," John said.

"So, how long until we know if this'll work?" Eve asked, sitting in John's office chair. Jean was standing next to the monitors, looking at the empty glass boxes where Jack and the others had begun learning what each of them were capable of.

"We'll have the results later on this afternoon," Jean replied. "I'll call you when Alex has them."

Eve stood up and almost lost her balance.

"Here, sorry," Jean said, handing Eve what looked like an EpiPen. Eve took it and found out what it was from Jean's mind.

"Thanks," she said.

Eve took the pen in her hand and removed the cap, revealing the small needle. She took the cap off and injected herself, mid-neck. The relief was almost instant; her pain from the day's testing, poking with needles and having all those tubes stuck in her was gone now.

"This is what you've come up with from John's blood, some kind of EpiPen?" she asked, taking the needle out and replacing the cap.

Jean grinned. "We've only been able to make half a dozen of those but they work really well," she replied. "We aim to make more but it takes time. The ones that we've made are all we'll have until next month"

"Until more EpiPens come in," Eve finished.

Jean smiled unconvincingly. Eve could see and hear that she was not like the others and didn't much care for her mind being 'invaded' as she described it; in her head, of course. Eve decided that seeing as Jean was nice she wouldn't use her ability on her, *unless she annoys me*, she thought and this made her smile.

Jean took the smile as a friendly one.

"You know, we had more but Alex used one yesterday to see how effective it was when someone wasn't hurt," Jean stopped talking and grabbed Eve's hand. Eve remembered what had happened to Jack and John, she saw what happened to Alex in Jean's head and began running with Jean to the woman's locker room.

Just as Eve opened the door to the shower it started. "Please don't be offended," Jean said as she pushed Eve into the shower and closed the door.

In the midst of bodily noises, running water and clothing hitting the floor or walls was a half spoken, "Thank you."

Jean waited a few minutes and knocked on the shower door. "Eve?"

She heard coughing from the other side, then, "Jean, could you please get hold of John and ask him to ask Lisa to come?"

"Sure. No problem, I'll go call him," she replied.

"Thanks again," Eve said. Jean went out of the locker room and made her way back to the lab. The door opened on her and she jumped in shock.

"Oops, sorry," Patrick said as he walked past. Jean had a hand on her heart and with the other she held the open door. She motioned to Patrick that she was fine and walked past him into the lab. She didn't look back, focusing on getting to John's office so she could close the door. Patrick hadn't stopped to watch her like she had thought; he went to the lift and pressed the button, laughing to himself about scaring two scientists in as many minutes.

Inside John's office Jean found Alex, sitting in John's chair.

"Alex?" Jean asked.

"Oh, hey," he replied. She moved the chair he was in so that she could get to the phone; she picked it up and pressed the speed dial button one. John answered after a few rings. Jean told him what had happened and asked him to quietly get Lisa to bring Eve some new clothes.

"Sure, I'll go find her. You really should have waited for the results before giving Eve one of the pens. I'll ask Lisa to go see her. Jean, make sure the first person with those results calls me, okay." Jean agreed, apologized and put the phone down.

"Well, you've told John what you've been up to. I'll tell you what has happened in your absence," Alex said to her as she half turned to face him.

"Patrick?" she asked.

"He knows we're re-testing Eve. He wasn't happy that we've ruled him out for more testing and he wants us to find a way to give him John's ability," Alex said, holding up his hands in disbelief.

"Well, we can have a look at one or two ways we have discussed and show him the results. I know that won't make him happy but if it proves that he can't have what he wants, maybe he will settle for a few EpiPens," Jean said and walked towards the door, taking Alex's hand and pulling him out of the chair.

John walked over to the table. Lisa had just finished writing down her request for lunch and was handing the paper back to Jack. She looked up and saw John standing a few metres away. He motioned with his head for her to come over. She walked past Jim and Luke and made her way over to John.

Jack watched her out of the corner of his eye. He lowered his head to make it look like he was reading the list and used his ability to read John's thoughts. After he was done and knew what was going on with poor Eve, he decided not to listen in any more and that he would ask Jean about it later. He took a step back from the table, closed his eyes and disappeared.

Lisa walked into Eve's room and got some clothes for her. "Poor girl," she was thinking. She knew what had happened to John and Jack the day they had gotten their abilities; to them it was a funny story. Now they knew that Eve had been through the same ordeal they would make fun of her, surely. Eve would retaliate in some way, that would be certain. Lisa would look forward to that.

She gathered everything she thought Eve would need and teleported.

Inside the room she walked towards the shower room door. "Eve?" she said, tapping on the door.

"Hey, Thanks for coming. I'm decent, come in." Lisa pushed open the door and saw her sitting on a chair in the corner. Lisa could see there were a few subtle differences; her hair was a little longer and her face looked a little younger.

"You look a little different," Lisa said, walking over and handing her the clothes.

"Really, I feel great. What's different?" she asked.

"Well, you look a little younger and, is it just me, or is your hair slightly different?" Lisa asked, stepping back to look at her properly. Eve stood up and walked over to the mirror on the other side of the room. As she looked at her reflection she noticed what Lisa had.

"I see." she said. Eve turned to the side and clearly saw that her hair was a bit longer and looked healthier. Her face was the slightest bit rounder and her skin was a little clearer.

"Eve?" Lisa asked.

"Oh! No, Hun, it's okay The shower got rid of all the-mess. It goes to show that I've always been quite healthy." She blushed. Lisa knew that Eve had seen that she didn't want to hear the details and so she changed the subject.

"Is this permanent?" she asked.

"I don't know, I hope so," Eve replied.

Eve got changed while she told Lisa about what she had been doing all morning in the lab. Lisa was happy, getting answers; John's vague tale had given her a few questions and for a brief moment, she started thinking about what would happen to her.

"Lisa, Alex and Jean are running tests again. I don't know how this could affect you."

"I don't think it would affect me permanently," Lisa replied. "You and Jack are very rare. If Jack can change people and we think he will be able to change most, they will only be able to sustain a single ability. I'll go see Alex after lunch. Oh, lunch!" She held out her hand.

"Can I brush my teeth first?" Eve asked. Lisa nodded, Eve took her hand and they disappeared.

Jack was just about done; lunch was all packed and ready to take back. He had a quick thought about Eve and how a treat would hopefully make her feel a little better; after all, she would have had to ask people for a few favours. Jack knew that Eve liked being independent, asking for help wasn't something she enjoyed. He decided to revisit a little coffee shop he'd visited in Switzerland one day when the others wanted something different for lunch;

Eve had said that their chocolate brownies were the best she'd ever tasted.

Jack said goodbye to the lady who owned the restaurant he was in and walked outside. It was a beautiful day. The town was quiet; the only people around were those who were visiting either for the first time, or those who had stumbled upon the quaint, quiet village and now frequented the place on every opportunity they had, or those who lived nearby.

The alleyway next to the restaurant was home to a number of wooden pallets, beer barrels and wheelie bins. He walked past a few, turned round to make sure that no one was watching and teleported.

Jack appeared from the same alleyway he had used before. Although he did not like using his telepathy, some of the places he had visited purely from picking through people's memories had left him very grateful. Switzerland has always been known for its chocolate and now the group looked forward to Jack bringing it back for them.

With already one large bag of food, Jack ordered the freshly made brownies he saw on the shelf. The boy working there packed them up for him, put his transaction through and wished him a good day. *Right, now back to the mad house,* Jack thought.

Eve and Lisa appeared in the garden area of the living quarters. Now that the weather wasn't quite as nice as previously, people didn't stay here much. Eve wanted to brush her teeth quickly and Lisa was the quickest way back and forth.

They leisurely walked to Eve's apartment, chatting about what Jack had said he would get for lunch and how nice it was that he would get almost every meal without fuss.

"Do you think he does it because it nice to get away or more likely; he likes to get to see the world, even if it only means on a food basis?" Lisa asked Eve as she was brushing.

"I know he likes to get out and about, but it's more of the fact he likes to see how different places smell."

Lisa could see what Jack would find appealing, but she didn't think that would be a contributing factor to him going to get them food every day. "I can understand that," she replied.

Eve could hear the questioning tone in her reply. "Well, that's how he saw it a while ago. I used to be able to dip into his thoughts whenever I liked, but for the last month or so he's kept me out. Perhaps there is more to it or he prefers to make me ask him questions, rather than letting me rummage through his head." Eve could see in Lisa's face that the latter was the more likely option.

"So, how are things between you and Luke?" Eve asked.

"Well, when we worked together it was nice and simple; he liked me and I could get more work done, knowing he would give me a hand if needed. It was clear that he liked me but I didn't want anything to interfere with the work we were doing, so I kept my mind on the job at hand. Now that we spend every day together, it's hard to ignore. To be honest, I'm not sure how I feel. We've been working lots and the jobs we do I'm usually with Patrick or Jim. Luke works mostly with you or John. Tomorrow will be the first job that we've all worked on together. It should be quite fun. Jim has asked me to stay with you and the client all day. We've been worked into the security detail, right?" Eve nodded. "I'm not a big fan of suits but I'm looking forward to tomorrow," she finished, just as Eve had finished rinsing and put her toothbrush back.

"Shall we?" Lisa asked holding out her hand. Eve felt better but she now realized how hungry she was. She took Lisa's hand again and they disappeared.

John had gotten the table ready. Jack was back with the food. He was setting out what people had asked for and had stored the brownies safely in the box he had used before they had moved. Jim was on the phone and Patrick was walking from the lift when the girls appeared. He stopped and turned round.

"And how has your day been, Eve?" he asked.

"Fine, thanks. I've been with Alex and Jean all day," she replied.

Eve dipped into Patrick's thoughts and did not like what she saw; the day she'd had was not news to him and he had an agenda she wasn't happy with.

"I see the benefits in what the lab geeks have created. It's taken a few years off you."

"Thanks," she replied. She planned to talk to him about his thoughts, later.

They walked towards the table where the only one missing was Luke.

"Right, everything is set out, I'll go see what's taking Water Boy so long," Jack said. He disappeared and the others all sat down where their order was waiting for them.

Jack found Luke getting changed in the pool area. "And how did your experiment go?" he asked. Luke was struggling to put his T-shirt back on. He'd lost track of time, even though there was a big clock on the end wall that Jim had put up especially.

"It went quite well," a muffled voice came from somewhere in the tangled clothing.

"Let me help," Jack said and pulled a knotted bit of shirt that had somehow been tucked into one of the sleeves. Luke's head popped out and Jack heard Luke sigh in relief.

"Come on, chap, lunch is getting cold."

He took Luke's hand and they disappeared.

Lunch was eaten in much the same way they'd become accustomed to; the main topic of conversation was mostly work; Jack would make a few jokes about how a few tempting opportunities had arisen to make people look silly on the jobs he been on. Thankfully, Jim knew Jack would not do anything untoward and some of the things he thought of doing were entertaining. Eve would pick out things she'd thought of working in future, they didn't use their abilities to rig elections or votes but there were a few things she wanted to put past Jim.

"What if we could help out in countries where the best person for the job keeps losing?" she asked. Jim looked over and wiped his mouth with a napkin.

"Eve, we shouldn't do anything like that. People should have the right to make their own decisions, after all it is really the only absolute freedom anyone has. Unless you have anything to say about it, of course," he joked. She rolled her eyes while the others laughed at his statement.

"What I mean is, can't we at least make sure that some votes are not rigged?" she asked.

"That would take a very long time, Eve. Could you listen in to all the people's heads that are counting the ballot papers, or those that use computers to tally up, quite a few people look over the organization of elections or votes. Quite frankly, the only way I can see us making any difference that way is for you and Jack to manipulate the majority of a town, city, state or country to vote the way we see as the best way they can be served by the right person at the right moment. That could work, but then the people that work for the person who's running for office could have bad people working for them. I have thought of that but I don't see a way of cheating fairly."

John cleared his throat.

"What about sports?" he suggested.

"I've thought of that!" Patrick said. "I would become the best at everything, besides golf," John half choked on his food.

"Very funny' Jim said.

"I'd become an epic goalkeeper!" Luke said, laughing. Patrick patted him on the back.

"That's thinking a bit small," Jack commented. "I'd win every golf tournament with holes in one. In fact, I'd even try it, blindfolded. Or I'd go up against the SAS and become the world's hide and seek champion." Everyone joined in, laughing. Eve threw a fork at Jack, who spun it around his head and sent it back into Eve's hand.

They weighed up work that they had done, what work Jim had lined up, and things they could continue to do on their own. Illegal power plants were next for Jim to divide up between them. A few more around the world had come to his attention. There would be no money for these jobs but they all agreed that something had to be done. They talked about tomorrow's job and were all pretty happy about what they each had to do.

"Thanks for lunch, Jack," Luke said, moving the empty plates towards the bin. The others said their thanks or gave appreciative nods. Jack smiled and bowed as a gentleman would.

"Dessert, anyone?" he asked. Eve saw what he had brought back for her and Jack saw her face light up. "As you know, Eve, we've all noticed the change you've experienced today and we thought this would be a good time to indulge in one of your favourite desserts," he lied. She knew he'd done it off his own bat. The others thought it was a nice gesture and, in unison, they said that she looked amazing.

"So, how do you feel?" John asked.

"Fantastic," she said. Eve thought for a moment. Everybody was waiting for more but Eve thought that one word was the only one that could sum up how she felt. Younger, vibrant, youthful, energetic, more confident, were just some of the things she felt but 'fantastic' seemed to sum it up best.

The group asked questions in turn. The mocking that she'd expected never came. Jack kept his mind closed from her, but he said nothing untoward, or even laughed while people asked questions.

They finished the brownies, Eve having more than the others, to no one's surprise. She insisted on clearing the table afterwards, giving those who tried to help stern looks. Luke ignored the look and started clearing his side of the table. Eve cleared her throat and when Luke turned; the look he got was all that was needed to stop him.

John received a call from Alex soon after the table was cleared. He, Eve and Jim made their way to the lab to look over the results.

Alex and Jean were waiting for them in John's office when they walked in.

"Good work, guys," John said, taking the folder Jean was holding. He and Jim looked over what was written. Eve went through everyone's head, deciphering what she wanted to know.

"These are conclusive?" John asked, looking at Alex.

"They are," he replied and Jean nodded with excitement.

"So, Eve now has John's ability?" Jim asked Alex.

"Not exactly," John said, still reading. "She appears to have something different." Jim looked between the three scientists with a curious look.

"Jack's ability is a direct copy of mine. He is able to give and take things from people, whether it be their ability or the person's energy," Alex said, as he could see John was reading. "Eve's body has changed itself to take in

John's blood as a welcomed virus. It's taken the changes and come up with something to suit itself. She'll heal the same when she's injured and her body has returned to when it was healthiest, but unlike John and Jack, she will continue to change. Her menstrual cycle, for example will continue as normal. Her body will stay as it is. Her ageing will eventually stop like John's and Jack's will, but her body will continue to change even after that. We think she will live as long as they will, but her body will have a normal cycle until it decides to stop. It's impossible to tell when that will be though."

"So I could still have children?" Eve asked.

"Yes, and we believe you'll give birth to children with natural abilities," Jean answered.

"I think your menstrual cycle will last quite a while, Eve," John said, closing the file and handing it to Jim. He looked through the file with Eve and John pointed out what each test meant.

"So basically, I'll have a normal life but over an extended period of time?" she asked.

"In a nut shell," John replied.

"Cool," she said handing back the file. She felt so happy, the smile on her face was now a grin. She would live as long as the others and could still have the option of children if she wanted to, but they would possibly be born like her, different, special. This was all theoretic. Only she would know what would happen, as she was the only one this would happen to. She was again excited about the future.

Chapter Eight

Working as a Team

Eve had told the others about what had happened with Jean and Alex. The only one not to give words of encouragement was Patrick. He spent the whole time sitting quietly, pretending to read the paper. Every now and then, someone would look over to where he was sitting. Patrick would half smile and nod, they would smile back and go back to talking with Eve. After a while, he stood up and walked out of the room, throwing his paper in the bin. Jim watched him walk off. He looked unhappy about something, and Jim was sure that Patrick would have some discussion with the scientists soon, if he hadn't already. Eve saw Patrick leaving and saw in Jim's head what would happen next. She would talk to him when the time was right.

"We've got work tomorrow, so how about we call it a night?" Jim suggested.

Jack and Lisa took them to the residence and after a little further discussion, they all went off to their apartments.

"Patrick will be okay?" Eve asked Jim. It was just him and Eve now on the grass.

"You know what I think and what I'm hoping for, Eve. Only you, Jack and Patrick himself know what the truth is. I hope we don't have to stop him from doing something that will cause problems. Anyway, good night," he said, patting her elbow, and turned towards his apartment.

"I guess we'll see," Eve said, far too low for anyone to hear, and walked towards her door.

Jim was the first one up. He made his way to the café that he and Jack went to the first time they got food for everyone.

The café was empty, from what Jim could see when he walked past, but a shadow he saw from the corner of his eye caught his attention. Jim half smiled and made his way to the door. He opened it and walked inside.

"Good morning, Mrs Cluckworth. Could I have two filter coffees when you've got a moment?" Jim said to the café owner, who was still preparing the café for customers.

"Patrick. You're here very early. I didn't hear you leave this morning," Jim said, sitting down at the corner table Patrick occupied. Patrick crossed his arms on the table.

"That's because I didn't go back to the residence. I've been thinking for a while." Patrick didn't look tired. His face was one of frustration. Whatever he'd spent the night thinking about was clearly bothering him. "I want what they have, sir. I want it more than anything. The white coats say it's not possible but I don't believe them. Isn't there always a way around?" He was leaning forward now. The frustration had turned to anger.

"Patrick, I honestly don't know. John, Lisa and Luke will have a look when I ask them and I'm sure that if there is a way to do it, they will make it so."

Mrs Cluckworth walked over with a fresh pot of coffee. The two men turned over their cups and gave her an appreciative smile as she served them their coffee. "Is there anything else I can get for you, gentlemen?" she asked.

"Some scrambled eggs on toast would be nice, ma'am," Patrick said. Jim nodded when she looked at him.

"Coming right up," she said.

Lisa woke up. She blinked a few times and turned to look at the clock on her bedside table. The time was six thirty. "Ahh," she grumbled and pulled the cover off. She made her way to her closet and selected a swimming costume at random. After she changed, she picked up a towel and closed her eyes.

Eve and Jack had gotten up at six and gone for a run around the facility. John and Luke decided that they would leave them to it and take advantage of the shooting range being free.

"I've no idea where Jim and Patrick are, but it's nice to have the place free for a change, isn't it?" Luke said as they were selecting a gun from off the wall each and getting the ammo ready.

"I think Jim went for coffee and I'm betting Patrick is with him," John said. He'd selected a desert eagle, the same gun Patrick had been teaching him to use, and was walking towards the ear defenders. John reached for one and saw the one next to it lift off the wall and start moving to where Luke was standing.

"I hope today goes well," Luke said as the ear defenders reached his hand. John walked back over and put his defenders on.

"Yup. I do, too," he said and fired off a round.

"So, we get there at eight thirty?" Jack asked Eve as they began their second lap of the facility.

"That's the plan," Eve replied. "Can we finish this lap and then you send me back to my apartment so I can get a few laps of the pool in before we leave?" she asked.

"You read my mind," Jack replied and increased his pace before Eve could punch him. She burst into a full sprint, determinedly overtaking him. The new ability she had meant that anything physical was now almost effortless. Sprinting felt the same but her muscles didn't get tired and her heart could easily cope with whatever she was doing.

"Ha!" She said as she ran past Jack, slapping the back of his leg. Jack skipped, holding his thigh. Eve turned back and started laughing. Jack sprinted off after her.

They all met up on the grass just before eight thirty and Jim went through, for the last time, who was doing what for the day. "So, we're all clear?" Everyone nodded back.

"Good. Lisa, Jack if you would, please."

Jack, John and Eve took each other's hands while Lisa took Jim, Patrick and Luke.

The seven of them appeared in a small group of hedges, a few feet from each other. Jim had had Jack and Lisa come here beforehand and Jack moved a few bushes around for convenience.

The park was still closed, but there were security men running around and guys in suits checking last minute details.

The park was full of sunshine. The early spring had the flowers in blossom; the birds nesting in the trees were singing their songs. The ground was clean and the morning dew made the whole place look like it was out of a children's book. Lisa looked around and for a moment felt like she was Dorothy, following the yellow brick road.

"Okay, let's get to it," Jim said, walking past Lisa and towards the man he had been told where and when to meet.

Jim and a man called Aaron dispatched them to different sections of the secret service team and other parts of the park. Lisa and Eve were with the president as she made her way around the park. They didn't move more than twenty feet from wherever she and her family were. They dressed in civilian clothing and blended in well. Patrick and Jim went into the CCTV suite and monitored everything from there. John and Luke stayed close to the president's family, who were in a different part of the park for the morning. Jack moved ahead, according to where the president's family wanted to go, whether they went on rides or to the rest rooms or restaurants. Their thoughts helped him decide where needed looking at and where to tell Jim there were heading.

"We're off to Fright Tower now, Jim," Jack said, moving at the front of the group.

"Roger that," Jim replied over the radio.

"Ah, I wanted to go on that one," Eve's voice came over the radio.

"Eve," Jim's voice came back.

"Boss, it's still not on," she said back. *I'll make her go later on*, Eve thought.

The president was walking around the park, security surrounding her. She was admiring the work that had been done in preparation for their day out. Fans and supporters were kept at an arm's length for the most part, but when the president wanted to shake people's hands and say hello, there wasn't much security could do but watch and pray no one tried anything. They found it a little odd that people were not rushing through or trying to get right up close. Eve had them all well behaved. Jack had come back to give her a hand while the First Family were on the rides. John and Luke were with them, along with enough security to keep the whole ride well behaved. Thanks, there are a lot of people here to keep up with, Eve thought to where she could sense Jack. *No problem,* she heard back. *I'll keep them from the guy in the red if that works?*

Let's not keep them too organized. Security's getting a bit confused, Eve thought back. She now saw Jack, who was juggling apples. *Show off,* she thought.

Jack went back and forth whenever it was needed throughout the day. The park was very busy but well behaved. The president re-joined her family after a few hours. They went on Fright Tower twice. Jim assumed and Jack knew that Eve had wanted to go again. The president asked the staff if they didn't mind her and her family going on once more. Obviously they allowed them and the people in line were kept from complaining. Jim called Eve on the radio. She tried to protest her innocence, but to no avail.

The meal time was hardest of all to deal with. Normal people had a hard time getting seats. For the seven that made up the First Family, a bench marked 'reserved' proved to be difficult to keep clear. Security did their best to keep people away, while Jack and Eve kept the staff honest and the food clean for everyone to eat.

Eve walked over to Jack and Luke, who were behind the First Family.

"Busy day, hopefully it won't be too much longer now," Jack started to answer her when they both turned to someone in the back, who was thinking something they didn't like.

A man stood up from his seat. The people he was with seemed to not know him or know why he was standing up. A gun appeared from his pocket. Jack was over behind him before the first person to notice could say anything. Jack grabbed the hand holding the butt of the gun and pulled down with too much force. The man's arm made a loud pop as the shoulder came out of its socket. The man began to scream in pain as Jack pushed a burger into his mouth, stuffing out any noise. The shoulder went back in as Jack slammed it into the wooden pillar he was standing next to. The man passed out. Jack didn't quite pick him up but

171

started moving him off and this was when people started standing up. All anyone could see was, a man in plain clothes, carrying out an unconscious man from the restaurant. Mild chatter started before Eve took care of those who'd noticed.

Jack got outside and walked behind the first wall he could find, and turned to make sure that he wasn't being watched. He wasn't. Jack closed his eyes and disappeared.

Jim and Patrick were inside the CCTV suite with the head of secret service when Jack came into the room. Jim turned round as the door opened. In walked Jack, in his left hand was an unconscious man with half a cheeseburger hanging out of his mouth and a large pistol poking out from the top of his jeans.

"Colonel, this idiot was about to do something silly in the local Burger King. Shall I leave him here to be questioned?" Jack asked. Jim sat back in his chair and looked at the head of secret service.

"Did you want to deal with this or shall we?"

The man looked, dumbfounded, at Jack. He put his hand to the microphone on his tie.

"Status report on 'Falcon', someone." A second went past.

"Location secure," Lisa's voice came back over the radio. Jim put his hand on the man's shoulder.

"Aaron, this is why we were hired. Jack, there is a police van downstairs. Take him there and make sure the police secure him. Make sure you get as much information you can when he wakes up." Aaron looked back to Jim, barely turning his head and back to Jack, still comfortably holding up the unconscious man with one hand.

"Sure, colonel, I'll have a chat with him later on," he said, not taking his eyes off Jack.

"Will do, colonel." Jack turned his head. "Aaron," he said, nodding once, walking out of the room.

Outside Jack met up with an officer standing by the police van.

"Officer." The man turned round. "Secure this man. He has a gun in his waistband. Secret service will be along after the president is finished to question him, okay?" The officer took the man and struggled to hold his weight.

"And who are you?" he asked.

"Don't worry about that, mate," he replied and walked towards the alleyway he'd come from. The officer quickly put on a set of handcuffs onto the man, who was starting to wake up, and sat him into the back of the van. He put the gun into an evidence bag and closed the door. The officer turned round and watched Jack walking off. A moment of thought came over his face and the officer started walking after Jack. Jack could hear the officer's thoughts and a smile appeared on his face. Jack walked towards the first alleyway he could see. Once there he closed his eyes.

The officer saw him walking round the corner and once he'd lost view, he ran towards the alley as fast as he could. He rounded only the corner to find the place empty.

"Who the hell was that?" he said out loud.

Eve was standing next to secret service, talking about the day and how long the visit was going to last.

"So, who do you guys work for?" the agent asked.

"We're on training," she said. "Secret service course," she added.

"Oh, well, I hope you guys pass."

Eve smiled "I think we're doing okay, today. But thanks. Excuse me a second," The man she was standing next to nodded. Eve was tired of listening to the man's thoughts about how good she looked and if she was single.

Jack walked back to his position and winked at her as he walked past. *Very funny,* she thought. Jack was looking as inconspicuous as he was able to, leaning against a lamp post. Eve gave him a nod; Jack stood up straight and walked over.

"Hey, how are things going here?" he asked. Eve gave him a sarcastic look.

"Nice job earlier. I had to change three people's thoughts on what they saw but aside from that, you managed to get that done safely and quietly. Well done." Jack gave her a mocking bow

"I'm glad you're slightly impressed," he said, flashing a crooked smile.

"Next one is on me," she said. Eve looked off, listening to something a few tables away that bothered her. A man was arguing a little nosily with his family. Not so much that the neighbouring tables would be disturbed, but the conversation, along with the group's thoughts, had caught Eve's attention. The conversation was about the same-sex marriage law that had just been passed. The men of the group were arguing against the law, while the women were arguing in favour; all this only four tables away from the president who had signed it.

Eve listened for a short while, picking up on a few things that the man who was being the loudest contributor was thinking. Jack was also in on this. "Got it," Eve said and turned for the table. Jack could see what she had planned and gave her a thumbs up for what she was about to achieve.

"Hi," Eve said, interrupting. "Could we speak about this outside? I couldn't help overhearing your conversation and would like to hear about your opinions in further detail. I'm with the president's advance party." The man leaned back in his chair; in an attempt at creating an over imposing posture.

"Sure, why don't we go outside and I can tell you where the president is failing the American public," the man said.

"After you," Eve said, showing the man and his family the exit. They had long since finished their meals, so they stood up in unison and walked towards the exit. Eve watched as the man gave way to his wife and daughters before his son, and then to Eve. She accepted his invitation and walked out with the others.

Outside she was greeted by brilliant sunshine. The sun was illuminating everything with an orange glow. She stopped for a moment and Eve thought how no one could possibly be in a bad mood on a day as magnificent as this.

"Where does your president get off-?" The man blurted out.

Eve turned to face him, slightly annoyed that he had spoiled the admiration she was holding for the beautiful tranquillity he had failed to notice. Eve invaded his mind. Against her natural reaction she decided to do this man a favour. *You will go about your day, along with your family and will do nothing but encourage them to have a spectacular day, filled with fun and love. This challenge you will accept gladly, for the people you are with, are the very purpose of your being.* She gave him back his thoughts and crossed her arms, looking at him and waiting for his brain to take in its new way of thinking. The man blinked a few times and with a slightly confused look smiled at her, turned and hugged his family.

"Come on guys, I'll race you to Thunder Mountain. Last one there has to hold the bags," and he took off, running. His family looked a little confused at first but wasted no time in running to catch up with him

Eve turned to walk back into the restaurant. Jack was standing there; watching her. He was cross legged and leaning against a pillar that was in front of the doors.

"That's quite possibly the nicest thing I've ever seen someone manipulate anyone into doing," he said and gave her a prolonged bow of respect and before he fell over, walked over to her.

"He almost spoiled my day," she said. "If it wasn't for the lovely weather, I'm sure that I would have given him a prolonged nightmare, one which I would have trapped him in for an hour or two." Jack stopped a few feet from her. He had a strange smile on his face. One she'd not seen on him before.

"Eve, today…" he trailed off. He wanted to share how good the day had been. He just couldn't think of how to tell her, without making her laugh at him or say anything to make things awkward between them. They knew how they felt about each other. They just didn't want to be the first to bring up the subject or make the first move.

"Working on a day like this; seeing all of these people enjoying a day out with those whom they love has made me think. You know, if I were to be given one wish -" he took her hand. She had her head to the side, listening to each word he said. "- it would be to remain at your side, repeating this day and its infinite splendour. It is a day I'd gladly spend an eternity, sharing with you. I can think of nothing more that would fill my soul with happiness." He reached out and with the back of his other hand stroked the side of her face. Eve closed her eyes and for the first time, she could hardly notice the sun kissing her skin.

"Eve, Jack," they heard over the radio. "The First Family are moving." Jack took hold of his microphone, without taking his eyes off Eve's.

"Thanks, Luke, we're waiting outside," they continued looking into one another's eyes while Eve spoke into her microphone.

"They will be leaving soon, one more ride and then we can call it a day."

"Okay, guys. We're about to start moving out," Lisa came back over the radio.

"Roger that," Eve replied. Jack looked almost lost in her eyes. She didn't think it would be possible to grow tired of looking into his odd but beautiful eyes. She was reading the look on his face. "Later," she said and turned round to face the doors. Jack's smile grew and he faced the doors just as a woman in jeans and a fitted T-shirt, sunglasses and a transparent earpiece, which only came into view when the breeze blew her hair, opened and held the doors for the First Family.

The president walked outside, followed by her family and secret service. There were no cordoned off areas so the public and security mixed quite well.

Jack and Eve moved into the crowd and escorted them to what was to be the last ride of the day. The ride was a log flume. The grandchildren had wanted to go on the ride first, but the president wanted to go on the only mystery ride the amusement park had, first. The day had been quite good as they had gotten to go on thirteen rides in five hours. The lines had been very short, but secret service had gotten the family onto the first sections on every ride, which helped get more out of the day. Luke and Eve went on the ride with the family. Once the ride had finished and everyone was off, they escorted everyone to the exits. Jack walked with Eve behind everyone. They were listening to the thoughts of those on their respective sides. Jack had a listen to Luke's thoughts and he drew the conclusion that Luke had enjoyed the ride more than everyone else, which wasn't supposed to be part of the working day, but Jack thought that Jim would take that as a happy coincidence. Eve was listening to the president's thoughts, against Jim's instructions. She was happy to hear that the Americans had elected someone she could see was a good person. Then, Eve heard a familiar person coming from behind them. Patrick had gotten bored and broken ranks to see what Jack and Eve could hear. The day was pretty much over as they were escorting their clients to the motorcade.

Eve turned to see Patrick walking behind Jack, who had chosen to ignore his presence and concentrate on the last part of the job.

"Patrick," Eve said in a confused, slightly annoyed tone. "What are you playing at?" Patrick smiled and winked at her.

"What's the president thinking?" he asked, walking side by side with her.

"Jim specifically said we were not to do that," Eve replied.

"You didn't answer me," he retorted. Eve didn't turn to look at him.

"Quite right, and unless you want to spend the rest of the day thinking you're a five-year-old girl, I'd leave it at that." Patrick raised his hands in submission and turned back to where Jack was. He slowed his pace to match Jack's.

"Patrick, Eve was serious about what she said, mate. Don't ask me to start snooping about inside people's heads. Let's just get the job finished." Jack was looking ahead, but keeping Patrick where he could see him.

"That's fair enough, mate. Just tell me later on if you do hear anything, okay?" With that, he patted Jack on the shoulder and walked away in the opposite direction.

Jim was waiting by the motorcade when they arrived. Aaron broke off and walked towards him. The agents got the First Family into their respective cars and joined them for the drive to the airport. "Thanks, colonel, it's not a bad team you've got here. I'll send you the report later on," he said, putting out his hand.

"Thanks, Aaron. I'll look forward to reading it. It's good to see you again. Let's make sure it's not as long 'til our next meeting," He took his hand and the two shook firmly before Aaron nodded to his old boss and joined the president in their car. Patrick walked over to Jim and stood beside him as the two of them watched the blacked-out vehicles drive off to the airport.

"So, that was a waste of time. Aren't you as bored as I am now of the constant babysitting jobs?" Patrick asked in a low voice, close to Jim's ear. He turned his head to look at Patrick.

"It's the quiet jobs I like doing most of all, Patrick. The blood lust and need for action passed me a long time ago, as one day it will to you. Don't go looking for trouble." He put his hand on Patrick's shoulder as he walked over to where the others were standing.

"Let's go," he said, taking Lisa's outstretched hand. She was holding Luke's hand; she knew he was looking a little too happy about it. Jim took Lisa's hand and the three of them disappeared. Patrick walked over to the group; the sunglasses on his face made him look more imposing than usual. Eve could see that he was happy about something so she decided to have a snoop around. *I wonder how that geek is getting on; he should have finished by now. I'll visit him after I debrief.* Eve had heard enough.

"Patrick, what's going on?" she asked. Jack and John were standing next to her, ready to go home. They looked at her, then at each other, and took a step closer to Patrick.

"I thought I could feel you, rummaging around in my head, naughty girl," he said without missing a step. He was surprised she'd taken this long to find out. "I'm sick of being left out of the healing squad. First, you," he said, pointing at John, "get the most useful ability of us all. Then, Jack does his photocopying ability crap, and now, the little annoying one gets it." The three of them were looking unimpressed at him. Jack took off his sunglasses

"What, being stronger, faster and tougher then you could ever have hoped to be, isn't enough, Patrick?"

Jack respected the fact that Patrick wasn't trying to hide his actions. He should have known something like this would happen.

"The scientists aren't there for you to bully into doing whatever ideas strike you. They've already done more than I'd ever dreamed of and they continue to work for me after I told them we'd give them a decent settlement and work. Now that the project has been finished, they want to see what else they can accomplish. You come and talk to me, first," John said, quite angrily. Patrick took off his sunglasses.

"Relax, John. If I want to talk to them I will. You wouldn't dare get in my way," he said, towering over him.

Patrick's right knee gave out and he fell onto his back. He strained like he was trying to get up but couldn't. Eve smiled at him.

"I'm getting good at this. Bully one more person and you'll regret it." Patrick was furious now and was glaring at her. She let him have control over his body back and Patrick jumped up. He said nothing and walked over to Jack, who already knew what he wanted. Jack took his hand and disappeared. A few seconds later he was back and took John's and Eve's hands.

"Leave him to it, Eve. I'll go see Alex and see what they've done." Eve looked at Jack and he could see that she had no intention of leaving Patrick to it. As far as she was concerned, he didn't deserve to have an ability any more and couldn't be trusted. John looked at them both.

"You'd better run this past Jim, first mate. I don't see this going well at all." Jack nodded with quite a solemn look on his face. They disappeared and arrived where the others were waiting by the table. Eve looked around and couldn't see Patrick. She looked over her shoulder but Jack wasn't there. Jim was sitting down at the table, looking through some paperwork. She walked over to him.

It didn't take Jack too long to find Patrick. He was in the lab, talking quite calmly to Alex and Jean. Jack moved to a position where he could take off his suit and became invisible.

"So, what you're telling me is that you've synthesized a way to make the healing process permanent?" Patrick said, putting his hands in his pockets. Jean took a step back and looked between Patrick and Alex.

"Well, perhaps not permanent. But you should be able to go a couple of days before the effects wear off. What you've asked for just isn't possible, Patrick. It's only the rarest of blood deformities that can accept an additional ability. What Jack can do, we never thought a person could do. Quite frankly, I have to stop myself from asking him to change me every time I see him. You're very lucky to have something," Alex said. Jack could see that he was very much intimidated by Patrick, then again, who wouldn't be? Seeing him more often had perhaps taken away some of the fear factor, or perhaps he wanted to look a little tougher in front of Jean. Patrick put one of his hands on his face in thought.

"What happened to that kid we had at the beginning that was originally in charge, Nathan something?"

Alex looked automatically at Jean in surprise.

"He was very early on and quite mad, I must say," Jean said in response. "John took him on because he was top of John's original class. He was quite brilliant but he didn't want the same thing as us. He wanted to develop something completely for himself. John had to let him go." She stopped before Patrick could ask any more "I don't think any of us know where he went after the initial stages. He never came here. You could look in the university but I

181

doubt he would have gone back there." Patrick smiled and turned round.

"Thanks," was all he said.

Jack watched Patrick walk off and out into the corridor. Once he heard the lift open and close he came back into view and walked over to where Jean and Alex were now in quiet conversation.

"Guys, please tell me about this Nathan bloke?"

Alex sat on the table and adjusted his glasses "well," he began.

It turned out that Nathan and Patrick shared the same goal when it came to what abilities were to be sought after and what sort of people should get them. Patrick was now after Nathan and hoping that he had continued the work John had started all those years ago.

"Well, good thing Patrick has to get to the university by human means," Jack said.

"Jack, mate, think about all the time you've spent with Patrick. He might be a brute but he's intelligent and very resourceful. If he wants to find Nathan, he will."

Jack thought about this for a moment and the realization hit him quickly.

"Thanks, guys. I'll go sort it out," he said.

Jim had in his office a top-of-the-line system. All Patrick needed to do was to go through the employment records and find Nathan's last name. From there it would take him minutes to find his last known address and place of employment. Jack disappeared and found himself in Jim's office. It was in darkness. The computer was off but Jack could feel the heat coming off the screens. They had been used and turned off recently. He thought about it and knew there was no other way around it; he had to tell the others.

The others were all sitting at the table, listening to Jim, when Jack appeared in the corner he usually sat at. Lisa let out a squeak at his sudden appearance. The others turned round and Jim stopped talking.

"Houston, we may have a problem," he said.

Jack filled them in on the situation at hand. Jim had his head cocked to the side, resting it on one hand. John had walked a little distance off to think, and Eve was driving herself mad, going through every thought she could hear from the guards outside, trying to see if one of them had spotted Patrick leaving. Jack was impressed as to how developed her ability had become. He would plan on talking to her about it later on.

"Anything?" Jack asked Eve. She looked up and the look on her face was all he needed.

"I should have seen this coming," Jim said standing. "Lisa," he said taking her hand. "My office, please." She nodded and took his hand. The disappeared and John walked back over.

"Ah, crap. They need to hear this," he said.

Jack held out his hand. "Then let's go." he said. Lisa and Jim were walking over to Jim's desk when the others arrived.

"Jim," John said as Jim was booting up the systems. "Nathan wouldn't have gotten along as far as us, but with Patrick's DNA, he could create something. He's a bright lad, and ambitious."

Jim wasn't listening. He stood up and turned to face the others. Lisa did the same. "He's crashed the system. I can fix it but it's going to take a while."

Chapter Nine

Nathan Gabriel

Patrick knew the others would have figured out that he had crashed the system and would be well on the way to fixing it by now. He knew it was only a matter of time before one of them got past his encryption and found out what he already knew. He had made good use of the four-hour head start. Luckily, Dr Nathan Gabriel didn't live too far away. Patrick was off the plane now and in a taxi en route to his home address. *I wonder why this guy lives so close to an airport?* Patrick thought. He'd already given the taxi driver twice the quoted price, to ensure this journey was kept off their books. He knew slowing Jim down was all Patrick could do. The taxi pulled up outside a large house. It was in need of restoration but it didn't look like it was quite ready to fall down. Something didn't look quite right to him. The front garden was overgrown and undisturbed. The front door was missing lines of paint and the grass leading up to it was completely undisturbed. Patrick looked at the mail box, which looked fairly new, so someone had been collecting mail for this place. Patrick decided to have a walk around and see if he could spot a path someone would have used. He made his way round to the side of the house.

The fence was intact, though slightly mouldy, so he went to the back of the house which was separated from its neighbour's by a thin alleyway. He made his way down and spotted a used path, which stopped by a secure wooden door. A heavy duty padlock was on the outside, which had rust on it. Patrick could see a bit of fence which to a normal person, wouldn't look too out of place. He tapped the sides and heard which parts were hollow and slid the bit of wood aside to reveal a number lock and intercom. Patrick shook his head and rummaged around in his pocket. He pulled out a pen and unscrewed the end to reveal a torch. He waved the green light over the keypad to see if fingerprints would be visible. They were. He knelt down and examined the prints. The five and two buttons seemed to be used quite a lot so Patrick thought back to Dr Gabriel's file. He punched in Nathan's mother's date of birth and a mechanical 'ping' was heard from the other side. The door slid back and Patrick could see a metal hatch at his thigh level. He pulled it up and started walking down the metal staircase. *Not bad for a geek,* he thought. Then there was a pop and Patrick dropped to one knee.

"Ha! Close, but no cigar!" he heard a voice cry. The initial shock was nothing to him now, so Patrick pulled the still-pulsing pins out of his skin and pulled to see where they were coming from. He threw them in the direction the gun was and heard the stun gun drop to the floor as Nathan had attempted to shield his face. Patrick walked quickly over and grabbed a handful of shirt and skin. Nathan grunted in pain. Patrick pulled him to the light and threw him onto the floor.

"Nathan Gabriel, I presume," he said, smiling.

"Right, everything is up and running, we've gotten through the encryption," Lisa said as the others all gathered round. Jim patted her on the shoulder.

"That's five hours he's got on us now," Eve said to Jack.

"We'll get him back," Jack said, trying to calm her down.

Lisa and Luke had been working on the computer while John was calling around his old contacts. Nathan had left quite a trail behind him since John had taken him off the project. Three professors had taken him on and failed to help him with his research. Nathan had gotten quite far but not having a working sample, he had hit a dead end. John knew he wouldn't quit and now he had Patrick helping him. There was little they could do until Jack and John went to get him.

"Right, here are all the addresses he's associated with," Lisa said, turning the screen so the others could see. "I'll pull up the map, so we can leave now," Lisa and Jack had a good look around the area and decided on the alleyway behind the house.

"No heroics, just bring them both here. We'll secure them in quarantine for now," Jim said.

"Understood," Jack and John said together. Eve and Lisa went off to where Nathan worked, while John and Jack went to his home address.

They appeared in the alleyway, which was deserted. Jack closed his eyes and tried to pick up Patrick's thoughts. "I can't hear anything," he said.

"I'll go over the fence and let you know what I see, if you don't mind giving me a boost?" John asked. Jack put his back to the fence and cupped his hands for John to put his foot into. He didn't quite expect what happened. John stood on Jack's hand and peered over the fence. Jack, thinking he couldn't see enough, raised his hands quickly enough that John was half somersaulted over and landed shoulder first on the metal hatch, with a thud. Jack turned round at the sound and went to pull the fence down when he heard John get to his feet.

"It's a metal hatch, Jack," he said, rotating his once-sore shoulder. John leaned over the fence and put his arm over so Jack could use him as rope. Once on the other side, they opened the hatch door and Jack listened to see what he could hear.

Lisa and Eve appeared in the refuse collection area and made their way to the front door of the Armtek building that had Nathan listed as an employee. They watched two employees finish their cigarettes and followed them through the security door; they made their way to the floor listings on the side.

"Can I help you?" a security guard said, standing next to the turnstiles. Eve turned to him and told him that he hadn't seen them.

"Right, third floor," Lisa said as they turned round to face the oblivious guard. Let us through, Eve put into his head and the guard swiped them in without a word. They pushed a small green button on the wall and the lift came down silently and levelled up with the spotless marble floor they were standing on. They pressed level three and the doors closed.

"So, who do we not want to see come through that door?" Nathan asked as one of his machines spun round at high velocity, with several test tubes inside it.

"A young bloke with strange eyes or an angry little redhead. If either of them come for us, we're done."

"Not quite" Nathan said, handing him a rather solid-looking pair of head phones. "These should help against telepaths." They put them on and he pressed a button on a large single speaker that faced the only door to the room. Patrick could feel the massive volume passing him but he could not hear a thing. *Clever bloke,* he thought.

Eve and Lisa were outside the laboratory Nathan worked in, when a sound neither of them had ever heard before knocked them to their knees. They clamped their hands over their ears, screaming in pain. They were on the floor for what felt like an eternity when Lisa grabbed Eve's hand and they disappeared.

Jim and Luke were still in Jim's office when two bodies appeared on the floor in front of them. Eve was still covering her ears and Lisa was bleeding from one of hers. Jim ran over, grabbing a small rectangular bag from under the desktop. He dropped to his knees beside Lisa, took out one of the EpiPens and injected it into her neck. Lisa's eyes were still watering and she was still dazed, but once the needle had entered her skin, she knew what was happening around her and her body started to feel the effects. Once Jim took out the needle, she smiled at him and disappeared.

Eve got to her feet, still panting as if she'd been running. "She's okay, she's in her apartment. It's a good thing you have those here," she said, pointing to the little bag he was wrapping up.

"I've got them in every room, Eve, even the apartments. It goes to show; you can't be too prepared." He put his hand on her shoulder. "I assume you've found Patrick and Dr Gabriel."

"John, we should go back and see -..." Jack stopped talking. His phone was vibrating in his pocket. He fumbled it out and quickly answered it, "Eve?" he said.

"It's Jim. The girls found them, they're in Nathan's lab. He's using a megaphone so powerful, the girls came straight back here with their ears bleeding. I suggest coming back here and taking some of the ear defenders with you. They will only muffle the sound, but hopefully enough so you can get in there and deal with the situation."

Jack turned to John and held out his hand without saying a word. John took it and they disappeared.

They arrived in the shooting range and Jack could hear Lisa thinking in her room, he could see her remembering the laboratory where she and Eve found Nathan. He took a pair of ear defenders off the wall. He turned to John, who had a worried look on his face. "Jim will explain," he said and disappeared.

Jack appeared outside the lab. The noise was almost unbearable; even with the ear defenders on, he had to put his hands over his head. He looked down and saw a few drops of blood on the floor. Jack focused on the lab door and with three strides, he kicked one of the doors clean off its hinges, snapping the lock along with it.

The noise that bellowed out dropped him to one knee and put his hands back over the defenders. His healing started to numb out some of the pain and he stood up. Patrick was running towards him, hoping to get a decent strike to Jack's head before he recovered, but Jack saw him coming and teleported behind him, just in time to pull his headphones off before Patrick could get the punch to make contact. Jack threw the headphones as hard as he could at the speaker. They rebounded without making any difference. Jack didn't bother to see if Patrick was down or not, he walked over, pointing at Nathan, who, with his hands up, moved over to the speaker and switched it off.

"I don't want any trouble," Nathan said, taking off his headphones. Jack took them off him and picked up the others, which were lying on the floor.

"Come with me," he said, turning round to pick up Patrick, who was trying to walk towards the lift. Jack had hold of Nathan by his sleeve and with his other hand he took hold of Patrick by the wrist. Patrick went stiff and violently collided with the railings which overlooked the lobby. It had been a long time since Jack had taken someone's energy from them, it was a pleasant feeling and once he had enough from Patrick he closed his eyes, took Nathan by the neck and the three of them disappeared.

Jack appeared in front of the two glass cubes he had first used his ability in. He put Patrick into the one with restraints that worked and put Nathan in the other. No sooner he had them in the cubes, than the doors sealed closed. Jack turned to look at the camera over his shoulder. "Just like old times," he whispered.

Lisa appeared next to him. "Where are the others?" Jack asked.

"They can take the lift," she replied, glaring into the box Patrick was in. "What did you do to him?" she asked.

"I had to take his energy. It was the only way I could get them both back," he replied. Patrick slowly got to his knees and feebly pulled himself into the chair. Even as weak as he was, Jack was impressed he could move at all.

"You 'had' to take his energy?" Lisa asked, looking at Jack while crossing her arms. He turned and she saw his crooked smile.

Jack and Lisa turned as they heard the lift doors open. They saw Eve and Luke come round the corner first, followed by John. Jim was last, strolling towards them. He didn't look happy.

"Eve!" Jack said catching her face and turning it towards his so that he could stop her from trapping the two caged men in some terrible world they could never escape.

"Please, just look at me, honey. Don't overreact," he whispered, his face an inch from hers. Eve closed her eyes and rested her head against his shoulder, which progressed into a full on embrace. Lisa and Luke looked at them and just as Luke reached to take Lisa's hand, John walked past them and went straight to see Nathan.

"It's good to see you, Nathan," he said. Nathan merely shrugged and sat on the floor. Jim walked silently over to Patrick and tapped on the glass. Patrick looked up, saw Jim's face and rolled his head over the back of the chair.

"We need to have a chat, don't we?" Jim said, knowing Patrick was angry he got caught. Jim turned to John, who was still looking at Nathan.

"John," Jim said a little sternly. John turned round.

"Yes, colonel?" he replied automatically.

"I'd like you, Lisa and Luke to go and make out what Nathan was working on."

Without a word he turned and walked over to Lisa and Luke, who were already holding hands. He took Lisa's free hand and they vanished.

Jim walked over to Nathan's box and as he did, Nathan looked up and shrunk into the smallest seated position he could.

"Son, co-operate, and you'll be fine," Jim said. He looked quietly at Nathan for a moment and turned to face Eve, who was walking over to Patrick's box.

"I could, you know, and I want to," she whispered to Patrick, who was looking dead into her eyes.

"Then why waste time?" he said and took hold of one of the arm restraints, trying to snap it off, but to no avail. He wheezed with effort and frustration, so much it brought tears to his eyes.

"What have you done?" Eve whispered so low that even Jack missed it. She turned to Jack, who was walking over with Jim. Patrick was still trying with all his might to break off a piece of metal but nothing happened.

"This is interesting," Eve said.

"So, it seems you can remove abilities as well," Jim announced, putting a hand up to his chin.

191

"So it would seem," Jack said. He couldn't resist his crooked smile creeping over his face. Patrick slumped into the chair, half sobbing, looking at his hands which were now bruised from the effort. What was he thinking? John asked himself while looking through the data on Nathan's machines. "This looks like something the army would have wanted to use. This could have been disastrous." John had gone through most of the paperwork he'd found while Lisa and Luke had gathered the vials Nathan had been using.

"We need almost everything here," Lisa said, looking around at the equipment she and the other scientists had developed themselves, with little input from Nathan. "He's copied a lot of our equipment, God only knows who else has this stuff," she said, unplugging and dragging machines into the centre of the room. Luke joined her and together they managed to get everything they wanted into order for Lisa to take back.

"'I'll gather the files. You guys make a start on...'" John looked up to see they had already finished what he was about to ask them to do. "Well, good to see you're organized," he said, going back to reading.

Before long, Lisa and Luke had taken the equipment back to the lab, to do more extensive testing. John was in his office, reading through Nathan's work again. The other scientists were curious to start working on what Nathan had been trying to accomplish. They had started plugging everything in when Jim cleared his throat.

"Everyone. The first instance that you come across anything harmful, it's to be destroyed. Is that understood?" A communal 'yes' came from all those who Jim made eye contact with.

"I think you've achieved quite enough to be proud of. Let's quit while we're ahead", he said, walking into John's office and closing the door. "Well, how bad is it?" he asked.

"Bad," replied John, not looking up. "He was trying to, basically, turn humans back into primitive man; acting on instinct alone. Some with intelligence, so an army of people, altered as he saw fit, would go into an area and kill everything that moved." John looked up. "And with Patrick's DNA he could have done it." Jim walked out of the office and back to where the scientists were working.

"Destroy it all," he said loudly. Everyone stopped and looked at one another.

"But, sir, just because it's a mess now, doesn't mean that-" Alex began, but Jim cut him off.

"Does it look like this subject is up for debate?" He looked around at the now silent faces. "Destroy it all, now," He stood there while they started packing up everything to be destroyed. John came out of his office and walked around the scientists, telling them what he thought. "Guys, it's beyond rescuing. The whole thing is a mess. Quite frankly, I was thinking the same thing as the colonel before he told you guys to destroy the lot. Can you please sterilize everything he used? We can see if his equipment can be of any use here."

John walked round, talking and patting each person before he went back to his office. For the sake of morale, he was going to stay there, just like he did before all the changes happened.

John told Brian to get the vials into their box so that they could be incinerated at once, safely. Brian packed them all in, but found that there was one too many. Simon watched with interest as Brian moved the vials around so he could squeeze the last one in.

"I know the colonel wants the lot destroyed, but I think that keeping one would be a good idea. You know, just in case, kinda thing, we keep a finished sample on ice?" Brian said to Simon.

Simon nodded, took the extra vial and walked toward the freezer. Simon moved the vials inside around so that this one could be put at the back where Patrick's blood sample was, out of the way and wouldn't be taken by accident. "There, nice and safe," he muttered and closed the door.

After the samples were destroyed, the equipment was cleaned and put back together. John walked around, talking like he used to with the scientists. Jean even went to the vending machine and got him a mint latté. He wandered round, catching up on a few things and telling them what parts he could about the work he'd been doing and how far each person's ability had come. They laughed together and when John's drink was finished, he asked them all if they wanted to sit in the break room like they used to.

Jim, Eve and Jack were talking over the table about what to do with Nathan. His equipment was taken and none of his work could ever be replicated. He was harmless now. A little out of pocket and soon to lose his job, but they decided to pay him off and send him on a long vacation. Patrick, on the other hand, was now untrustworthy and would now have his memory altered to suit the best interests, and be put back in charge of security for the facility.

Eve walked over to where Patrick was still sitting.

"Are you going to torture me, sweet Eve?" Patrick said without moving his head to look at her.

She put a hand on the glass and whispered, "Not today. But I will. You can count on that."

Patrick looked up at her and stood. "Well, punish me now or set me free," he said, raising his arms in a biblical fashion. Eve took her hand off the glass and put them in her pockets, looked him in the eye and Patrick's world went dark. Eve went through his memories and took out everything that related to the work going on here and every reference to the group and their abilities. She then put Patrick to sleep while he was standing up and he dropped into the chair like a corpse. Eve could feel Jack inside her head and turned to face him.

Jack had been watching Eve with worry. Thankfully, she did exactly what they wanted to do with Patrick and now Jack could do the same to Nathan.

"What?" she asked and walked away. Jack blew her a kiss which she mockingly caught, pretended to shred and threw it back at him. Jack gave her a jokingly hurt look, which made her smile and she carried on walking.

"She's kinda hot" Nathan said when Eve was out of earshot.

"She is, yes, but she wouldn't hesitate to turn your life into a living nightmare if you even so much as looked at her funny," Jack said as he turned to face him. Nathan gave him a smug look. "Eve, Nathan is being disrespectful," Jack said, still facing the box.

Nathan then lost his right footing and at the same time slapped himself in the face before toppling over. Jack started grinning and turned to look at Eve, who had a blank expression on her face. "I've heard worse thoughts then his" she said. "Could you?" she asked and walked over with her right hand outstretched. Jack took her hand and she vanished. Nathan, who was still getting over the shock of what had just happened to him, looked at Jack in amazement.

"It's a good thing you won't remember this soon, mate," Jack said and closed his eyes.

Nathan's expression was one of blank humour as he adjusted his belt in preparation for the trip Jack had seen in his mind while making him forget. Nathan was told that he was going off to Africa for a while. He was off to do the safari trip he'd always dreamed of but never had time to do. Jack had made sure that he had enough money and correct paperwork, before sending him off to a hiking shop to get supplies and then off to the airport. Nathan didn't say much, just took in all the information Jack was giving him before sending him on his way.

"He's ready," Eve said and Jack took his hand. Nathan vanished. Patrick didn't look surprised at what had just happened. Eve had made it so that Patrick wouldn't wake up from his trance until someone said, 'What time is it, boss?' seeing as a guard known as Trumpy was on shift today and this was an expression he used often as a way of asking for a cigarette break, this would get Patrick right back into the swing of a normal shift. Jack took Patrick's hand and he vanished.

"What time is it, boss?" Patrick heard. He blinked a few times and looked up. There in front of him was an ageing fellow, who was younger than he looked. He was wearing his immaculate uniform with distinction.

"You need another break, Trumpy?" he said and reached for his newspaper, which was always kept in the crease between the filing cabinet and the table. "Here you go," he said, handing it to him.

"Thanks, boss," Trumpy said and shuffled away.

Things carried on that way for a few weeks. Jim got some more close protection work for them to do. Eve helped out with some missing person cases and Luke got quite involved with Lisa in jobs she wanted to do back home. The economy was crumbling and she needed to help fix it. Where she couldn't make a difference, Eve and Jack would (against Jim's wishes) help out where they could. Jim asked Jack every now and then to take him to a remote town in central North Carolina and Jack did so without question. The incident with Patrick was hard on Jim, as he was the one who misplaced his trust and was betrayed by someone he felt very close to.

Patrick was in Jim's office one day, when he noticed a bag, bound and taped to the underside of the desk, where no one else would notice it. He took it out and unravelled it. Inside were three white EpiPens. He took one and replaced the bag where he found it. "I wonder if this is what he's been working on," Patrick said to himself and walked back to the reception desk.

Jim was sitting on a porch with an ice cold beer in his hand. The weather had been perfect today; not a cloud in the sky but there was a refreshing breeze blowing through the trees. The porch looked over a small lake in a town that held no more than eight thousand people. He'd come here a long time ago, for a bit of peace and quiet. He'd left another life in Texas, one he could never go back to, but this small town reminded him of his past life. Jim closed his eyes when he heard a voice from inside the house.

"Daddy, are you gonna stay for supper?"

He leaned round to see where the voice had come from. Inside the house was his daughter. Nikki was in the kitchen, which was shouting distance from the porch.

"I can't today, Honey, I promised your momma I'd just stick around for this afternoon then head back to the office when my assistant gets back."

"Aw," he heard her soft voice as she walked out onto the porch and put an arm around his shoulders.

"Well, at least we got to see each other every day this week," she said.

"We did indeed, sweetie," he replied. Just as he'd finished talking, he saw the red pickup truck he'd been expecting to arrive.

"Yo, boss" Jack said in his version of a southern accent, pulling into the driveway. He had a checked shirt on which had the sleeves rolled up and his left elbow poking out in full view of the sunshine.

"Hey, Jack," Nikki called out.

"Hey, Nikki, sorry we've got to shoot off now, I'm sure your dad would like to stay longer."

Nikki walked round and pulled Jim out of the chair. "Be good, Daddy," she said kissing him on the cheek.

"You too, Honey," Jim replied, wrapping an arm around his daughter.

Jim got into the truck and Jack reversed out, with a bit of wheel spin.

"Jack, every time?" Jim said, half looking in his direction.

"Yes, boss," he replied.

"You know you sound ridiculous, Jack," Jim said putting his arm out of the window.

"I blend in well, cowboy." Jack retorted.

He parked the truck in the same spot he stole it from every time and threw the keys back at the old man who owned it. "I'll have to fill it up the next time I 'borrow' his truck" Jack joked as they walked to the street corner he would always teleport to. "That's a good lad," Jim said, taking his hand.

Patrick had been holding on to the EpiPen for a few weeks now. He was at the hotel he sometimes rented rooms out of when he wanted to get away. "Ah, what the hell," he said and jabbed the needle into the side of his neck. He felt the change immediately. The bowel noises got him rushing to the shower, undressed, just in time as everything started happening

He cleaned the shower until the evidence was erased. He felt embarrassed and the best he'd ever felt at the same time and he started to get flashbacks of what Eve had made him forget. The first time he'd gotten to see Jack and Eve, their awakening, the news, Jim inviting him to meet them, the change, the jobs they did, Nathan. Everything came rushing back. He was so overwhelmed by the flurry of information that he fell over in the shower. 'Okay, things are making sense now. I won't tell them their shots erase her silly mind tricks. First patrol tomorrow, I'll pop in and walk around the lab. See if anything has survived. I wonder how I can get my ability back. God, it's good having my memory back. That girl has had me in a half coma for three months.' Patrick picked himself up and got out of the shower.

The next day, first patrol, Patrick was walking round the lab as if he were still oblivious to everything. He spotted the fridge the samples were kept in. He opened it up and immediately spotted his name on one of the vials. "Literally, mine," he said, taking it and a syringe from the tray next to it. *Let's see if this works,* he thought, walking out and into the men's toilets.

Eve and Lisa were having a morning swim when Jack and Jim got back. "Oh, Jim's back," Eve said, almost jumping out of the pool.

"Eve, he's not going anywhere today," Lisa reminded her, turning for another lap. Eve was caught in two minds until she heard Lisa's thoughts. *Race ya*, she heard and dived under the water and swam after her.

"Jack, where's John?" Jim asked.

"I dropped him off in Niger earlier today. He's trying out something which might help the locals. Why, what did you have planned for today?" Jack said, turning round.

"Nothing, I've got no work today, I was going to see if he fancied a game of chess," Jim replied. Jack turned round and Jim could see the look on his face, suggesting he wanted to play, you always cheat," Jim said, crossing his arms.

Jack looked at him, a little hurt. "I don't think so, Jim," he said.

Jim stood up. "Really?" Jim asked. Jack pouted and put his hands up in disbelief. "How about the time I had to 'king' you when we last played draughts? You wanted your kings to move eight spaces. I had to do what you wanted until Eve got bored and saved me. Or how about last week, when you forced me to take my own queen, because you were losing? Or the time before that, when you convinced me you had six kings and were unbeatable? For once, Jack, I'd like to play a game where no one stands a chance of cheating. Against you, it's fun until the game changes to 'let's torment Jim'. No more," Jim said, walking towards the pool, where he knew Lisa would be.

"There's just no trust any more. A few little tricks and people think you're cheating," Jack said, walking over to the table. "Right solitaire, prepare to get cut," he said, sitting down, and chuckled to himself.

Lisa had just won her second race against Eve, who wouldn't stop until she won one, but Jim approaching stopped her and she caught hold of Lisa's foot.

"Eve, that hurts. What is it?" Lisa asked, while hopping in the water.

"Jim wants to see if you'll play chess," Eve said, letting go of her foot.

"Well, two birds, one stone," Lisa said, jumping out of the water. Eve followed her, after telling Jim they would meet him upstairs.

Jim was watching Jack lose every game of chess he played against the computer. "I keep telling you, Jim. I'm only after the moral victory today. It's not the winning, it's the - No! Not my queen again!" He said, almost pleading with the computer to change its mind and go after one of his pawns. Jim looked sympathetically at him. Jack looked from up from his game.

"False sense of security. I've got him right where I want him."

Jim got up and patted Jack's head.

"Afternoon, girls. Lisa, Jack's about to finish -"

"Nooo!" he heard from behind.

"Correction, he's finished now, fancy a friendly game?"

"Sure. It's nice to play against someone who can't cheat," she said at Jack as he walked past them.

"Moral victory," she heard him mutter.

Jack was walking into his apartment, ready to have a well-deserved nap when his phone started ringing. It was John.

"International taxi service," he said, getting up off the bed.

"Yes please, mate. For two," John said. Jack closed his eyes. He arrived at John's makeshift medical unit that he insisted on using on his trips around the world.

"Would you like a hand folding your mobile NHS or shall we burn it and get you a new one?" John turned to face him; John had started growing a beard. It suited him but it was well in need of trimming now. Jack watched as he started rolling up one of the sides.

"It's okay, mate. I'm coming back here tomorrow."

Jack walked over and gave him a hand.

"You do realize I don't give out frequent flyer points," they laughed while they folded the sides up and Luke was getting the boxes packed away. Once they were done, they walked round the back of the tent and disappeared.

"It'll be okay there?" Jack asked, getting out his notebook so that he could take the dinner orders for the evening.

"It should be. Luke has taken the boxes, so all there's left is the tent." Jack nodded and opened his book.

"Shall we go see the others and find out what their food demands are for tonight?"

Luke came back from the lab they were standing outside of. "What shall we have to eat tonight?" he asked. Jack and John shared a look and Jack took his hand, while holding the other out for Luke.

"Oh, a surprise?" he asked and took Jack's hand.

The others were all sitting around the table when Jack, Luke and John arrived. They were already dipping into various cardboard boxes with chopsticks.

"Lisa and Eve fancied Chinese food tonight. I hope you're all hungry, they've gone a little over the top," Jim said, without turning round to talk to them. Jack put the notebook back in his pocket. He was slightly relieved that the girls had sorted out food for the evening. Jim had a large amount of various steaming foods on a big napkin in front of him. John and Luke walked over to their seats and started getting together beers and napkins for those who needed a first helping and for those running out. Jack sat in his seat and thanked the others for getting the place ready and for getting the food.

"So, what's good?" he asked.

"Everything," Eve and Lisa said at the same time. Eve had a half-finished mouthful and Lisa had another load in her chopsticks.

Jack looked around and spotted the food he recognized and liked, so he decided to get a helping of the food that was in abundance instead. "It is important, to always try new things," he had never forgotten his mother saying.

They ate a remarkable load each as the food was fresh and full of flavour. The always-free portion of prawn crackers were all that was left and John said that Alex always liked them, so he would leave the bag on his desk for the morning.

"Africa again tomorrow, John?" Jim asked. John nodded, finishing his last mouthful of beer. "Would you like a hand? I don't start in London until Thursday," Jim asked.

"Well, Luke and Jack are very helpful to have around, but another pair of hands would be good, thanks." Jim started helping Eve tidy up and Jack started wiping the table down.

"One night, we'll have to eat out in a restaurant. Just for a change," Lisa said, collecting the empty bottles from the table. They all stopped and turned to face her. It had escaped all their attentions that they had not gone out for a single group dinner since the start of all of this, almost twelve months ago.

"Why have we not done that?" Eve asked. "I guess we have just slipped into this comfortable pattern of eating in. But tomorrow, we shall go somewhere nice. I remember Paris and Rome having some very fine restaurants. Let's all meet back here in a few hours and make a decision."

Patrick was sitting in reception, an earpiece in one ear and an inner ear headphone in the other. He'd installed a small microphone in the smoke detector above the table. A small smile crept over one side of his mouth.

They all went and did their own activities for a while. Jim was in his apartment, reading. Luke and John went to the shooting range, and Jack went for a run in the room next to theirs. Eve and Lisa went for a swim. They had wanted to talk about where they wanted to go tomorrow and the pool was the only place the guys left to talk. "I like the idea of Paris," Eve said. Lisa had just finished another lap and was taking the break she was thinking of.

"That sounds nice. I can't believe we've not gone out after all this time. Not that we haven't indulged in wonderful food from all over the world. Even some strange things that Patrick and Jim have recommended from their time in the forces." They shared a look. Patrick had made a monumental mistake and had deserved his punishment, but they had spent a long time with him and now that he was out and had his memory altered, they still felt bad for him.

"Should we invite him?" Lisa asked. Eve thought for a minute. He was a laugh at times and she knew what she had done was the right thing to do but, how they would ask him, and what would he think of sitting with a bunch of strangers in a restaurant?

"No, there is too much that he wouldn't know and it would be too complicated. I miss having him around too, but he's a liability and not the kind of person we were led to believe." Lisa nodded and took in a deep breath. Eve did the same and they went under the water.

They all met at the table once more and sat down. Jack was already there. He was finishing a game of chess. "Queen Takes Rook Pawn." The computer beeped. "And that's checkmate," Jack said quietly. Jim gave him a thumb-up and Eve rolled her eyes.

"So, have we all decided on Paris?" Jim asked. He looked around the table at all the grinning faces. The girls were the most excited and Jim could see it in their faces. "Okay, good. I'll make a call tomorrow and let you all know what I've arranged." They all stood up and made their own way to the apartment level.

Luke woke up and got out of bed. He stretched and flinched when his joints cracked. He flicked on the TV and went for a shower. John and Jim were waiting for him when he had finally gotten his life together and joined them on the grass. "Where's Jack?" he asked. Jim looked at his watch.

"He'll be back in three, two, one ..." and Jack appeared.

"All set up and ready, Colonel," he said, saluting Jim as best he could manage.

"Poor posture, terrible dress code and you're unshaven, private," Jim said, smiling.

"All in a day's work, sir," Jack said back, winking. They all made a circle, holding hands, and disappeared.

Eve and Lisa were working on the computer. Lisa was typing up what she needed to do in Ireland tomorrow, while Eve was looking around at the restaurant that Jim had selected, without saying anything out loud.

"So, what's the restaurant like?" Lisa said, finishing her paragraph. Eve looked up from the restaurants home page.

"I just hope he's paying," she said. Eve gave Lisa the address for the restaurant so she could look for a good place to take them.

"Well, the closest I can get us is half a mile away. That should provide us with a nice walk," she said. Eve looked around for shops that would be nearby and she started thinking of asking Jim to get back a little earlier than he'd planned, so that she and Lisa could get some shopping done.

"Look at the boutiques they have near the place," she said, flicking some images across the table. Lisa pulled them in front of her and started flicking through the images and the street view map Eve had sent her.

"We'll call Jim?" she asked, looking at Eve, who smiled and took out her satellite phone.

The guys were all inside the NHS tent with patients when Jim's phone started ringing. Jim patted the man he had injected and Jack took him to the room where they collected the chemical waste.

"Hello, Eve," he said, answering.

"Jim, could we leave a few hours before we eat? Lisa and I would love it if we could get some shopping done beforehand," Jim swapped hands.

"Well, why don't the two of you go there when you've finished what you're doing today, and we'll meet you at the restaurant?" Jim said, not surprised at all that Eve already knew where and when they were going.

"Okay, thanks, Jim," Eve said hanging up the phone and putting it back in her bag. "They've got a full day there but seeing as we're having a day off, how about we go there today and have a good look around? We could look for a salon and have a real girly day?" she asked.

Lisa smiled and started looking online. "How about we do it the old fashioned way and just get ready and go?" Lisa asked. Eve closed the web page.

"Okay, shall we go soon?"

Lisa saved her work and closed the application. She logged off the computer and stood up.

"I'll meet you in your apartment in twenty minutes" she said and started walking to the lift. Eve looked at Lisa as if to ask if she was really going to go from one floor to another normally. She saw the look and rolled her eyes.

"What? It's been a while since I last used it," she said.

"Got the key?" Eve asked and stopped walking. Lisa stopped and turned round, holding out her hand. Eve walked forwards, took it and they disappeared.

They arrived on a secluded alleyway behind a restaurant in Paris. Eve looked out, past all the rubbish and could see people walking round with expensive shopping bags and clothing to match. *This is going to be a good day,* she thought. She was still holding Lisa's hand as they stepped outside. "Ooohh!" Eve exclaimed and Lisa turned to see what she had gotten excited about. They both started walking quickly to a Christian Louboutin outlet.

"What time are we eating, Jim?" John asked as he closed the last box and Luke stacked it with the others.

"Our reservation is for eight o'clock," Jim said, folding away one of the sections.

"Right, so that's in twenty minutes?" John said, looking at his watch.

"Correct," Jim said. Luke and Jack looked at each other and nodded. Jim and John left the floor and moved away from the tent. The left and right hand sides came together and the boxes lifted off the floor and went towards Luke's feet. The roof and sides all fitted as they should and the safety line locked itself in place. Luke bent down and put his hands on the boxes, which vanished.

"I'd like to shower and change first," he said, looking at Jim, who was standing there with his hands behind his back.

"Then let's go," he said. Jack stood still, but raised his hands in an over exaggerated way to make it look like he was some form of messiah. The men all looked at him like he was crazy, but his kind of behaviour they were well used to by now. Jim and Luke took hold of a hand each while John put his hand on Jack's face. Jack laughed.

"Face five!" he shouted and they all disappeared.

The guys got back to find the girls in Eve's apartment, looking through their new wardrobes. They looked up when the guys walked in.

"Hey, you're back early," Eve said, looking at her watch.

"We've got twenty minutes to get ready, ladies," Luke said. Eve looked again at her watch and from looking through Jim's mind, she realized that she'd set her watch to the wrong time.

"But we've got a half mile walk," said Lisa, grabbing what she'd already decided on wearing to dinner.

"Nope, we'll use the manager's office to arrive in, seeing as she knows me well and won't bother asking questions." The girls looked at each other and stood up.

"We'll meet you on the grass," Eve said. Lisa picked herself up and went towards her bathroom. Eve walked out with her bags and the guys moved out of her way. Jack disappeared, leaving the others to make their own way to their apartments.

They all met up on the grass ten minutes later. John and Jack were discussing how late the girls were going to make them when they appeared next to them. They were wearing body hugging dinner dresses. Eve's was black, with a thin white stripe going down one side to a slit that came up to her mid-thigh. She had on a pair of classic Christian Louboutins in black, which Jack noticed made her legs look even longer and more toned. She had her hair neatly combed back; it flowed perfectly down her spine. Lisa had on a dark grey dress which had a corset criss-cross style ribbon down the back. She'd teamed her outfit with a pair of light grey Gucci sandals, which she liked because of their simplicity. Her hair was in a French plait which matched in length and thickness with her dress. The guys were star struck with what they had done in such a short time.

"Wow," Jack and Luke said quietly. The girls smiled at them and disappeared.

"Eve and Lisa know where we are going and will meet us there," Jack said looking at Jim and John who were in neatly ironed shirts and dark trousers.

"They do look good," John said. The others took Jack's hands and they disappeared.

Patrick was watching a small portable TV which was showing the grass area behind where he was sitting. He stood up and walked over to the lift and pressed the button, the door opened and he selected B3.

Patrick walked onto the floor and unsurprisingly, it wasn't empty. He walked over to where Brian was sitting, reading through some paperwork which he seemed to be musing over.

"Something you'd like to discuss with me?" he asked. Brian looked up and slowly started folding the paper away from view. "I know what you and Simon have stored away, Brian. I know you've been running tests you shouldn't have; on something that shouldn't exist." Brian looked guiltily. "Don't worry about it. What results have you had from this? It can't be good news or you'd have gone to John with it."

Brian looked over to Simon, who was talking with the others and didn't see his look of desperation. Brian looked back at Patrick, who had changed his expression to a smile and had his arms crossed over his chest. Patrick put one hand out and moved it in a way that put Brian a little at ease.

"We've had some results from the tests and we're not sure if it good or bad. The strain that Nathan made is unstable. We don't know for sure what this would do to a person. But what we do know is that the cells within the blood stream would change drastically. They don't quite multiply into identical cells but they do generate cells that match in some ways and differ in others."

"So they behave similarly to John's cells?" Patrick asked him.

Brian looked back at him; a worried look on his face. "In a way," he replied and Patrick crossed his arms again. Another smile appeared on his face.

The manager's office was empty when the guys arrived. Eve and Lisa were waiting for them.

"Right, let's go and check in," Jim said and opened the door leading to the main restaurant foyer.

"Jim!" A soft French accent said. A tall, slim woman in a dark, feminine suit came over and hugged Jim. They conversed in French for a while. Jim turned and introduced the others.

"This is Adele, a very dear friend of mine," he said. Eve stepped forward and Adele hugged her. Eve was a little uncomfortable with this but she returned the embrace regardless; the others all got their turn.

"It is lovely to meet you all," Adele said. "Please, you must be hungry," she said and took them into the restaurant. They walked for a few moments and she sat them at a large oak table with seven dark red chairs around it. "Christophe will be with you shortly," she said. Adele and Jim kissed each other's cheeks and spoke again in French before she walked off, presumably to her office.

"This place is amazing," Lisa said, looking around.

"Adele owns this place, it's all hers and she makes a very good living from it. She's joining us tonight," Jim said. A few minutes later, Adele returned with a very handsome man in a grey and white suit, carrying six menus. He handed the menus around before he pulled out the one remaining empty chair and Adele sat down.

"Would you like to look at the drinks menu?" Christophe asked, looking down at Jim. He nodded and took the menu from Christophe. The others all took one and perused it. Christophe stayed in silence and took each order down as they came. When everyone had ordered, he left the table and they all began talking to Adele, asking her things about her business.

"You do have a beautiful restaurant," Lisa said to her, taking a sip from the water which was already on the table.

"Oh, *merci*," Adele said. "You are too kind. I adore your dress, Lisa. Is it a Christian Dior?" Lisa smiled back at her. "*Magnifique,*" Adele said. She turned to Eve and looked at her dress. "And yours is one of Giorgio Armani's?" Eve already knew she had seen both dresses and she liked Adele's flattering thoughts toward her and Lisa.

"It is. I bought it today," Eve replied.

"Like you, it is beautiful," Adele complimented.

"Thank you. And your lovely suit?" Eve asked.

"Oh, a friend made it for me; it's one of my favourites," Adele responded.

Christophe returned with the drinks they had ordered and placed each drink in front of them.

Eve knew that Adele's suit was made by Yves Saint Laurent and it was indeed custom made. "Please, *excusez-moi*" Adele said and stood up. The men all stood as she rose. They sat once she had left the table.

Eve turned to Lisa. "Yves Saint Laurent made her suit. A handmade, one of a kind. I'd be telling the world if I was given something like that!"

Lisa's eyes bulged. "That was very kind of him," she said.

"Friends will always be kind to their friends," Jim said, picking up his beer and taking a sip.

"And you two met where?" Eve asked. The others all turned to Jim.

"We were on the board of directors for a small company, back when it was small. Once the profits got to a stage where we felt we should step aside and let new blood take the reins, we did. I think we did quite well from our time there. We went our separate ways and worked in fields where we would be happiest. She has this place and I have you guys," he said, raising his bottle. "Thanks for the past twelve months." They raised their glasses and bottles and repeated his statement.

"We're not there yet," John said, putting his glass down after taking a sip.

"John, it's been seven years to the week that you first agreed to take on this task. We've finally finished and enjoyed the benefits of your brilliant mind, leadership and success, your family are right to be proud of you."

John smiled, his eyes were glazed over. "Thanks," he said, taking his glass again and took a sip.

Lisa and Luke raised their glasses. "Thanks, boss," they said, almost together.

"I'm very thankful and proud of you two. I'm sure I'd still be struggling, if it wasn't for your dedication. So, thanks to you guys as well."

The four turned and looked at Jack and Eve. "Thank you, for the new beginning, fresh start and saving my life," Jack said, raising his bottle.

Eve took her glass and raised it half as high as Jack did his bottle. "I guess I'd still be in my coma, if it wasn't for you. I am happy in this life, but I do miss my old one, which I hope to return to soon. Thank you for helping me," she said. The others raised their drinks and then they all took a sip.

Adele and Christophe returned the others ordered more drinks. Christophe remembered the orders, went away and returned quickly with them.

The evening went pleasantly; they laughed at jokes, they discussed things that the media had reported on, conversed about past experiences, they discussed where they had travelled and what they would like to do in future.

Dessert came and went; they stayed long past when the restaurant had closed, drinking fine spirits and coffee.

"Oh, crap. We forgot to settle the bill," Eve said in a moment of semi-drunken realization. Her new ability made it almost impossible to get drunk, but a full bottle of Johnny Walker Blue had given her the kick she was after. Adele started laughing.

"*Mes amis*, you have already paid me compliments and shared your company. To pay me any more would be too much. Please, Jim is a wonderful friend of mine and now he has shared some of his closest with me." She looked at the clock on the wall behind Jack. Jim did the same. "I must say *adieu*, though, but please do come again." She stood and the others stood up, some finishing their drinks. Eve and Lisa were the first to hug Adele and say their farewells. Jim and Adele walked towards the front door where her chauffeur was waiting in her car. They embraced. She turned to a man in a white suit, who was standing next to the front door, smiling and trying not to look impatient, although his thoughts were the exact opposite. Adele spoke to him in French, asking him to thank the remaining staff, who were finishing up in the kitchen. He did as he was asked, trying not to pay any attention to the strange group of people he hadn't noticed coming in this evening. Eve and Jack noticed this, then watched Adele get into her car. Jim closed her door and raised his hand to shoulder height as the car drove off. He walked inside and the others were standing in a corner, waiting. Jim walked over and took Lisa's hand.

The group spent many a pleasant evening with Adele. She became quite attached to Eve, and she felt the same. Eve loved how Adele's mind worked. She rarely had anything that Eve found unpleasant inside, and her love for fashion without compromise appealed to her in a way that she had never found before. Shopping with her and Lisa in Paris made her feel happier and carefree, something she never thought would happen to her. Jack occasionally joined them but more for a break from working than anything to do with fashion. Luke joined them a few times too, more to try and fit in than anything else. Lisa helped him choose some new clothes and everything was fine until it came to pay for the items. "How much?" he asked once and only once, while they were doing a quick shop before going for lunch. Eve quickly silenced him with one of her looks and Adele looked at him as one would look at a young child trying to figure out something rather simple.

"Luke, you have to look at the price before you take them to the till," Lisa said in his ear.

"But I've never spent that kind of money on clothes. Rent, yes, but not clothes," he replied.

"We can now," Eve said and then walked off to investigate something that had caught her eye.

Luke begrudgingly handed over his card and the pretty girl behind the counter smiled and put the transaction through. Luke didn't even know how much was in his account now. Money wasn't something he thought about now. But he still had the same frame of mind about what he thought was a reasonable price for things. Jack, on the other hand, was having fun trying on clothes Eve was picking out for herself and trying to get her to look at whichever feminine clothing he currently had on.

"I'm not playing your silly game," she said with her back to him.

"But look how pretty I am," she heard from behind her. Eve sighed and turned. Almost twenty minutes of this was starting to get annoying and she thought shutting him up by looking would make her trip today easier.

Eve turned round to see Jack admiring himself in a mirror wearing a skin tight black dress that was meant for evening wear. "I think it shows off my good side," he said just as a sales assistant walked over. The woman half stopped where Eve was, thinking she should just ignore Jack and then she changed her mind. Jack very rarely used his ability, preferring to try and talk his way out of situations rather than 'cheating' as he liked to put it.

"Excuse me, sir," the young lady said.

Jack turned around. "Yes, I shall," he said. "By the way, do you happen to have this in green? I don't think the black suits me."

The lady gave him a scornful look and put her hands on her hips. "Sir, that's an eight hundred Euro dress. And you're stretching it."

"I'm sorry," Jack said and took it off, there in front of her. Eve watched in horror and the only thing stopping her was that Jack had bothered to put on underwear. "Here, I'm sorry. It's as good as new now," he said. The lady took the dress in both hands and looked it over. Remarkably, there were no damaged threads on the item. Jack had made sure every strand was how it was before he started messing around. Eve tutted and went back to the Ralph Lauren collection she'd spotted. Jack chuckled to himself and disappeared once the young lady's back was turned.

Later on that week they went out again to Adele's restaurant. Eve wanted to surprise Jack for his birthday. And seeing as she was the only one he couldn't get anything out of, Jim left her to arrange all the details.

"But you know I don't like surprises," Jack protested while Eve was getting ready. "And where are the others? I've not seen or heard anyone for hours." Eve looked at him and raised her eyebrows. "They're waiting for us, aren't they?" he said, sitting on her bed.

"Yes, they are, so be quiet and do as you're told," she said putting her hair in a neat plait.

"Really, Eve, you're bossing me around on my birthday?"

Eve turned to face him. She smiled and walked over and placed a soft kiss on his head. "Every day, no exceptions," she said and held his face side on to her chest. "Now, please be nice to everyone. They want you to have a good evening and I've got a nice surprise for you when we've finished dinner." Jack looked up at her, grinned and winked. "Not that nice" she said, patting his face and pulling him to his feet.

"Where in Adele's would you like me to take us?" he asked.

"'Her office, please," she replied and took his hand.

They appeared at the back of Adele's office. In the week that had passed she'd had the office half changed. The desk and the items on it were all that was the same from their last visit.

"It's changed again," Jack said, picking up a cushion on the black leather sofa, which used to be a green felt one.

Eve was looking around, admiring. "I do like her taste," she said and then refocused and took Jack's hand.

"Really? A surprise party?" Jack whispered.

"Ssssshh," Eve said and opened the door. The room was full of balloons and party poppers, the black oak table was covered with colourful decorations, which suited the table and the crackers laid out in a triangle in the centre. They walked into the room. Jack's left hand shot up out of reflex and his head moved slightly to the right as a foam ball, shot at a great velocity, struck his hand, which clenched and tore the ball in two.

"Nice try, Jim," Jack said, throwing the remains of the ball where he guessed Jim was standing. The ball came to a halt in mid-air and Jim reappeared.

"Almost got you," Jack said as Jim walked toward him and handed him the ball.

"You are always welcome to try again," Jim said, smiling.

"Isn't it a bit risky, using our abilities around other people?" Lisa asked Jim while she gave Jack a hug and handed him a little blue present. Adele was over the other side of the room talking to John. Eve tapped Lisa on the shoulder.

"I thought we'd agreed ... oh. That's a good idea," she said, turning to Jim, leaving Jack a little confused. "Look, Adele has far more important things on her mind and she's a mutual friend of ours, who I thought could join us. I wanted to talk to you two first before the others and see what you think, as you've spent so much time together over the past few weeks."

Lisa looked to Eve, who looked a little ambivalent.

"You didn't see this coming?" she asked Eve.

"I guess I've let my game slip a little," she replied. "Jim, I really like her -"

"As do I," Lisa echoed. "But why would she want to change her life style?" Lisa asked while Eve fell silent.

"He wants to replace Patrick and Adele wants a more fulfilling life. Jim has told her what we have been doing and she wants to join us. Tonight he showed her what he can do and has told her Jack can make her like us. But it's been agreed by them both that the group will make a decision as to whether an addition to the team is needed," Eve said to Lisa while Jack was next to her.

"Putting it that way, Jim doesn't really give us much of a choice. Don't get me wrong, she's a lovely woman and she's nice to talk to, but could she do the things we've done?" Jack asked, keeping his voice low.

"She'll be fine," Eve said. Jim nodded.

"If you guys think she'll be okay doing this, then I don't have a problem with having another girl on the team,"

Lisa said. She patted Jack on the shoulder and walked toward Luke, who was now talking with John and Adele.

"They are currently discussing," Eve said to Jim and Jack.

"The others look quite happy with it also," Jim said.

"They're talking about places in South America we can have a look at helping," Jack said. Jim looked a little puzzled. "I don't use it often. But I'm curious," Jack said, answering his unspoken question and started walking off toward the others. "I didn't say thank you," he said to Eve and Jim before leaving.

"That's the first time in over a month I've heard of him using that ability," Jim said to Eve.

"He likes to leave that part up to me," she said, "and besides, I like using it, whereas he isn't too comfy going through people's heads." Jim smiled at her.

"Whereas you don't have that problem." Eve didn't say anything. She merely smiled and walked over to where the others were.

"As long as everyone else is fine with an addition, I'd like to discuss it further," Adele finished saying as the others joined them.

"Happy birthday, mate," John said, giving Jack a hug. Luke did the same and the rest all gave their 'happy birthdays' and hugs. They conversed for a few minutes and then made their way next door where a buffet was being put out for them.

"Thank you," Jack said to Adele. She smiled and gave him a hug. They all went to the buffet and started helping themselves. On the table behind the buffet was an open bar table, with a young man behind it. On display was an assortment of fine spirits, liquors, whiskeys and mixers to suit everyone's taste. *This could go well,* Jack thought.

Eve woke up. She rubbed her eyes and came to realize she wasn't alone. She reluctantly looked to her left and saw Jack. His shirt was all crinkled, his trousers were on the floor and he still had one sock on. She looked at him peacefully for a few moments, until his mouth opened and he started to snore softly. She smiled and slapped him. Eve watched almost in slow motion as Jack's face took the impact and watched his eyes open almost instantly, his hands went up to hold his face.

"Good morning to you, too," he mumbled and scrunched his eyes closed. Her smile widened and she leaned towards his face. She kissed his nose softy.

"Good morning, honey. Now get out," she said quietly. Jack opened his eyes and looked into hers.

"And they say romance is dead," he said, cracking a smile. Eve pushed his shoulder and Jack rolled over, he shuffled a foot further and put his feet on the carpet. Jack stretched and groaned as his muscles started to obey and stood up, rotating the shoulder he had been sleeping on. "And how many dates do we need to have before we can-you know?" Jack said, winking at her and smiling.

"Only a thousand," Eve replied back, putting her head back on the pillow. "Did you have a good birthday?" she asked.

"I did, thank you. I'm a little sad that we don't get hangovers any more."

Eve doubled the duvet under her chin and moved up onto her pillow.

"I was never a fan of hangovers. So I'm glad they're no longer an issue. I'll go to work then, I guess," Jack said while hopping around trying to put his trousers on, which still had the sock stuck in one leg. He stopped hopping, to look at Eve for a reaction.

"Call me," Eve said, turned and slid back under the duvet. She closed her eyes.

"Sure," Jack said and picked up one of Eve's socks. He threw it at the area he knew Eve's head was and opened the door. He stopped short, as Luke and John were both walking towards him.

"Good morning," Luke said.

"I wish it was what it looks like," Jack replied to John's look, while he attempted pulling out the sock from the bottom of his trouser leg.

"Well, either way. I hope you had a good night. We lost you after you started singing and tried dancing with the guy serving us drinks. How is it when you heal as fast as we do, you can still act like you're drunk?" John said.

"Just a talent I have," Jack said back. John patted him on the shoulder and Luke walked between them.

"It's our last day in Africa, mate," John said, pulling a bread stick from the back of Jack's trousers. "We've done a lot of good, helped thousands of people, set up some stable housing and hopefully it will make a lasting difference and it'll stay like it is for a long time," John continued; he was admiring Jack's just out of bed hair. Jack heard his thoughts and started using his hands to try and sort out the mess on his head. "Much better," John said without even the littlest bit of sincerity on his face and held out his hand.

"Off we go then," Jack said, took their hands and disappeared.

He and Luke went to get the boxes and took them to where John was setting up shop for what would be the last time.

Jack's phone started ringing, an hour into their day. He didn't recognize the number. "Hello?" he said.

"Jack, it's Jim. Patrick hasn't shown up for shift, can you come back and give me a hand finding him? I'm in reception. There is no one here."

Jack hung up the phone and walked over to John and Luke. "Guys, Patrick hasn't shown up for work so I'll be with Jim and I'll be back when we've found him." John and Luke nodded in silent agreement and then looked at each other apprehensively. Jack walked to the back of the tent and the others watched him.

"Do you think he's okay? I don't think it's a good thing at all, Patrick hasn't missed a shift in his life and I hope he's okay" Luke looked back to see Jack but he wasn't there. "I guess we'll just have to hope," he said. They shared another look and slowly went back to their patients.

Jim was standing in reception when Jack arrived. "First time, ever," Jim said, walking to his office.

"Jim, I thought-" Jack got cut off.

"I just want to look at his accounts, quickly. Something is not quite adding up," Jim said, opening the door.

Inside, all the computers were on, along with the main lights. Jim walked in without stopping and looked at his computer, which had two screens open. "Son of a bitch," Jim said and Jack ran to his side. One screen was a word document with, 'I remember everything' typed on it; the other screen was open with Patrick's personal banking. A recent transaction was from an ATM in New York. That morning he'd paid for and gotten on the first flight out.

"What's he doing in New York?" Jack asked. Jim didn't answer and opened up a map of New York. The ATM was inside a hospital.

Jim looked down and closed his eyes, thinking. His eyes opened a few seconds later. "The lab, now!" he said taking Jack's hand. They appeared in the lab and Alex jumped, knocking papers off the desk he was sitting on.

"Wow," Alex choked.

"Alex, did you destroy every sample that Patrick and Nathan were working on?" Jim asked very firmly.

"It's important, Alex," Jack said, putting a hand on his shoulder. Alex looked over at Jean, who was staring at him.

"Yes, I gave Brian the task of destroying them. He and Simon told me they incinerated everything."

Jim looked at Jack.

"They don't know anything, Jim," he said.

"Wait," Jack began and walked over to Simon's desk. "Jim, you might want to come here," he said. On Simon's desk was a folder they used for important results and on the cover was his name in large letters. Jim grabbed the folder and opened it.

Inside was a statement from Simon, co-signed by Brian. They read the documents enclosed and the looks on their faces said it all. None of it was good news.

"We need to get to New York," Jim said and Jack took his hand.

They appeared in a corridor next to the hospital's fire exit. "It's the best I could see," Jack said and they opened the doors, setting off the alarm. They ignored it and ran towards the main entrance where the ATM was. They ran through the open doors and saw Patrick standing at the machine. He was in his work uniform, eating an apple. There was another one in his other hand.

"The forbidden fruit, so legend tells us," he said. "It's a good thing I found the EpiPens under your desk or I would never have gotten my memory back. There should be time. Give me what I once had and I'll tell you where the vial is."

Jack walked over and took him by the arm, almost lifting him off the floor. It looked painful but Patrick's face hardly moved at the tightness of his grip. They didn't say anything to one another and Jim followed them outside.

Jack took Patrick round to the alleyway he and Jim had teleported to just a few minutes ago.

"Okay, Jack, tell me what's going on," Jim said, once they were out of earshot. Jack let Patrick go.

"Jim, he's taken the vial and put it into a syringe." Jim looked gobsmacked at Patrick, who just stared blankly back at him.

"Where is it now?" Jim asked.

"He's injected it into himself, Jim. He's changing as we speak. I can't quite make out his thoughts any more." Patrick's body was trembling like he was cold.

"How long have you been like this?" Jim asked.

"An hour, I guess. The results those guys got were not what I'd expected but I am starting to feel the effects."

"Why did you choose the hospital?" Jim asked. Patrick smiled.

"Jim, I can't hear anything. Best we get him back to the facility." Jim took his hand and took Patrick's but he snatched his hand away and Jim lost his balance, due to the power of his actions. Jack caught Jim and grabbed hold of Patrick and managed to hold on to his arm but only just. They disappeared.

Inside the facility, Jack sent Jim to John's office and held Patrick as best he could in the box. The door quickly slid shut and Jack teleported to the other side of the glass. He watched as Patrick stood there, panting. His shoulders hunched. Staring at him, Jack moved to his left and Patrick snapped in the same direction.

"Jim," Jack said out loud and Patrick's stare became a smile.

"I can hear you, Jack," Jim's voice came over the speakers. Patrick's gaze broke; he looked around for the person he couldn't see.

"Call John, please, he needs to know," Jack said and the sound of his voice automatically got Patrick's attention.

"I'm on the phone to him now," Jim said.

John's phone started ringing as he and Luke were having a bite to eat. "It's Jim," he said, picking up the phone. "Hey Jim-" he started saying.

"John, we have a serious problem," Jim said. "Get back here now. I'll call Lisa and get her to come get you both. Pack what you can and get back." The phone went dead.

"Luke, start packing up, something is seriously wrong," John said. Luke dropped his sandwich and started making the boxes fly around, packing themselves up as if by magic.

Eve's phone started ringing and she pulled it out in annoyance "Jim, I'm working -" she started before Jim cut her off.

"You and Lisa need to go get John and Luke. When you've got them, come back here and meet me in John's office. I need you back here now," and the phone went dead.

Eve got up out of her seat and walked off without saying anything. The three men she was in a meeting with soon forgot she was there and she walked to the next room where Lisa was. "I missed a call from Jim and now he won't answer," Lisa said, holding her phone.

"We need to go get the boys," Eve said. The look on her face worried Lisa.

"So, they made a protein based regenerative serum," John said, reading the paperwork Brian and Simon had left for Jack.

"So it seems," Lisa said. She had read the paperwork first, as John wanted to speak to Jim about what had happened. "Patrick has it in his system and now is not acting right at all." They all looked at the cameras. Patrick was standing in the corner of the box, looking out, not moving. His eyes fixed on nothing, he didn't even seem to be thinking.

"So we have no idea what's happening to him. I can't hear anything or even make sense of how his brain is working," Eve said.

Jack hadn't said much since the others had gotten back. "All Patrick did was stare. It was like he was thinking I was something to eat. He didn't say anything to me and I couldn't get him to do or say anything. His mind is completely blank." Jim was watching Patrick on the camera.

"Since you left he hasn't taken his eyes off where you were last standing. I'd like to go down. Would one of you be so kind as to send me behind him, please?" Lisa walked over and took Jim's hand.

Jim appeared behind Patrick, who spun round and charged the glass; he ran with what looked like a wild animal's hunting pace. The box wasn't large enough for him to get any decent speed but somehow he did and without any hesitation, Patrick ran straight into the glass, hitting it face first. His body carried on going and he ended up flat against the glass then toppled over, landing on the floor. The glass remained intact but the noise echoed around the room. Jim didn't really react as Patrick struck the glass, only putting a hand over his face. Patrick was stunned for a few seconds and got to his feet, breathing heavily for a short period and then began breathing normally. This got Jim's attention and as Patrick stood he could see the anger in his eyes.

"Patrick," Jim said and that sent him off into a fury of punches against the glass, making blood-curdling noises with every blow. The glass absorbed the impact, but the noise bounced around the room. Jim disappeared from view and Patrick stopped. He kept looking at the spot Jim was and just stood there breathing, his hands red raw from hitting the glass. The skin on his hands was broken and had stained the glass. Jim reappeared behind Patrick, who didn't notice him standing there. As Jim moved around the box, Patrick noticed his presence and spun round. Jim kept walking around the box and Patrick followed him.

"What's happened to him?" Eve asked. None could answer her. They all had their eyes fixed on the screen, watching Patrick, who was now watching an empty space once more.

Unbeknown to the group, while Eve was in a meeting and Lisa was taking notes, Jim and Jack were reading the file that had been left and John was with Luke, helping others and taking samples, Patrick was walking round the hospital. He had a vial in his pocket, already transferred into a syringe. He found a room where he could inject himself with the regenerative serum Brian and Simon had developed but strictly told him not to do anything with until the trials they had started were finished. Patrick had no intention of wasting an opportunity and took it from the secure storage and left for New York, where he could use this. After injecting himself, he started getting huge migraines and heart palpitations. Wandering downstairs, he spotted an opportunity; he walked into a room that had a sign on the door saying, 'nil by mouth before surgery' and injected it into a woman who was lying in her bed, unconscious and waiting to be moved. He paid no attention to her, just injected it into her foot, pressed down on the plunger and walked away.

Going downstairs, he started feeling better, even helped himself to a few apples from the lunch trolley. *I bet they'll be here soon*, he thought. *I'll go to the ATM and wait. Hopefully this thing will kick in soon and I'll be ready to take them both on.* He stood there waiting; all the while his humanity was slowly draining from his body, the ever-increasing migraine taking over his mind, Patrick stood there, smiling.

Chapter Ten

I Don't Like What's Happening

Doctors in surgical overalls and face masks were working hard, trying to save a middle-aged woman on their table. She'd been in hospital for almost two weeks in preparation for an operation to remove a growth that was in between two vertebrae. Every precaution had been taken and they'd even given her drugs to settle her because she suffered panic attacks. Less than an hour into the surgery they had lost her. All her vital signs were normal one second and gone the next. The anaesthesiologist was at a loss for words as her readings did the same.

"Get the crash cart over here now!" one doctor shouted to a nursing student who was only in there to witness a routine surgery. As the poor lad hesitated, one of the nurses grabbed the cart and moved the lad out of the way. The machine buzzed into life, the doctor rubbed the contact gel onto the pads, shouted "Clear," and gave the woman lying dead on his table a jolt of electric current.

"She's flat lined, doctor," said the other surgeon in the room.

The doctor holding the pads looked up at him and then the equipment that showed no sign of life on its monitor.

"What the hell happened, Jeff?" he said. He tried five more attempts with the crash cart while everyone else slowed down their mad rush; they eventually just stood there, watching him, before he gave in to reality.

"I don't know," said Jeff as he started taking his gloves off.

The other surgeon pulled his mask off and looked at the big clock on the wall. "Time of death 7:22 PM. Nurse?" The nurse who brought over the crash cart looked up at him.

"Frank?" she replied. "Can you close her up, please? I've got to go and talk to her family." Frank walked off, his head down, slowly taking his gloves off. The nurses in the room watched him walk out to the scrub room and the door closed behind him. Without talking, the nurses all started clearing up the operating room and the nurse who had been asked to started stitching the woman's back together.

They all thought it was a tragic end to their shift, but something else was playing on their minds.

Luke was looking at the pile of food and waste all over floor in the box. "So he's just eating the meat," he said.

Eve was standing in the corner of John's office, looking at the camera screen they had been staring at for the past two days.

"He just wants the meat, the rarer the better," she said.

John had been going through everything he could with the group he'd pulled in to try and fix what was wrong with Patrick. "We need to get Simon and Brian back here, if we can get hold of them that is," Jean said. John and Jim had gone through their bank accounts and looked at any information they could to try and find them, but seeing as they were two of the best he could find with technology, tracking them down just kept leading them to dead ends.

"They're not coming back any time soon. They did leave everything they worked on here but to talk it through with them would be handy," John said, reading their work for what felt like the millionth time.

All the work made sense and they could see what they'd done. It was just how they came to the conclusions and what tissue samples they used that was preventing them from coming up with an antidote. They tried using the EpiPens which made no difference. Jack injected Patrick several times with them and each time it only annoyed him. Jack had even tried taking Patrick's energy from him; he jolted in pain and Jack let go. It seemed Patrick's condition had now fully taken over his body and they were, for the first time, running out of options.

"Did you ever come up with anything promising with anyone else's blood?" John asked Jean.

"We'd have told you," she replied.

"What about my blood?" Jack asked, knowing they'd run a few tests using his DNA and kept the results from John, because of how lethal they were.

"We can't use that, Jack," Jean said in an almost deadpan voice. John looked over at her and she explained that Jack's blood would take over any sample they would introduce it to and cause almost instantaneous death.

"People have called me toxic before but I guess it's actually true now," he said.

"What about testing the unforgivable?" Jack asked.

John and Jean had been thinking the same thing. Jack was the only one who would say it out loud. "I'll go and get Luke," Jack said after John and Jean both agreed in their minds but remained quiet.

Luke was sitting with Lisa, running through the paperwork and new results they had gotten from the latest batch, which wasn't looking promising. "Luke, I need you to help me get all the samples you and the others need to run my DNA and Patrick's together," Jack said without hesitation. Both Luke and Lisa looked at him like he was speaking a foreign language. "It's the only thing we haven't tried yet and we're all trying to ignore the possibility it might work," Jack said after a few moments of silence. Luke stood up and nodded.

Lisa watched them walk off together, discussing how they would go about holding Patrick down. "Anaesthesia won't work on him so we'll just have to be quick and try not to prolong his suffering," Luke said and Jack nodded. They went to the lab and Luke gathered all the equipment he would need.

"Okay, are we ready?" Jack asked and Luke remained still as if frozen.

"Have you gone insane?" Eve asked, walking behind him. Jack waved his hand in front of Luke's face, which remained frozen.

"Nice trick," Jack said, ignoring her question.

"You're lucky I can't get into your head or you'd be in serious trouble," she said, walking over.

"It's the only thing we haven't tried and it's the one thing we're scared of trying," he said.

"And you know why," she replied. Jack walked over to her and put his hand on her shoulder.

"It'll be tested safely and I'll make sure it goes no further than the testing stage," he said.

"I've already done that," she said. "Not a single scientist or one of us can or will even try and test this in an unstable way," she said.

Jack looked at her with a little admiration but more concern. "You've told them they can't?" he asked knowing exactly what she'd done.

"No. I've made sure there won't be another Patrick while they're working," she almost shouted back. "Things were fine here. I was happy and then this mess erupted and things have gone from bad to worse. I can't believe what's happened to Patrick and it will not happen again," she said.

"It won't," Jack said and Luke turned round.

"Eve, when did you get here?" he asked.

"Just now. I thought I'd come make sure you two don't get carried away and decide to try and take his kidney out or something," she said and patted Jack's face.

"Be careful," she said and walked back toward the lift.

"Jack, are we ready?" Luke asked. Jack gave him a nod and took his hand.

They appeared outside the box and Patrick started staring at them both. His breathing seemed to move his whole body up and down.

"I'll hold him," Jack said and put his hand on Luke's neck.

Luke reappeared behind Patrick, who turned and lunged at Luke so quickly, Luke barely had time to react. He moved his arm instinctively, shielding his head. Patrick's flight path diverted as if he'd been hit side on by a missile. His body struck the side of the box so hard it cracked. Patrick's body fell to the floor like a stuffed toy. Jack caught him before he hit the floor. He placed him flat and checked for signs of life. Unbelievably, Patrick was still breathing.

"That was lucky, mate. You could have killed him," Jack said, putting Patrick on his side so Luke could pull up his shirt.

"I need you to hold him while I take these," Luke said, taking out a syringe and a very long needle. Jack kept him still while Luke worked on him and he glanced at Patrick's hands. He was expecting to see them all bruised and cut from where he'd been punching the glass but they looked normal.

"That's interesting," he remarked.

Luke looked up from behind him as he pulled the long needle from Patrick's spine. He looked over and noticed his hands too. Jack stopped concentrating temporarily and when Patrick woke up he could move just enough to scare Luke. Jack got him back under control and Luke finished up taking samples from his very unwilling patient. "There's not a mark on him, look," he said and Jack looked over Patrick's body. Over his torso there wasn't any indication that he'd just been thrown into a glass wall.

"There were slight marks earlier but now there isn't a trace of it" he said, putting his shirt down. Jack had put Patrick into a recovery position and kept him there so that he couldn't struggle during their observation of him. Jim and John were there now too, they wanted to see how he was doing and John wanted to help Luke.

"Well, he looks the same man," Jim said, standing. He'd been kneeling beside him, looking over the man he once knew.

"But I don't know what's going through his head. It's almost like he's reacting on instinct only now," Eve said, coming from behind them. She was with Lisa, who was keeping her distance from the man lying on the floor, looking more peaceful then he had for the few days he'd been locked up.

"How secure are those 'clean' rooms you had me and Eve in, you know, the ones we woke up in?" Jack asked John.

"Not as strong as these," Jim said. "If he wanted to, he could break out of those in a day or two. But here, he'd die of old age before he broke the glass enough to get out. Even now, with the crack up there -" Jim said, looking up and they all did the same; "- it would still take him weeks to break out. I say we keep him here until we know more, or at least know what it is that's happened to him. Not three days ago, he was still able to talk and now, he's more like an animal." The others looked down at Patrick, who had his eyes shut, not through choice but Jack thought he looked a bit less threatening like this. The same thing happens with crocodiles; once their eyes are shut off from any source of daylight, they remain in a placid state. This had the same effect on Patrick.

"What do with him now then?" Lisa asked once the samples were taken and Patrick was, once again, left alone.

"I'm not sure," said Eve. Jack looked at the screen and then turned away. There was a thought in his head he was glad no one else could hear, because it was unthinkable to him and he thought the others would be upset if he were to share it. Unbeknown to Jack, he wasn't the only one thinking it.

The hospital morgue was as quiet as always. The mortician was on lunch and had popped out for a cigarette. The strobe lights overhead needed changing, which gave it an even spookier atmosphere. Most people at the hospital didn't like going in there at the best of times. You could have heard a pin drop over the dull noise of the refrigeration units. There were three body bags which were yet to go into units before the families came to collect them for burial. As one of the lights flickered, you could be forgiven for thinking your eyes were playing tricks on you but the truth of the matter remained; one of the bags started moving.

Jim had taken John to the shooting range for his opinion on what to do with Patrick now he was completely out of sync with reality and was now left with no humanity at all.

"We'll just have to be patient and see what results we can come up with," John said. He had his hands in his pockets and didn't want to tell Jim he thought all hope was lost and they might have to do the unthinkable with Patrick. Jim had already considered the option, but was trusting his belief that the scientists could possibly save him. Patrick was after all, still a good friend and a good soldier. All other options had to be exhausted before he would reconsider the unthinkable.

Eve had lost interest in swimming. She enjoyed her daily exercise and was happy to be back in shape, but today she couldn't focus and wanted to do something else to take her mind off the situation at hand. She knew where Jim and John were and decided that she'd join them. It had been a few weeks since she'd been to the range and today she thought it would be a good idea to go; hopefully it would take her mind off things. She made her way down to the range and opened the door. Jim half expected her, but John did not. Eve heard John's panicked thoughts; his brain was going a mile a minute and she didn't want to even try and keep up. Eve walked over and looked John in the eye. He knew she knew and that it was okay; they were all thinking it, and, as Jim said, they might find a cure.

"So, who's up for a bit of a competition?" she asked. Jim patted her on the shoulder and walked to the cabinet to get her gun.

Jack and Luke were outside the facility, having a walk in the sun, discussing things they'd been working on and what they thought about the goings-on with Patrick, when Lisa appeared in front of them, making them both jump. "Nice," Jack complimented, while Luke was so startled he was holding his chest, trying to catch his breath.

"Luke, you really should be more accustomed to this kind of lifestyle now. You've been in some pretty bad situations now and shouldn't be this jumpy," she said, walking between them.

"I've gotten a lot better, thank you. And for the record, I didn't react like I did the last time I was startled," he remarked. Lisa remembered watching Patrick launching himself at a defenceless looking Luke, who reacted and sent him flying into bulletproof glass.

"Fair point, well put," she said and they walked around the back of the building discussing what was going on with the scientists and how things were going.

"So, it's not looking promising?" Jack asked.

"I've never seen anything like it. When we first started, we came up with an antidote within hours. But once it's introduced, his blood adapts to the antidote, modifying it to be useful in its own survival. Radiation has the same effect on it. His blood uses the rays to make itself multiply. It's almost like his own blood has become a living organism, and is determined to fight everything that gets introduced to it, at times using it to make itself more efficient." Jack took all this in, but biology was never his strongest suit.

"So we can't kill it?" Jack asked.

"I'm afraid Patrick has become it," she said. They all walked in silence for what felt like hours. None wanted to admit the facts: Patrick was no longer himself. He wanted to kill everyone, he wouldn't eat anything but raw meat and all attempts to find a cure so far had failed. Patrick was lost to them. They only had a few options left, none of them good.

"Does John know?" Luke asked.

"I've just been up and seen him. He's got all the results, he and Jim are going through them. Eve has gone to see Patrick once more to see if she can get into his head. She really won't accept defeat," Lisa said lowering her head. Lisa knew Eve would do everything she could to cure Patrick, but she knew it was a waste of her time now. Lisa was starting to fear the worst.

"She doesn't like the fact she's defenceless against him now," Jack said. The others knew he was right. Eve and John could heal now and were therefore able to get away, regardless of the physical onslaught he could throw at them. But apart from that, Jack was right; Patrick was beyond human and anyone normal would not stand a chance against him.

I don't get it, I just don't get it, Eve thought. Nothing she tried worked. Patrick just sat there, unresponsive and without thought. She had been stood behind him for almost twenty minutes and had tried everything she'd learnt to get him to do or think something. "It's not going to work," Jack said, walking up behind her.

"I heard you coming," she said. Patrick spun round and launched himself at the glass, hitting the side and rebounded, landing awkwardly on his hip.

"Well, at least he'd not able to outthink anyone," Eve said, approaching the glass. Patrick got to his feet and ran over to the glass. He and Eve were only a few feet apart. Patrick started punching the glass once more. Eve looked at him without reacting to it at all; she simply crossed her arms and watched him.

"It's annoying I can't do anything to him. And a blessing that glass is as strong as it is. I mean, look at him. What kind of human would be able to defend themselves against him?" Eve turned her back on him and walked over to Jack who was standing there, watching the man in the glass box punching furiously away.

"Jack. You're letting me in and I don't like what you're thinking," she said.

"I'm just curious to see if he is still capable of fear. I could use a challenge and we need to see for certain if there is anything in there at all." He looked at Eve, who was not happy with the idea and wanted him to at least talk it through with Jim first.

"Where are they?" he asked.

"Waiting for us in the shooting range," she replied and took his hand.

Lisa and Jim were having a loud debate when Eve and Jack joined them. "You can't know for sure! You've only been running tests for three days!" They'd not heard Jim shouting for a long time and they didn't like the sound of it.

"Jim, I understand what you're thinking and it's not unreasonable to come to that conclusion, but we have run everything we've sampled and everything we've used in the past to get where we are today, which is over twenty years' worth of studies and trials. All our tests so far have not just failed but impressively failed. I've never been scared of DNA but I am of his. Nothing will cure him. He has become the virus now and, unfortunately, we only have a few options left. And for the record, I don't like any of them but we must face reality. I really am sorry, Jim," she said. Jim was standing against the second section of the range and Lisa was right next to him. John and Luke had taken a few steps back when Jim started raising his voice but Lisa understood how to put her argument across and Jim had refused to face reality. Someone had to help him see sense.

"I'm sorry, Lisa. I didn't mean to lose focus. I'm sorry I raised my voice," Jim said, slumping back against a cool steel ledge and putting a hand against the back of his neck.

Lisa walked over to him and put a hand on his shoulder. "We need to discuss what we're going to do now."

Jim looked down at her. "I know. I just hoped a solution would arise and we could help him."

Eve walked over to Jim and he turned to look at her. "Jack has an idea. I don't like it and I doubt you will either.

237

But I don't think it's an idea we can ignore. We have to look at this from all angles," she said.

"What are you thinking of trying, Jack?" Jim asked.

Chapter Eleven

Things are Changing for the Worse

It had been almost three days since Dr Frank Jager lost his last patient. He was a brilliant surgeon who didn't make mistakes and had zero malpractice suits against him in the last thirty years. Leaving surgery, he'd had an odd feeling in the back of his head that he couldn't shake off. He'd spoken to the family, which was difficult, but he assured them that a full investigation would take place and the cause be determined. He'd told staff that he was finished for the day and had left to go home. It had been a double shift and he could do no more. That night he'd eaten, caught up on what his wife and kids had done that week and gone to bed. He had started getting a headache a day after the operation and it had gotten so bad that after two days he'd been bedridden. His wife, who was a nurse, couldn't tell what was causing it. She was starting to get a headache of her own, as well as her children. *This is a nasty virus that's going around*, she thought. Forty miles away, the family her husband had spoken to were suffering as well.

Little did everyone know, but what Patrick and the others had created was the start of something that would reshape how the world worked. Brian and Simon had fled because they knew what would happen after Patrick had stolen the vials and departed the facility; they knew it was time to run. They knew who would be affected and what it would mean for them when Jim and John discovered what they'd created. If they had known what Patrick would do with the other vial, they might not have run. Or they might have run faster than they already had.

Two weeks after Dr Jager was bedridden, the whole state of New York was in the grip of this virus. It turned out that once an exposed person died, the virus became contagious. Dr Jager contracted the virus, along with everyone else present when their patient died during surgery. The virus would have been easily contained but as all viruses do, it modified itself once with a new host. This person would suffer after twenty-four hours with headaches that could not be eased. They would die a few days later. Their blood would prevent the organs from working properly and once the person was dead, it would spend a few more days changing the insides, then reactivate the body as a vessel. The sole purpose of the body now was to spread its virus to other organisms. There wasn't a laboratory on the planet that could have contained the outbreak. People wouldn't know they were exposed for twenty-four hours and by then it was too late. The papers had called it 'Gorman's' virus, derived from the first family to go on television, warning people to stay in their homes and not leave, so as to avoid the virus.

What started out as a control measure for New York soon became a cause for panic, as people discovered that simple human contact was the root cause for the uncontrollable spread of the virus.

Effects went from panic buying and stripping supermarkets of water and dried foods to the freeways being overrun with people and their vehicles, trying to flee the city.

Hospitals were packed full of people suffering from the effects and doctors were powerless to stop it. They ran syntheses to try and analyse it and discovered that the virus changed whenever an antidote was introduced. Some actually accelerated the process, causing the patient in some cases to die within hours. This caused further problems when the dead came back to life, showing no signs of normal behaviour. They were aggressive, emotionless and only seemed to be driven by the most basic of needs: the need to feed. When the infected started attacking, police and members of the public took matters into their own hands, defending themselves at all cost. Fights broke out, buildings became war zones; civilization was beginning to go out of the window as people lost their trust in their fellow men.

Authorities had tried to lock the state down by taking out bridges and tunnels. They policed roads and tracks, but the sheer number of people was uncontrollable. The virus was unstoppable. Within a month of the Gorman family appearing on television, New York, its surrounding islands and Virginia were taken over. As news channels started shutting down across New England, the rest of the country started taking precautions, but because the infection was now on planes and trains it wasn't long before the rest of America, Canada and Mexico were showing signs of infection. The airports were shut down but news of the virus was in England, France and spreading across Europe. Things were not looking good for mankind.

There was an incident in South Carolina where police and army troops had set up a blockade and had to stop infected people by deadly force. This type of incident became more frequent as the virus progressed across the globe and the public started living in fear. Three months after the Gormans went on television, infected people were starting to outnumber those who hadn't been infected and the lucky few who didn't seem to get infected by the virus started hiding wherever they could.

"Right, so what does this mean?" Jack asked, knowing full well what was going on and he was tired of asking the same questions without getting a straight answer from people's mouths. "Okay, so he's not going to get better, we all know this by now but how does this help us?" Jim asked, pointing over to the machine that Jean and Alex had been working on for the last few days.

The two of them had been working round the clock to get one of the machines that they'd gotten from Nathan's lab. It was apparent to them that given a bit of work the machine could be useful. But they'd never thought that something like this would ever happen in their lifetime. They had stayed, worked and slept in the lab for ten days now. The rest of the scientists had done almost as many hours, but John had sent them home to rest when some mistakes started to occur.

"Jack, the machine is a dispersal machine that can now send up a projectile, which mixes with the environmental factor and uses the weather system to deliver a payload into the atmosphere, which mixes with the natural occurrences …"

Eve stopped her in her tracks. "Please just tell us the end result, Jean. The whole World has started getting sick and we can't do anything to help. The work being done by you and your team has been confusing to say the least, but it's about time you told us what it is that's been developed, and how it will help us contain the outbreak."

Jean looked at John and at Alex. "It can't be contained," she said flatly and looked back at Eve.

Eve ignored that part. "'What can Jack's blood do now then?" she asked.

"We've managed to combine it with the Gorman virus and the results are very encouraging." The whole group were together now as Lisa and Luke came back into the lab. "It's moving across Tennessee and the south now. A virus of this kind will more than likely wipe out most of America by the time we get this ready."

Jack hadn't said much since he'd been in the room. Dancing around the subject had gotten him in a bad mood. Eve knew as much as he did, but she was being more optimistic about what they had planned. He didn't think shooting up some kind of device that mixed with the weather and when it hit the right pressure system, sent down rain, blended with their combination of his DNA and the Gorman virus was going to work. They had theorized that this would be like the rain acting in the same way his ability did. Jack wasn't happy with his ability changing people at random. But it would be the only way to stop everyone turning into people like Patrick.

Jack didn't know that there were people out there, just like his team, who wouldn't get infected. Everyone was worried about contracting the virus. So much so, it was a big reason none of the scientists wanted to leave the facility. John wanted them to get some rest and he knew that the surrounding areas hadn't shown any signs of the virus getting near them. He'd planned for them to be able to stay out and be free until he and Jim had no choice but to lock the facility down, which wouldn't be too long now. Jim wanted it locked down now, but because of how things were he'd given in to John's request and wouldn't act until he knew they had no choice.

"Fine, when do you want to start lift-off?" Jack asked, while the others were still discussing the details of how the equipment would work. They all turned and looked at him with a little anger that he was using this as a joke.

"I know this is no time to joke around, but it's not the time to just stand by while the planet we live on is being taken over by something we helped create. I do not like my ability being used this way and somehow I see it making things worse. Let's just get things straight, okay? Will it work? Yes. Should we take action? Yes. So when do we launch?"

He crossed his arms and watched everyone turn to everyone else, looking for an answer they hadn't really focused on. Finally, after Jack and Eve waited patiently, the scientists refocused and did some number crunching in their heads. It was Chris who answered, after what seemed like a long time.

"We can be ready with the first launch in a week."

The others nodded in agreement and Eve could see in their heads that it would take around twenty of these launches to cover enough ground to stop the virus from changing everyone into mindless creatures.

"We'd best get things ready," Lisa said, taking Luke by the hand and they disappeared. Eve saw they were going to start getting things moving in the lab and were in more of a rush then the others to get things done.

Since the incident Patrick had caused, the group had tried to stop the virus from spreading. Jack and John had gone over and tried to contain the outbreak, but the virus spread too quickly. They'd taken five people out of the area who were in different stages of infection. It turned out that a person only needed to be in contact with someone infected for a few minutes. Breathing in the skin people shed naturally was how the virus spread and a person only needed inhale a few times to become infected. First a person would feel unwell, then the headache started. After a few days they would be very ill, showing almost no life signs. Most people died within a week. The virus would reactivate the body after three days, which shocked them. It was only luck that saved the facility. The incinerator was down and until John fixed it, the bodies were kept in the quarantine room Eve stayed in. They broke out of their body bags and started turning on each other before the only surviving one tried escaping. They were angry, violent people who looked like they were after something to eat. When the large man broke out, Jack could hear the commotion going on and went to investigate. The door snapped off its hinges and the man ran straight at Jack, who caught the man by the neck and snapped it before he could try and get away. Afterwards the scientists took every precaution to prevent the virus spreading. Jack destroyed the bodies once the incinerator was fixed. He spent a few days in the room and it became clear he was immune to the virus. He cleaned every trace of the virus, taking everything to the incinerator until the room was bare. The building was locked down. Everything went to ensuring the prevention of the virus getting back in. They had all watched in horror as the virus took over everyone in the surrounding area and then moved on from county to county, and then from state to state. There was no controlling it. All they could do was watch in horror.

Not even a day had passed when the scientists started working on every possible cure to this. But their efforts were unsuccessful. Jean had been working on Jack's mimicking ability and come up short. His ability to alter people did come up with some results, but the effects would wear off. Mixing it with the Gorman virus did bring promising results. People would be permanently changed but as with Jack's ability, knowing what that person would get was unpredictable and that was what Jack did not like. Those who were luckily unaffected could be in danger from people getting an ability they couldn't control or worse still, people who would abuse it. There wasn't another choice. The mix wouldn't change anyone already infected, or those who, like the group that Jack had changed, could not catch the Gorman virus.

Adele was in her house, door locked and all the provisions Jim had recommended she have before one of his team would come to get her, were already packed. The virus hadn't gotten over to France yet and was still in the early stages of its journey across the planet. Jim had wanted to get her and Nikki safe before it was too late.

She jumped when Jack appeared in front of her. "Oh! Adele, I'm sorry," he said, taking a big step back. "That's the first time I've teleported that close, I guess it was bound to happen. Goodness, I wonder what would have happened if I'd teleported into you. That would suck, wouldn't it?" he said and she laughed so hard, she had to hold her chest. Jack laughed as well, but didn't think his joke was that funny. He guessed it was more the shock then the joke but he was glad to see she was okay.

"Ready when you are," he said, taking both fully packed suitcases in one hand and holding out the other.

"I'm sorry," Adele said, catching her breath and walked toward him. "Let's go," she said, taking his hand.

They appeared just outside the apartments and Jack showed her to the one she'd be sharing with Lisa. It was a choice between her and Eve, but the fact that Eve liked to listen in on people's dreams meant that she'd never get a good night's sleep. Lisa was already there, making sure that she could welcome and show her around.

"Hey!" she beamed and walked over for a hug. Adele had a huge smile on her face and walked over with her arms out. Jack turned round and jumped; Eve was standing behind him

"Jeez, babe. Sneak much?" he said.

Eve smiled at him. "You're going to have to get better at knowing when someone's behind you. Now, move. I want to say hi," she said, almost pushing past him in the narrow doorway.

"Of course, Your Majesty," he said and bowed to her as he stood to her side. She poked her tongue out and him and winked.

"Hey, Adele," she said, walking over and the three were in a group hug. Jack smiled at their embrace and disappeared.

Jack had gotten Jim's daughter after getting Adele. She was still adjusting to the new place, which she found creepy, but she loved being with her dad and his friends were nice, so she was getting used to it. The news of everything had frightened her but she'd done what Jim had said; she'd stayed home and not gone outside. The windows and doors were secure and she'd been on her own for two days before Jack came to get her. Jim wanted the tests and the bodies disposed of before bringing his daughter into the facility.

The group were all sitting round the table that evening, having eaten, and discussed that in less than a week they would launch the first pod into the atmosphere. The weather coming would help cover most of north America that was not affected yet, and then they would start getting the next pod ready to shoot over mainland Europe. England had already put measures in place and would be next on their list. The virus was now in mainland Africa and was already in Asia. News in Australasia was that they'd closed off all borders and it was the same story with every island left unaffected. Luke had done some research with John and they'd concluded that after enough people were infected, the virus would be unstoppable. It really had become a pandemic. They'd discussed when to change Adele and Nikki, along with the scientists, so that they could all be safe from getting infected. Security for the facility had all quit, so the whole building was locked down. The scientists had beds in the locker rooms now and the place was surprisingly comfortable.

"I guess we'll start tomorrow then," Eve said, looking across at Jack, who was just picking up another spring roll. He nodded and went back to eating. *Such a charmer,* she thought. Jim was sitting next to Nikki and Adele was on his other side. They were both ready to start tomorrow, but were nervous about getting changed. They both expected it would hurt. Jack and Jim had both talked at length with them about what to expect, which helped a little, but it was still unnerving to them.

Lisa and Luke were discussing how and where to launch on Thursday. John was going through the results and the configurations they'd decided, on the table that they'd put the information on so he could use and edit when needed.

The evening passed slowly for everyone, same as every evening they had now, seeing as they couldn't go anywhere or do anything to help for the first time in nearly two years. At around eleven o'clock they all made their way to their respective apartments. Nikki was staying in Jim's room. She had brought everything she thought she might need and Lisa had helped her settle in. Nikki liked Lisa and she did like Eve, but the way Eve could read her mind made Nikki a little afraid of her. She didn't get much sleep that night.

The next morning, they woke up at different times. Jim woke up at his usual time of five thirty. He got up, went for a run, worked out in the gym, all the while trying to find things on the news or via radio. He got some news from a pirate radio station that seemed to be running on a loop. According to this station, there were a group of people who were unaffected by the virus in Manhattan, who claimed to have made a fort. They welcomed others and they would apparently be well protected. Knowing what he did, and with his experience, Jim knew this was not going to be true for long, if at all.

Eve woke up and went straight to the pool. She wanted to be alone this morning and the pool was always a wonderful distraction. Jack got up and went to the gun range with Luke. They too wanted a distraction. Lisa went to the lab and chatted to the scientists, who were getting things ready for Thursday. The programs were running; it was the mixture that was taking time to complete. The machine was ready and had been tested. They only had a few things left to run and then they would be able to make enough of the mixture to spread into the different air pressure cycles on the planet, eventually changing everyone who was left.

Today Adele and Nikki weren't sure how to feel. They didn't really want get hurt. They had been assured by Jack and Jim that it wouldn't be too uncomfortable. Jack had lots of experience by now and said that they shouldn't worry. They still did though.

They were in the glass box where the group had held Patrick for nearly a week. It had been determined that he would not get better and they couldn't fix him. Drugs didn't work on Patrick, so they had no choice but to give in and to accept Jack's idea. They put him into one of the glass tubes and decided to keep him there, slowly filtering through his blood, until they could get a better understanding on how to fix him. The heart-breaking moment was when Jack had to engage in a fight with Patrick. The idea was to teleport in, knock him out and teleport him out to where the rest of the team would be waiting. They figured they could get the process started before he woke up, but he was very quick and Jack had to engage him. Eve and Jim had to watch them fight. Jack was trying not to hurt Patrick, but he had no choice. Two hits to the head and Patrick was out cold. John and Luke worked on putting Patrick under and once his blood was drained, he was put on life support and secured. They decided that they didn't want to see Patrick in the glass; John switched to black light so that he was hidden from view. This made it a bit easier for everyone, but they still knew he was there, perhaps to stay in perpetual suspended animation.

Adele was first to sit in the box. Jack was with her and as per the procedure, once they were in, the pole shot up and the box was sealed. "Have a seat," he said. Adele sat down. The restraints snapped in place. She jumped, but remained in place. "Are you ready to begin?" he asked. She smiled nervously but he could see in her mind that she was ready. He took her hands and the welcoming feeling of pins and needles came back to his body. Adele's convulsed instantly as it began. Jack closed his eyes, focused and her body relaxed. Nikki, who was watching this, held Jim's hand. Jim looked down and gave her a reassuring look.

"See, it's not too bad," he said. Nikki didn't say anything. She looked back at him with an 'easy for you to say' look on her face. She looked back at the box. *I can do this,* she thought.

The familiar feeling was almost over and Jack started to relax. No sooner had he opened his eyes, than he looked down at his hands in amazement. Adele fell out of the chair. Her hands and arms slipped out unscathed through the restraints while her feet did the same. Her shorts moved through them like a gust of wind would blow your shirt sleeve. Luke reacted so quickly that the rest of the group, including Eve, thought it was Adele's new ability. She hung in the air and Luke made it appear she was standing on her feet. After she had regained her senses she stood on her own and Luke left her to regain control

"Oh, *mon Dieu,*" she said looking at her hands and then at Jack. "*Comment avez-vous...?*" she asked.

"Well, this is an interesting one," he said and looked at her. "Don't worry; it takes a little getting used to." Then John's voice came over the speakers

"Is it safe to open?" he asked. Jack nodded and raised his hand up to where John could see. He sat Adele down in the chair and she cooperated willingly, as she was still a little shocked. Jim made his way over to the box and leaned against the wall, just inside so that the others, who were congregating behind him, could see but couldn't get in.

"How do you feel, Adele?" Nikki asked before anyone else had the chance to. She didn't really hear her, but answered more by reflex then by choice.

"I feel great. I don't know how he does this but I feel wonderful." She looked at Jack, who had crouched to her level and was grinning. "Thank you," she said.

He looked her in the eye and simply nodded. He mouthed the words "You're welcome," and stood so that the others could get in to see how she was. Jack walked outside where John was now coming into the room.

"Hey John, we've now got someone who can literally walk through walls," John beamed and increased his pace. He held out his hand to shake Jack's hand and it went straight through. John half stumbled and after looking at his hand and back to Jack, whose cheeky smile had widened, started grinning back. He put his hand out and firmly shook John's hand. He turned and patted him on the back and they walked toward the box that was now full of people talking to Adele.

"I've missed this," Jack said to John, who put his arm around his back while they walked.

"How does it feel when you've gone through things?"

"Can you put clothing through things as well?"

"What types of things can you do it to?"

Adele was getting bombarded with questions, so Eve took charge and made everyone silent. Once it was quiet, she gave everyone their minds back and they each asked a question in more of an organized manner. Jack and John were discussing the ability calmly outside the box and he would demonstrate it by putting his hand through and back out from the glass wall. His shirt sleeve would crumple against the glass, but stay where it should, while his skin moved easily through. Jack put his cuff over his hand and pushed through it and the glass.

"It looks like the ability is the same when it comes to affecting clothing as Jim's ability," Jack said matter-of-factly. He pulled off his shirt, revealing his running T-shirt, and went to put his elbow up against the glass. The fabric moved through. Not as quickly as the rest of his bare arm, but it still passed through. John moved back and put a hand to his chin. "How interesting," he remarked.

Jack felt a hand tapping him on the shoulder. He turned to see Nikki smiling at him. "Can we start in a minute?" she asked, more beaming than smiling. He smiled and patted her shoulder.

"How about we start now?" he said back. Nikki grinned and turned to get back to the box. *Cute kid*, Jack thought and turned to John, who could see what he was going to ask him. John took his hand and disappeared. Jack walked over to the box, where everyone had cleared out, and Nikki sat in the chair. Adele was with Lisa and Eve, using her ability on objects and she took off one shoe so she could test her body more. Jack walked into the box and closed the door. He walked over to Nikki, who jumped when the restraints closed in place. He smiled at her. "Are you ready to begin?"

Nikki showed great restraint during the transition; when he let go of her hands she opened her eyes and smiled at him.

Jack took a sharp step back. "Don't open the box," he said. Jim launched forward towards it.

"Jack? What's wrong?" he asked, trying to sound level and only just succeeding.

"Its best we stay in here for a minute, Jim. Her ability is quite a dangerous one," he responded and not a second after he said it the restraints on Nikki's body opened with a pop. "John?" Jim shouted, but Eve was right next to him.

"It's Nikki," she said and Jim looked at his daughter, who was still sitting in the chair, laughing.

"Thank you, Jack," she said but as she got distracted, a bolt of electrical current shot from her fingers and bounced around the glass, leaving scorch marks in its wake.

"Nikki, I'd like you to focus on keeping it running over your skin," Jack said to her and she placed a hand on the chair arm. The restraint snapped back and forth at her will, and she started laughing again.

"I'm sorry but it's so much fun," she said, standing up and looking at her hands as she made little ripples of electric current flow smoothly over her skin.

She got the hang of her ability like it had always been a part of her. The group's first reaction of her being unstable with it was unfounded and Nikki was able to use it right off the bat, making things turn off and on when she liked. She could shoot with quite good accuracy, depending on what it was she was aiming at; and she could shock people who touched her by surprise, which Luke found out the hard way when he patted her on the shoulder, trying to ask a question.

"So you can do everything we can do then?" Nikki asked Jack, who was helping her develop her ability in the shooting range. She was getting very accurate at a distance now. Jack thought her growing up with Jim around was a big contributor to this. "Wow, so you're pretty much unstoppable now," Nikki said matter-of-factly. She made this statement as he was loading up another clip. They were competing for the same target he'd taken back over sixty yards away. So far there wasn't much between the shots. Jack would put a bullet through the card and Nikki would try and burn the hole he'd made. So far she had only missed by a small margin. He stopped and reflected.

"I guess so," he said, laughing. "I've never really thought about it like that," he continued, loading the clip. "If I could do what you can do, I'd be having so much fun with it," Jack stopped and turned to face her.

"I guess most people would be getting up to all sorts if they could do the things we can do. Luckily, your dad has kept us busy using our abilities for good. So we've been taught to use them responsibly."

She looked at him and without taking her eyes away, shot a long bolt from her palm, which went through his bullet hole, almost leaving no trace on the card.

"You don't think I know about responsibility?" she said quite angrily. Jack thought that she really should use Eve's ability more.

"Holding back, were we, Nikki?" he asked.

"You don't use Eve's ability much and I like that. She scares me. I never know when she's inside my head." She turned and looked at her shot. Jack brought back the card so she could get a closer look at it. "I'm tired of restraint. I want, for once in my life, to go nuts. To be let off the leash that I've felt on me all my life. Daddy's trained me well and I'm so thankful for it, but he's always told me that I don't know my own strength and I'd hurt people if I lost control. I guess I'm more like him then I know." Jack looked at her and for the first time, could see what she was talking about. Her features were all very feminine and soft but if you really looked at her, you could see the muscle definition and how strong she really was. She trained and ran every day without fail, sometimes with Jim but mostly on her own.

"Be careful what you wish for, Nikki. Given how things are with the world now, you might get your dream quicker than you think." She smiled without looking at him.

"You never know," was all she said and cracked her knuckles. The sound echoed around the range. *None of us ever do*, he thought and they both grinned.

Wednesday arrived and the scientists had finished their work. There was more than enough of the mixture to cover the globe, and the machine they needed to disperse it was ready to use. They had even gotten the coordinates ready for where and when to launch. Jack was approached to run the machine and help two others, who turned out to be Luke and Lisa. They would work perfectly to the schedule that had been drawn up, based on weather and earth pressure patterns. They would run the machine constantly and using its GPS, would know how much mixture to disperse and when to start the next cycle. All that was to be done was to start it up tomorrow and work with the schedule that they had drawn up.

Jean was nervous and Jim could see it in her face. Eve was already aware of what was on her mind, and she knew that the others had all voted for her to be the spokesperson. "Jim," she said quietly. Jim turned to face her properly and smiled at her.

"Don't worry," he said and put a hand on her shoulder. "Once the process has been completed and Jack's back, you'll all get to become part of the team. The only things that I can ask you is if you want to get your ability from Jack like we all have, or if you'd rather gain one through the means that you've created. Do you want to be like everyone else on earth?" She looked up at him. "We've all decided we want to do it the safe way and if Jack doesn't mind, we'd like him to be the one to do it." Jim looked over at Eve, who was already playing that conversation in her head and trying to hear everyone else in the building to determine whether there was anyone up to no good. She'd gotten to know them all quite well, but Jim wanted to be sure. Eve was more than happy to help.

"Everything's fine, Jim," she said after a few minutes. He smiled at her and turned back to Jean.

"I'll ask him," he said.

Jack was in the lab with Lisa and Luke. They were teaching him what he needed to look out for on the machine's screens, but he wasn't really paying attention.

"So the big green button does what again?" he asked.

Lisa rolled her eyes. "There is no green button, Jack. Why must you make fun of what we're trying to teach you?" she asked.

He huffed at her and looked at them both in turn. "Because I know that you know that when it comes to things like this, it will go as follows. You teach me to use a nice new piece of tech, we go out to use said piece of tech and then, when it's time to use the blooming machine, I have to stand guard while you use it. If you're only teaching me so you can run through with each other and don't want to look stupid or paranoid, then fine. But if you're going to teach me this time, then when it comes to using it, I will make sure I do. Now, do I get to use it this time?"

There was a brief silence and then Luke looked at Lisa. "So, that's everything updated and ready to launch tomorrow?" he asked.

She looked back at Jack and gave him an apologetic smile. "Yes, Luke. I just wanted to make sure that everything is ready," Jack put his hands in his pockets.

"So I can help. I've been listening to you both cluck away like chickens. I got bored, so I went through everything you both were thinking and the machine does what it's been designed to do, everything you've been thinking of is updated and it's ready; all we have to do now is wait fourteen hours, activate it and then get into position. Are you both happy now? Can I go watch some paint dry because you two are driving me crazy?" and with that he walked off. Lisa and Luke watched him walk away. He was muttering to himself about playing chess, because it's the only thing people let him do on his own around here. She looked at Luke and shrugged.

"For a man who can do pretty much everything around here, he does get wound up easily," Luke snorted and covered his face, holding in his laughter.

"I heard that," they could hear Jack shout back at them.

Jim was talking to Eve when Jack walked past them. He hadn't used the lift in so long that seeing him walk out of it was a bit odd. "Jim, babe," he said, walking past. "It's not a problem. After I've helped Tweedledum and Tweedledee, I'll start with Jean then follow down the ranks until everyone is on the team," he said this without stopping, so the last bit sounded a bit muffled.

Jim looked at Eve. "He's in a strop because he won't get to use the machine," she said and Jim just shook his head at Jack, who walked over to the table and started a new chess game.

The rest of the day passed along very slowly for everyone. Lisa kept going back to the machine to check on things she knew were fine, and the rest of the scientists did the same. The living quarters got changed around so that everyone would be safely accommodated until they knew how things around the world had changed. They'd been in a meeting with the whole group and Jim went through the idea he had for everyone. They were to see Jack, who would give them the ability to help and then they were to split into groups and see what the situation was around the globe, being transported back every few days to report on the situation.

"Document and report." Jim made sure he got this drummed into their heads. "I want nothing more and nothing less. Remember that." He had looked each person in the eye while he said that. They all knew what he meant and Eve told Jim that none of them had any thoughts to suggest they would go off and try to play hero. Jack would head up the main parties in the most populated areas, which they knew would be high risk. The others would go out and see what the situation was. They would help those they could and if they were threatened, they were to get back to the facility.

"Are we all in agreement then?" Jean asked them while they had their own meeting. There weren't any confused faces before her, just looks of excitement and a few that looked understandably scared. "Then we'll start getting everyone ready for when they get back. They looked at one another, sharing the familiar looks that were mirrored on their faces. Jean herself could barely contain her excitement.

Jack and Eve were in his apartment, which was to soon be his and Luke's when they were due to get back and start getting the rest of the team ready. He was getting clothes sorted out into piles of things he didn't mind getting screwed up when he had to throw them to the bottom of the wardrobe. She was making a mental list of these clothes and she would sort them out while he was away. "Don't bother trying to sort them out. They'll be different when you return," she said, smiling.

"I know. But I like pretending I'm in charge of the clothes I wear," he said, throwing a shirt he rather liked into the wrong pile. She rolled her eyes at him and started sorting out his bedding. While she was distracted, he manipulated the shirt so that it moved to the correct pile.

"That's cheating," she said without bothering to turn round. He walked over and went to push her head first into the bed, but her shoulder muscles were very strong now and she caught herself just in time, and as she spun she caught a fistful of his shirt, effectively pulling him toward her. He played along and landed on her shoulder. His head was only a few inches away from her face. He looked into her eyes and smiled.

"I'll miss you," he said and brushed his nose against hers. She closed her eyes and smiled while he traced her nose with his. She opened her eyes after a while and looked into his.

"Come back in one piece. If you put yourself in harm's way, then you'll have me to deal with when you get back." Jack kissed her nose, which he knew would make her go cross-eyed for a second. She did as he predicted and brought his head up so she could focus on his face.

"Sounds fun," he said and winked. She punched him in the ribs and he mockingly rolled off her in pain. She grabbed the back of his shirt and turned him over.

"I mean it," she said, watching his expression. Jack moved closer to her face

"I know. And you know that I'll always come back to you," he said. She put her arms around his neck and hugged him close.

"You'd better," she whispered.

The next day, after no one slept properly, Jack, Lisa and Luke got dressed, had breakfast and after the morning debrief Jim had set up, got everything they needed ready and met up in the laboratory. Jack could see how focused they were and he was glad they were in their professional modes. How long that would last he wasn't sure. The next week of holding the machine in place, moving it to the next location and starting it all over again would be difficult, but this was going to even out the playing field and the new challenge ahead was a thrill.

Eve was going to help monitor things from here and get the scientists ready mentally. Eve and Jack had shared an intimate moment the night before and she was sad to see him leave. She worried that he would be in trouble, even though she knew he was the only person, alive or dead, who could deal with any situation now, but she still worried. Jack could see this and he knew how much he would miss being around her.

Lisa switched on the machine. All the dials activated and the machine started heating up.

"It's alive!" Jack joked. They all looked at him. "Wow, tough crowd," he mocked.

"Let's go to the first point," Luke said and they all took hold of the machine. Jack looked at Eve.

"Be good," she said. A tear formed in the corner of her eye. He smiled and winked at her. *This had better work*, he thought and they disappeared.